MOMENT
of WEAKNESS

KG MacGREGOR

BELLA
BOOKS
2017

Bella Books, Inc.
P.O. Box 10543
Tallahassee, FL 32302

Printed in the United States of America on acid-free paper.

First Bella Books Edition 2017

Editor: Katherine V. Forrest
Cover Designer: Linda Callaghan

ISBN: 978-1-59493-557-2

Other Bella Books By KG MacGregor

Acknowledgments

I'm always happy when I finish a book, but never more than one borne from a challenge. It's one thing to take readers out of a comfort zone. This book took me out of mine.

The genesis of *Moment of Weakness* was the desire to write a romantic novel that opened with a couple on the rocks. It was a book I'd get to someday, but never the book I wanted to write next. So I held it on the back burner while waiting for the characters to present themselves, for their conflict to materialize, for their themes to emerge. Truth be told, I don't even remember any of that happening. All of a sudden I had a manuscript.

But not a very good one. In fact, the first draft was so clumsy I almost ditched it. Fortunately I have an editor in Katherine V. Forrest who zeroed in on the strengths and drew them out. It's probably the most work I've ever done on a second draft, and there's a marvelous sense of satisfaction to cross a challenge off my list.

I have a great team behind all of my books. Besides Katherine, there's my partner Jenny, who reads it the way you would and tells me what you'll think. And finally, the professional team at Bella Books polishes it and puts it in your hands. What would I do without these great women?

About the Author

Lesbian romance author KG MacGregor is a former teacher and market research consultant, with a doctorate in media research. In 2002, she tried her hand at writing fan fiction for the *Xena: Warrior Princess* fandom, and found her true bliss. Three years later, she signed with Bella Books and kicked off her third career. An award-winning author of 24 books, she served as president of the board of trustees for Lambda Literary, the world's premier organization for LGBT literature. She and her partner make their home in the Blue Ridge Mountains. Visit her on the web at www.kgmacgregor.com.

CHAPTER ONE

Zann Redeker closed the conference room door behind her and blew out a sigh of relief. After months of twisting in the wind, something finally had broken her way.

It helped a lot that the mayor himself had vouched for her. A longtime family friend, Willard "Ham" Hammerick had helped plead her case with the town manager, all but offering his personal guarantee that she'd be a model employee from this day forward. Now he jostled her shoulder with a fatherly hand. "I know you're glad this nightmare's over, Zann. Come Monday morning everything goes back to normal, like it never even happened."

She appreciated the sentiment but her life was still light years away from normal. At least getting her job back gave her a fighting chance. "Thanks for sticking your neck out, Ham. I promise I won't screw up again."

"I know you won't. I'm just sorry we had to put you through all this rigmarole." Always the gentleman, he helped her into her heavy parka as they walked toward the lobby. "Used to be when you made a mistake, you apologized and everybody moved on. Now the first thing people do is call a lawyer to see how much money they can get."

"This was nobody's fault but mine." She would be forever embarrassed for the trouble she'd caused her bosses at town hall. In a rural hamlet like Colfax, Vermont, even the tiniest scandal was front page news. It wasn't long ago that the townspeople were cheering her return from Afghanistan as a war hero. Now they probably thought her just another combat veteran with mental health issues. A walking cliché.

"Don't be too hard on yourself, Zann. You made a mistake but you paid the price fair and square. It all comes out in the wash." Ham's masterful empathy and habitual use of folksy idioms endeared him to local voters, making his continuous reelection a foregone conclusion.

"Getting my job back…at least that takes the pressure off. Now all I have to do is sort this mess out with Marleigh and catch up on our bills."

He gave her a grim half smile. "I was sorry to hear you'd moved back home with your mom and pop. What's going on with the house?"

Zann cringed to think how many people in the closely-knit town knew of their marital problems. "Marleigh got an offer from the real estate agent but she needs me to sign the papers too. Maybe now that I'm going back to work, we won't have to sell. I'm heading over there right now to try to talk her out of it."

It wasn't only their house that needed saving. Marleigh didn't trust her anymore, and like everything else, that too was her fault.

"Good luck, hon. We're all pulling for you."

Feeling exposed under his watchful eye, she thanked him again and skated tentatively across the icy parking lot to her SUV, a rusted Jeep Grand Cherokee with 164,000 miles of wear and tear. As usual, the engine turned over several times before finally catching and sending a blast of frigid air up from the floorboard. With her fingers shaking from the cold—to say nothing of her gut-wrenching anxiety—she tapped out a text on her phone: *Just got big news can i come to your office?*

More than a week had passed since they last spoke by phone, which should have been enough time and distance for Marleigh to calm down and rethink her rash decision to sell the house. Instead she'd forged ahead and jumped on the very first offer, dropping the papers off for Zann's signature without even hanging around to talk.

The reply was devastating but not surprising. *Only if ur ready 2 sign contract.*

"Twist the knife, how 'bout it?" Zann pounded her steering wheel as she studied the ultimatum on her text screen. An open-handed slap would have been kinder.

Another fight about the house was the last thing they needed, especially with all of Marleigh's coworkers straining to hear. She'd bring the contract, all right, but that didn't mean she'd sign it. The house was all they had. If they sold it, what would bind them together?

It was after three o'clock, almost press time for the *Colfax Messenger*, the newspaper where Marleigh worked as city editor. They'd be winding down their workday.

On my way.

What choice did she have? With her back against the wall, there was nothing left to do but come clean. Marleigh had been right all along—Zann had hidden something from her since last May, a secret so explosive it could rock the very foundation of their marriage. But then keeping the secret had done that too.

Bottom line—she wasn't the person Marleigh thought she was.

"Goddamn it." This was it. The whole truth, nothing but the truth. It wasn't just the last three and a half years they stood to lose, but the rest of their lives too.

Her Jeep plowed through the slush onto Colfax's Main Street, now bustling with after-school traffic. Between the crosswalks and bus stops, it took almost ten minutes to travel a quarter of a mile to the newspaper office, a flat one-story building at the edge of the town's modest commercial district. The lined spaces near the door were reserved for customers, so she parked alongside Marleigh's gray sedan in the area designated for *Colfax Messenger* employees. Six cars…that was practically everyone on staff, making this a spectacle for all to see.

The stakes of her last-gasp appeal were high—if Marleigh said no this time, it really was over.

* * *

On my way, the text read.

The coffee turned to acid in Marleigh's throat. It wasn't in her nature to be so pigheaded, but Bridget had a point—pigheadedness was the only language Zann understood anymore. One of them had to be the adult. Now three months behind on their mortgage, they faced foreclosure by the bank within days if they didn't act.

Financial ruin wasn't even the worst of it. Even if they somehow staved off bankruptcy, their marriage had suffered a savage blow. Her heart still held out for a miracle but her rational side was quickly losing hope. The woman she'd married only three years ago had been a kind, peaceful soul whose love felt like the most precious thing in the world. Was it even possible for Zann to be that person again? Their love should have been for all time. Six months of nudging, begging and demanding hadn't worked. Zann was on a road to self-destruction and she was taking Marleigh down with her. With each day that passed, the end game looked more and more like divorce.

Divorce. She'd never even uttered the word aloud and now it seemed all but inevitable. It wasn't supposed to end this way. It wasn't supposed to end at all.

"Everything okay?" Bridget asked, peering from her adjacent desk over a pair of Oliver Peoples reading glasses that she didn't actually need. The lenses were the lowest possible strength, she'd explained. Apparently her boyfriend Luc thought they gave her a sophisticated flair.

"I just got a text from Zann. Says she has big news about something, asked if she could come by." Feeling guilty for her weakness, she quickly added, "But I told her only if she brought me the signed contract."

"Good for you. You need to hold the line on this, Marleigh. I'm here if you need backup. You're the one who taught me to stand up for myself."

"I think I can handle it," Marleigh muttered.

The heavy glass door swung wide, sending a gust of wintry air around the room. Editor Clay Teele entered and stomped his snow-covered shoes on a welcome mat that stretched all the way to the chest-high customer service counter. Though short and wiry, he always managed to overpower the room with his intensity. "What have you got, Anderhall?"

Marleigh held out her working versions of the day's assignments. "Suspicious garage fire on Highbridge. Owner of puppy mill pleads guilty to animal cruelty charge. I'm still working on the police blotter for tomorrow…couple of break-ins, vandalism at Hannaford's, and a hit-and-run on a parked car at the armory."

"Over a thousand expected for Winter Festival," Bridget said, adding her story to Clay's pile. "Plus I got some good snow pictures from Barry. And the high school honor roll's out. I went over this morning and got quotes from some of the kids."

Clay's shoulders drooped, his typical response to a slow news day. Scandalous drug busts, graphic vehicle accidents and raucous town council meetings sold more papers. That mattered a lot with all the ads running for Christmas sales. "Please tell me there's something exciting in sports."

Terry Henderson, whose desk sat behind Marleigh's in the back corner, continued typing as he answered, "Bruins won, Celtics lost. Got those off the wire. Colfax varsity plays Rutland tonight."

Marleigh, Bridget and Terry were all that remained of a local news staff that had withered from a dozen over the past six years amid a continuing downturn in newspaper readership. Clay culled national and state news from the wire services and wrote a daily column for the editorial page, answering directly to the corporate office in Burlington.

Tammy Hatch, the youngest *Messenger* employee at twenty-four, handled advertising sales. Like Clay, she had a glass-enclosed office with a door, a blessing to everyone since she spent ninety percent of her time on the phone chattering with potential advertisers.

Though Clay was editor and boss, it was Fran Crippen who kept the place going. A widow with Colfax roots going back to the American Revolution, she'd managed the customer service desk for almost forty years and knew every subscriber by name.

Marleigh punched up the lead on her puppy mill story and submitted the final version electronically to Terry's inbox for copy edits. She was ahead of schedule for a change—which gave her a few minutes to talk if Zann actually stopped by.

As Clay disappeared into his office, Bridget leaned over and murmured, "Is it my imagination or is he crankier than usual?"

"He's always like that when he gets back from a meeting at corporate. They're probably leaning on him for more budget cuts."

"Cripes, we're down to six people. It's all we can do to get the paper out as it is."

Marleigh worried every day the honchos in Burlington would decide to cut their losses on the cluster of small-town dailies and shut them all down. They'd folded a handful already and were hiring stringers to cover local news for the statewide Burlington edition. In fact, she'd taken on some freelance work in nearby Middlebury to make ends meet after Zann lost her job.

"Luc says I ought to try working at the *Montreal Gazette*," Bridget scoffed. "Like I'm just going to walk in there and get a job. I reminded him I'm not even Canadian."

After years of being emotionally and physically abused by her former husband, Bridget deserved someone who would lavish her with the finer things. That was Luc Michaux, a day trader from Montreal who had fallen in love with both Bridget and the small-town life of rural Vermont.

"What are you and Luc up to this weekend?"

Bridget scrunched her nose and shrugged. "Not sure. He's been in New York all week. He's been so busy...hasn't even called me in like, two days."

Marleigh briefly considered inviting her over to hang out, but she needed to finish packing. If their sales contract went through, she'd have only a couple of weeks to get out. The buyers were paying cash and wanted to close by the end of the month.

"Don't look now, but somebody's coming," Bridget said. Her desk afforded the best view of the entrance. "And I'll be damned...it looks like she's got the papers in her hand."

Just knowing Zann would walk through the door any moment filled Marleigh with both longing and dread. Longing for the thrill Zann had aroused since the first day they met, and dread that today could be the beginning of the end. The last time they spoke, Zann had warned of leaving Vermont once and for all if they split up. Sign on with a private military contractor and return to a war zone, she said. Threats like that were hard to swallow, but they only prolonged the suffering. Marleigh had to put her own feelings first for a change and let the chips fall.

At five-eleven, Zann was a formidable woman, no small thanks to the stiff posture ingrained through years of military life. Her usual swagger had faltered somewhat since her troubles started last summer. She glanced hesitantly at Marleigh's coworkers, peeled off her gloves and fleece cap, and shook out her shoulder-length dark hair. With a small wave to Fran she ambled closer, her aching smile threatening to break Marleigh's heart. In a gravelly voice, she said, "Hey...think we could go somewhere private and talk?"

The calm words were a welcome change from a month ago, the last time they'd stood face-to-face. Then, Zann had been desperate for a lifeline and anxious about having to move out of the house.

Marleigh stole a glance at the papers in her grip, confirming it was the contract with a 72-hour deadline she'd hand delivered to Zann's father three nights ago. The finality of signing over their house gripped her as she rolled her chair back and gestured toward the hallway leading to the restrooms and break area. "Let's get some coffee in the back."

The break area was barely large enough for the card table and four plastic chairs. A refrigerator stood against the far wall where a small window overlooked the employee parking lot. The counter held a cheap coffeemaker and an apartment-sized microwave, with storage cabinets above and below.

Zann shrugged off her parka and draped it over a chair, all without letting go of the papers. "You look great. As usual, I mean…you always look great to me."

Marleigh took the compliment in stride. There was nothing special about her appearance today. She wore old corduroy jeans and a black fleece pullover that zipped to her neck. Her caramel-colored hair, short and straight, was overdue for a cut. She suspected the compliment had more to do with Zann just being glad to see her. "What *you* look is tired, Zann. You taking care of yourself?"

"Best I can. It hasn't been easy…I know, not for you either. "

"Of course not. I hurt just as much as you do."

"I haven't signed these yet." Zann slapped the papers in her opposite hand, then drew in a deep breath and nearly choked as she let it out. "I'm so sorry for getting us into this mess. It kills me to think everything we worked so hard for could be gone forever just by writing my name on this stupid piece of paper. I'd do anything to keep that from happening. That's why I'm here, because I need to tell you something. Please just try to keep an open mind. If you hear me out and still decide this is what you really want, I'll go ahead and sign it."

"I appreciate that, Zann. I really do. We can't hold on any longer. At some point, we have to just…" She couldn't bring herself to say it—they were saying goodbye to their dream.

Zann's face fell, but she recovered instantly with the same strained smile as when she'd walked in the door. "There's still time to work this out. I promise I didn't come here to give you the same old shit again."

"We've already been through everything a million times. What's left to say?" The resignation in her voice had more to do with hopelessness than resistance. She could never *not* listen—that's why Bridget had urged her to avoid another bargaining session. Even after all they'd been through, she'd always be a slave to Zann's magnetism. "I'll listen, but don't expect it to change anything."

"That's all I'm asking. Thank you." Zann leaned against the counter and folded her arms, blowing out a nervous breath. "First of all, I just came from a meeting with Malcolm and Ham. I start back to work on Monday—same job, same salary. Everything back just like it was."

A part of her wanted to leap for joy. Zann had been suspended from work for the last five months, causing what had been an almost-manageable crisis at home to spin completely out of control. It had upended not only their financial stability but Zann's sense of purpose. In practical terms, this could put them back on solid ground.

But was it too little too late? It didn't fix the underlying problem—Zann was grappling with a personal demon from her past and refused even to say what it was.

"And now comes the big news," she went on, her wide green eyes showing a glint of cheerfulness that didn't jibe with the occasion. "I went for the psych eval like they asked...and like *you* asked. Turns out I'm not even all that crazy. Can you believe it?"

"I never thought you were. I just thought you needed to talk to somebody." Except she'd hoped that somebody would be her. Zann had kept her in the dark for too long.

"We set up three more sessions but he says we can go longer if I think I need it."

Marleigh wanted to cheer, but after so many empty promises there was no shaking the fear that this was purely an attempt to manipulate her into calling off the sale. Zann wasn't easy to trust anymore—she could very well keep her appointments but sabotage her progress and they'd be back where they started, especially if she lost her job again.

"Look, Marleigh…this is what you wanted, isn't it? Everything's going to be okay now. I love you."

"I know you do. And you know how much I wanted you to get help. But it doesn't change how much you hurt me."

"How many times do I have to say it? I'm sorry. All this crap I've been going through has nothing to do with you."

"It has *everything* to do with me if you shut me out. I've never given you a reason not to trust me, not once." Her voice rose with every word, enough that she forced herself to close her eyes and take a deep, hissing breath.

This was their pattern. Or rather, Marleigh's pattern. She started every conversation wanting badly to believe Zann was ready to turn the corner. In the end, the hurt would overwhelm her and she'd lash out. The issue wasn't only the lack of trust. Zann had ignored her pleas for so long that it began to feel like deliberate indifference to the toll it was taking on their marriage. The final straw came when Marleigh concluded that she was the only one who cared about saving what they had.

"You're the only person I've ever completely trusted in my whole life." Zann took a step toward her, holding her hands out as if begging to be believed. "It was never about you. Hell, I could barely stomach telling the psychologist, and he hears this kind of shit all the time. But I swear I'm ready to talk now. I'll tell you everything you want to know."

Marleigh couldn't deny her surge of hope that today might be the breakthrough Zann needed. That *they* needed. The fact that she'd finally confessed to someone had to be good news. "Whatever this is, Zann…I'm pulling for you. I want to see you happy again."

"I can't be happy if we aren't together. Simple as that. The reason I haven't told you…I was scared you wouldn't love me anymore."

Marleigh's arms opened automatically as Zann closed the distance between them and enveloped her in a hug. She was utterly powerless every time Zann reached for her.

"Can we hold off a little longer, Marleigh…please? I don't want to lose our house. We're supposed to grow old there. Give me one last chance to fix this. If I screw it up this time, I swear I won't fight you anymore. Just please don't throw us away yet."

As she buried her face in Zann's warm neck, strong arms tightened around her waist. And her heart responded the same way it always had. She wanted so, so badly to say yes, but…

The window casing shuddered from a change in air pressure, a faint signal that someone had entered the lobby. Marleigh broke their embrace. "Look, this isn't the time or place to—"

Two sharp pops erupted in the outer room.

Zann gripped her shoulders tightly and whispered, "Those were gunshots!"

CHAPTER TWO

June, three years earlier

Khaki combat boots were a bit overkill for lawn work but Zann's only other options were running shoes or the black corframs she wore with her service uniform. Her entire wardrobe needed a civilian overhaul.

"You don't have to do that," her mother yelled from the patio door. "Corey Hammerick only charges fifteen dollars for the whole yard."

Zann waved her off as the mower roared to life. She'd been sitting on her ass since returning to Colfax two weeks ago. No job, no prospects. Bored out of her mind. There wasn't much demand for experienced combat soldiers, especially one who couldn't even raise a weapon.

The Troy-Bilt mower was self-propelled with a motor on the front wheel that pulled it forward as long as she squeezed together two bars on the handle. Easier said than done, since the radial nerve in her left arm had been severed by a bullet from a Taliban fighter in Afghanistan—five months ago today. Now four surgeries later, she had only a trace of feeling in her thumb and index finger, and little control of her elbow or wrist. The physical therapist's most optimistic prognosis was a fifty percent recovery, a number that had drawn her a medical retirement from the Marine Corps after only eight years.

No way was she settling for fifty percent. The last surgery, a tendon transfer, had swapped the affected muscles to another nerve. Now all she had to do was train that nerve to do a new job. On any given day it meant three hours of repetitive therapy. The aggressive schedule was necessary—she'd been advised that recovery had to happen soon or the muscles would lose their tone forever. Six months from now she could be maxed out.

Mowing grass seemed to put all the right muscles to work, at least. Maybe the answer was to swallow her pride and sign on with a lawn service for the rest of the summer. That would buy her some time to decide on a new career. Surely someone had use for a Syracuse grad with the self-discipline of a Marine Corps officer.

"Zann!" Her mother dodged clumps of freshly-clipped grass as she picked her way across the lawn. "Did you forget about the interview? That reporter just called and said she'd be here at two o'clock."

"Ugh!" It was tradition, the editor had said, for the newspaper to profile the grand marshal of the town's Fourth of July parade. No one had ever declined the invitation. "You think it's too late to change my mind about this whole parade business? I'm going to look like an idiot."

"Oh, come on. It might be fun."

The parade gig had been Ham's idea. He'd just been elected mayor on a campaign of bringing back small-town values like family and patriotism. What better way for Colfax to celebrate Independence Day than to put a local face on the War on Terror?

She couldn't imagine anything worse than being the center of attention at a town parade, and would have flatly refused if not for her mom's gentle reminder that it would mean a lot to her father's friends and coworkers at town hall. Personal relationships mattered and Ham was a friend.

"I should be done by two o'clock," she shouted. And if she wasn't, the reporter could just cool her jets. Maybe she'd get bored and leave.

* * *

Marleigh crept along Fullmer Street, one hand on the wheel and the other on her scribbled directions. Most houses in the neighborhood were Cape Cods, two-story cubes with a pair of gables on the second floor. These were the established families of Colfax's professional class—doctors, attorneys, professors.

"Eight-seventeen," she said aloud as she rolled to a stop in front of a home that was markedly different, a small bungalow separated from its neighbor on one side by a row of juniper trees, and on the other by a tall wooden fence. Why would those neighbors feel the need to hide the house from their view? It was a small but tidy home, freshly painted in pale yellow with white trim and shutters, and surrounded by colorful petunias and mums. An American flag hung limply from a mount in observance of Independence Day, less than a week away. Clearly the Redekers were patriots.

The grass between the sidewalk and the street was freshly mowed, but a pair of grooves suggested this was where guests were expected to park. She checked the vanity mirror and applied a light coat of pink lip balm, the only makeup she wore in the summer.

This was a plum assignment, an in-depth profile of an interesting public figure. At thirty-four, Marleigh had earned the chance for more challenging work, having paid her dues reporting small-town news for the local afternoon newspaper, the *Colfax Messenger*. Community events, police blotter and traffic accidents. Not much else happened in rural Vermont.

Today's interview was special for more than just a professional opportunity. She was already in awe of her enigmatic subject, United States Marine Corps Captain Suzann Redeker, a returning war veteran who'd tried at first to shun the attention her heroic deeds warranted. That alone made her intriguing.

What kind of person eschewed the prestige and acclaim of her hometown? According to the commendation report, Redeker had been awarded the Bronze Star with V—one of the nation's highest medals for valor—after rushing headlong into a hostile dwelling to save another soldier. While her effort had been unsuccessful, she'd taken out four militants who'd amassed weapons for an imminent assault on Camp Leatherneck in the Helmand Province of Afghanistan, home to thousands of Marines.

Notepad and recorder in hand, Marleigh climbed the stairs and rang the bell, eager to meet the courageous Captain Redeker.

A sheer curtain wafted as someone inside checked her out. Then a middle-aged woman appeared at the door, the captain's mother Marleigh assumed. She wore the unofficial uniform of a housewife in summer, Capri pants with a knit top that proclaimed her World's Best Grandma. "You must be the reporter Suzann told us about."

In preparing for the interview, she'd learned Chuck Redeker worked in the town clerk's office as a property tax assessor. Modest income but at least recession-proof. His wife Leeann advertised in the Yellow Pages as a seamstress doing alterations out of her home.

"Yes, Marleigh Anderhall with the *Messenger*. Here to see Captain Redeker."

"Please come in. I'll get her."

From the entryway, she peered into the living room, as simple and neat as the exterior of the house. The furniture appeared worn but comfortable. Family photos lined the wall, including one of a smiling young couple with two small boys. The father in that photo had to be the Redekers' son, since he looked exactly like the woman who'd answered the door.

In the corner was a shrine-like exhibit that included a carved mahogany eagle on a pedestal. Beside it was a photo Marleigh recognized as her interview subject, probably taken years ago when she was first commissioned. Wearing Dress Blues with a white cap, she stared sternly at the camera with a glower of determination. Mounted on the wall beneath the portrait was a glass case that displayed two medals, which Marleigh surmised from this distance to be the Bronze Star and Purple Heart. According to Clay, the latter was why the good captain was now back in Colfax—a medical discharge for injuries sustained in combat.

The front door opened behind her, this time to Captain Redeker herself, now standing on the porch. She was taller than average and sturdily built, and her dark hair was pulled through the back of a Red Sox cap. A faded orange Syracuse University T-shirt, its long sleeves pushed to the elbows, was tucked neatly into worn jeans.

There was an instantaneous vibe about her, a stereotype Marleigh made a conscious effort to resist. A woman could be physically imposing without being gay.

And that would be a real shame. She'd always been a sucker for a strong woman in uniform, and her imagination raced to fill such a vision with the features of Captain Redeker.

The captain's face was lit with uncommonly pale green eyes and the faintest hint of a nervous smile. "Sorry, didn't mean to sneak up on you. I was out back and didn't want to track through the house."

Marleigh looked down to see tan combat boots covered in freshly clipped grass. A war hero who mowed her parents' lawn… humility personified. "It's okay. I'm here from the *Messenger*. Is today still good for our interview, Captain?"

"Yeah, sure. Would it be okay if we did this out here on the porch? Mom'll kill me if I get her rug dirty."

Her voice was more animated than Marleigh had expected, given her reluctance over the phone to the interview. *Messenger* readers were sure to find her fascinating.

Mrs. Redeker reappeared. "I have to go pick up some zippers and thread, Suzann. Don't forget your dad's grilling hamburgers for dinner. The Hammericks are coming over."

That had to be the mayor, Marleigh thought, since Hammerick wasn't a common surname in Colfax. It was curious to think of the Redekers, obviously a working-class family, hobnobbing with the town's power center.

The captain waited gallantly for Marleigh to choose the rocker before spreading herself in the center of the swing. With a tap of her foot, she started the gentle pendulum.

"I should properly introduce myself. My name's Marleigh Anderhall." She handed over a business card and placed her recorder on a side table between them. "If it's okay with you, I'd like to record this interview. This gadget's a whole lot better at taking notes than I am."

"Fine by me. Just don't ask me to sing."

She was instantly charmed by the hangdog smile—not that she needed more charming. Redeker's personal story had captivated her even before they met. "I feel like I ought to confess something, Captain. I've read your Bronze Star citation about a dozen times and I'm a little starstruck to meet you."

"Thank you…I guess," she mumbled sheepishly. "Like I said on the phone, I can't imagine why anybody would be interested in me. I'm a pretty boring person."

Surely she realized she'd done something extraordinary. "I spoke with someone yesterday at the town manager's office. He said they really had to twist your arm to get you to agree to be the grand marshal at the Fourth of July parade. Should I take that to mean you're modest? Or just shy?"

It wasn't the first question on Marleigh's list, but she needed to establish a conversational rapport to make the captain more forthcoming. Redeker had already explained that she couldn't say much on the record about her time in Afghanistan. Apparently most military actions were considered classified.

"I don't know that I'm either one," she answered with a shrug. "Some people might think what I did was a big deal, but it was just my job. Same as any other Marine. It's what we're trained to do."

"And right there—that's what makes it interesting. A woman who grew up right here in Colfax wins a Bronze Star, and we think she ought to lead the celebration on the most patriotic day of the year. But you're going to tell us why valor like yours is just another day at the office for the Marine Corps. Sound right to you, Captain?"

She finally grinned. "Call me Zann. I'm a civilian now. Or I will be if I can get a few more years in without being called back up. Not even a medical retirement gets you out of the reserves."

Zann. A stronger sounding name than Suzann, perhaps chosen by a girl who resisted frilly things.

"A civilian. How does that feel?"

"It's definitely going to take some getting used to. Yesterday I almost saluted the mailman."

Marleigh chuckled and leafed through a small stack of clippings, handing her the oldest one. "Here's something kind of interesting...turns out I've written about you before. I first came to work at the *Messenger* twelve years ago as a college intern. One of my assignments was to write blurbs about all the high school seniors who got scholarships. You were headed to Syracuse with the ROTC."

Zann smiled faintly as she studied it. "I remember this. Mom and Dad bought up about twenty copies of the paper and sent them to everyone they ever knew. You'd have thought I cured cancer or something."

"That's what proud parents do." There was a second article from four years later, a column about Colfax families with a military connection. Fresh out of college, Zann had joined the Marines as a second lieutenant. "I came across this one too, but it's not one of mine. Volunteering during wartime...even more impressive than a scholarship, if you ask me."

The smile dimmed as she silently scanned the words. "That was the deal I made when I accepted the scholarship."

Marleigh went on, "A lot of people were against the war but they respected the people who sacrificed by putting on the uniform and going into harm's way."

"Yeah, that was good while it lasted. Hard to sustain the support though when it drags out so long."

The reporter in Marleigh wanted to pursue that remark, but her assignment was to write a feel-good piece to celebrate a heroic soldier coming home, not a takedown of politicians or protesters. Opening a can of worms could derail her interview, perhaps causing her subject to clam up.

"So what was it that drew you to the Marine Corps instead of one of the other branches?"

Zann shifted and draped an arm on the back of the swing, a surprisingly relaxed posture for someone who'd been so reluctant to talk. "To be honest, ever since 9/11 I felt like busting some heads, and the Marines…they're all gung-ho, you know? The toughest, the first to get to where the trouble is. I guess the short answer is I wanted to be in the middle of the action. I thought my best shot was with the Marine Corps. Plus it's like a family. I'm sure you've heard that saying—once a Marine, always a Marine."

Knowing the recorder would capture their words, Marleigh was free to focus on her subject and her unusual combination of features—a strong, intimidating physique that was feminized by soft eyes, rounded lips and smooth-looking skin. The sharp jawline hardened her face somewhat, and her husky voice suggested she didn't suffer fools. It wasn't hard to imagine soldiers jumping at her orders.

"But the official policy of the Pentagon was not to allow women in combat. Were you thinking they might change that for the War on Terror?"

Zann rolled her eyes. "You'd think—especially after enlistments dried up. I waited four years to get deployed and ended up doing three tours in Afghanistan."

"Three tours…that sounds like a lot. But at least you were lucky you weren't sent to Iraq. The local National Guard unit got deployed there. One of them works at my hair salon now. She said it was like going through the back door to hell."

"Iraq, Afghanistan. It didn't really matter to me. If I learned anything in the Marines, it was to shut up and do as I was told. That whole argument over Iraq was for you guys to figure out."

Marleigh picked up a hint of rebuke. "Sorry, I didn't mean… I'm sure what they did over there was important."

"No, I get it. Some people say we shouldn't have been there in the first place, but the guys I knew felt pretty good about what they accomplished over there. On a personal level, I mean."

"So what did you do all that time while you were waiting to get deployed?"

"Two years advanced officer training at Quantico, two years instructing urban tactics at Camp Lejeune. Then I lucked out and got picked for one of the FETs. Gave me a chance to put my knowledge to work."

Marleigh recognized the acronym, sounded out to rhyme with *vets*. "I read about those, the Female Engagement Teams. Team Lioness, I think they called it."

"Talk about making a difference...we really did. All the FETs were attached to regular combat units that went out on patrol. We were combat soldiers too. They just wouldn't call us that because of the Pentagon policy."

"Pretty absurd, right?"

"Guess that's one word for it. Our job was to change hearts and minds. A typical FET was six or eight female soldiers paired up with a couple of dozen infantry. We'd go into villages—all of us carrying a full pack and M16s just like regular infantry—but our main mission was to talk to the women. The wives and daughters and mothers...see, they weren't comfortable around male soldiers. Just talking to a man could be humiliating for a Muslim woman. Imagine how they felt being patted down by one. They got so they'd hide from the patrol units, but we could see them sneaking around. It made everybody tense, trigger happy. We turned all that around by engaging with them... asking about their families, giving toys and candy to their kids. When you show people you care about them, that you respect their customs, they'll help you. They didn't want their kids getting blown up or going off to join the radicals. So they'd help us and tell us things we needed to know, like who was working with the Taliban, or what time a truck came through the village and how many men were on it. They knew we were there to keep them safe."

It was then she realized Zann had been waving her right hand as she talked, while the left lay still in her lap. Lifeless. Was that the reason for her Purple Heart? For leaving the Marines? "It sounds like dangerous work."

"Like I said, it was a job. The danger—being aware of it, focusing on it—that's what kept you alive."

* * *

The lingering gaze at her lap was subtle but certain. Marleigh Anderhall had noticed the weakened appendage hanging almost uselessly from her shoulder.

"I can tell you want to ask about my injury," she said evenly, resisting the urge to chuckle at Marleigh's blush, her second of the afternoon after the scornful remark about soldiers getting deployed to Iraq instead of Afghanistan. "Go ahead, I don't mind."

Marleigh was charming with a good mix of friendliness and professionalism. And attractive too, she admitted. Especially the brown eyes that smiled so much. It was tempting to read more into their connection, to entertain a certain vibe that they also were speaking to one another through a more personal undercurrent. Or maybe she was so flattered by Marleigh's respect and admiration that she mistook it for interest.

"Okay then…you were awarded a Purple Heart. Was that because of your arm?"

"I took a bullet here," she answered, drawing an imaginary line just above her left elbow, which was covered by her sleeve. "Right through the radial nerve, which it turns out is how you bend your elbow and wrist. I don't have a whole lot of strength in my hand but I'm still working on it."

"I'm guessing you planned on a career in the Marine Corps. How did you feel about being discharged?"

"Separated is what they call it…means exactly what it says," she added dismally. It was as if a wall had been dropped between her old life and where she was now. "They're there and I'm here. I wasn't happy about it if that's what you're asking. But I went through all the assessments fair and square—it was pretty clear I wasn't up to the job anymore. You can't take a gimpy arm onto the battlefield when you're responsible for other soldiers in your team. I would have been the weak link." She'd practiced those words in her head at the Naval Hospital at Camp Lejeune once she'd gotten word she was being recommended for medical retirement. The verdict didn't change just because she didn't want it to be true.

"So it was hard to accept."

"Most days I realize I'm damn lucky to be alive. I was wearing a tactical vest with ceramic plates. That's something you put on every time you leave camp, even if it's just to fetch a ball that gets thrown over the fence. It protects your major organs, which is the difference between life and death if somebody's shooting at you close-range with a semiautomatic rifle."

"The commendation says you were ambushed. That must have been terrifying. It scared me just to read about it. You were on patrol in the Helmand Province?"

She nodded. "What they put in the commendation...that's pretty much all I'm allowed to say about it. The particulars are still classified. Probably will be until fifty years after all of us are dead."

Marleigh wagged her pencil by her cheek the way Groucho did his cigar. "Well now, that's a problem, Captain Redeker... Zann. Because if I can't write about your wartime heroics, I'm going to have to write about *you*. And something tells me you don't like to talk about yourself much."

Zann chuckled. "You could end up with a very short article."

"Maybe...maybe not. How about you tell me what you're looking for out of life now that you've come home to Colfax?"

"You *would* have to start off with a hard question."

"What makes it so hard?" Marleigh narrowed her eyes and leaned forward, as if she thought the answer would be a whispered secret.

Which in some ways, it was. Zann hadn't discussed with anyone, not even her parents, her reservations about coming back to her hometown for good. She'd changed so much in the time she'd been gone, not only as a Marine but as a woman. In her mind, Colfax was only a stopover, a place to recover from her injury and buy some time to figure out what to do next. She doubted seriously the town could offer what she needed to feel at home.

CHAPTER THREE

Colfax Union High School was a sight for sore eyes, as it marked the end of the parade route and with it the end of Zann's ridiculous ride atop the backseat of a convertible. Her arm was tired from waving, her face permanently frozen in a plastic smile.

A parking attendant guided them to a stop amid a throng of parade participants who seemed as happy as she that the event was over. En masse, they peeled out of their outer layers of red, white and blue to reveal shorts and T-shirts appropriate for the summer heat.

That wasn't an option for Zann. She'd worn her Dress Blues for the occasion and couldn't wait to get home so she could change. Sweat poured down her back, causing the starched khaki shirt to stick to her skin and the pants to chafe her thighs. The black dress coat was hotter than body armor in Kandahar.

"Captain Redeker!" The exuberant voice belonged to Malcolm Shively, Colfax's town manager. A penguin-shaped, balding man in his mid-fifties, he wore a short-sleeved white shirt with a bowtie and suspenders. "Great job, Captain. It was a real honor to have you leading the parade this year. You did us all proud."

"I was happy to do it, sir," she lied. Halfway through the parade, it occurred to her that Shively's approval might come in handy if she applied for work with the town's police department.

"That was quite a story about you in the paper. The whole town's talking about it. You really took out four Taliban? All by yourself?"

"Yes, sir."

Marleigh's feature had included information from her commendation, but true to her word, none of the details of the incident. Instead she'd somehow coaxed Zann into talking about how her training had kicked in to produce an automatic response with no time for fear or panic.

It was fascinating to see her words woven into someone else's narrative. She'd managed to sound thoughtful and compassionate in her acknowledgment of having made several orphans and widows that day. The article ended with how she hoped to transition from military life to finding a worthwhile second career.

"And you're coming to the picnic, right?" Shively's invitation jolted her back to the moment. "We have a booth set up. It would be wonderful if you could sit behind a table, shake some hands maybe."

"Of course, sir." There wasn't anything she'd like less than sitting under a sweltering tent in the middle of a football field talking with strangers.

"Now you stop with that 'sir' business. You're home now, soldier." He pumped her hand with enthusiasm. "I'll let Connie know you'll be setting up at the booth."

As he toddled away, Zann tugged at her collar to get some air inside her coat. She could stand a couple more hours of feeling like a burrito if it helped with her job prospects.

* * *

With a bottled beer in each hand, Marleigh craned her neck in search of Bridget, who'd stood in another line for their hot dogs.

"Marleigh! Over here." Bridget Snyder, ten years younger at twenty-four, waved from the high school's back steps, a perch in the blazing sun. As cute and shapely as a coed, she wore cut-off denims and a clinging pink tank top with matching pink flip-flops. "Sorry, the only shade is over there by the building. Maxine Hurstburger's over there, and I *do not* want to hear another word about how awful it was we put her grandson's mug shot in the paper just for cooking meth."

"This'll do. I only want to sit long enough to eat. What did you put on them?"

"Just mustard. The relish looked like puked-up bird food."

Marleigh groaned. "Thanks so much for that visual."

"My pleasure. People always said I had a real way with words. Too bad Clay won't let me use any of them at work."

"Yeah, that AP style is so unimaginative," she replied drolly. In fact, Clay had spoken confidentially of letting Bridget go after only her first year on staff, but Marleigh had convinced him they needed someone at an entry level salary who would cover mundane events without complaining and grow as a writer as she gained more experience. All true, but the main reason she'd stood up for her underling was because she was the only other female reporter in the newsroom. If Bridget got canned, Marleigh would find herself back to covering social clubs, schools, craft fairs and the like—topics Clay would never dream of assigning to one of the men.

"There's Christopher." She pointed across the field to their compatriot, the summer intern who'd been tasked with collecting quotes from fair-goers while a local freelance photographer tagged along to document the festivities. "Remember having to do that when you were an intern?"

"Ugh. Clay gave me all the crap jobs on the weekend." Her mouth twisted and she visibly shuddered. "Always making me get photos and quotes so everybody would buy a paper to see if their name was in it."

It was a reliable trick for boosting sales, and it brought to mind Zann Redeker's remark about her mother purchasing multiple copies of her scholarship announcement to send to friends and family.

"Say, Bridget…what did you think of the grand marshal, that Marine I interviewed last week?" Zann had looked positively drool-worthy in her Dress Blues as her convertible passed. Unfortunately, the high school band had chosen that moment to strike up "Yankee Doddle Dandy," drowning out attempts to get her attention.

Bridget daintily licked mustard from her fingers. "My sister used to date her little brother. Payton Redeker, serious stud."

"He's married now. Two boys."

"I know. That was funny what she said about how they played army when they were kids and he always let her be the sergeant."

"You read my profile?"

"Of course. I read everything you write. Don't you read my stuff?"

Blindsided by the question, Marleigh felt the heat rush to her face. "Uh…not all of it. As much as I can though."

Bridget smacked her arm. "Get outta here! I'm your best friend. You're supposed to at least read my stuff. Every last boring word of it."

They were interrupted by the shrill ring of Bridget's phone.

"Shit, that's Rocky. I was supposed to be home an hour ago." She flipped the top and answered sweetly, "Hey, babe."

Marleigh tried not to listen, knowing it would only rile her to hear Bridget placate her boyfriend's childish tantrum. Why a woman who was so outgoing and friendly would hook up with a controlling SOB like Rocky Goodson was beyond her. The guy micromanaged her social life—checking her phone and private email account—and always insisted she come straight home from work every day. The only reason he tolerated Marleigh at all was because he knew she was gay and wouldn't take Bridget out cruising for guys.

"You want the rest of this?" Bridget asked, offering half a bottle of beer. "I need to get home."

"Pitch it. One's enough for me. I'll see you Monday."

Marleigh polished off her own beer and contemplated calling it a day. But then a crisp figure in uniform strode across the field and entered one of the exhibitor booths—Captain Zann Redeker. Smart, courageous, dashing. And for Marleigh, the sort of woman who made her want to go home and make sweet love to herself.

Since the captain had been kind enough to grant her an interview, the least she could do was say hello.

* * *

Sandy Cruder was several pounds heavier than she'd been in high school, but still had her double dimples and a mass of carefree blond curls that gave her an approachable air. Though she'd once been the object of a minor crush for Zann, there was no inkling of that today. Still, it was nice to see her and meet her six-year-old son.

The boy scowled as he looked Zann up and down. "That's a man's uniform. Girls are supposed to wear dresses."

Sandy's freckles ran together in a blush and she covered her mouth with horror.

Zann dismissed it with a wink. "You know, a little boy in Afghanistan once said the same thing to me. Except I was wearing camouflage that day...even on my helmet. But what surprised him most wasn't my uniform. It was my rifle."

"You had a rifle?"

She squatted so they were eye to eye. "You bet I did. All Marines carry rifles."

"Where is it?"

"Well, I don't need it here in Colfax. But I always take it when I go out on patrol."

As the boy chattered about his plans to join the air force someday, Zann caught sight of another familiar face.

Marleigh Anderhall, flushed from the heat, waved a hello from the sunny entrance to the canopy. She was dressed in shorts and a scoop-necked T-shirt. Wisps of hair peeked out from beneath a white cap, strawberry blond in the sun. "Good afternoon, Captain Zann."

Zann instinctively drew herself up and thrust her shoulders back, surprised at how glad she was to see Marleigh again.

"Sorry, I couldn't resist calling you that…seeing as how you don't look much like a civilian right now."

"It's just for today. Totally ceremonial." She said a polite goodbye to Sandy and her son and stepped outside the shade of the tent. "With any luck, this'll be my last appearance in uniform for the foreseeable future."

"Too bad. Looks good on you. In fact, I think it makes you look kind of…I shouldn't say."

Zann blocked her turn by stepping in front. "Oh, no. You can't start a sentence like that and not finish it. I look kind of what?"

Marleigh's mischievous look gave way to a grin. "Kind of amazing…but then I have a thing for women in uniform."

"Is that a fact?" Now giddy with interest, she congratulated herself on her initial instinct about Marleigh. "*Do* say yes, Miss Anderhall."

"Yes, it's a fact."

With mock seriousness, Zann nodded and asked, "And this uniform fetish of yours…is it perhaps something you'd like to discuss further? Assuming of course you're free to fraternize. I wouldn't want to be accused of conduct unbecoming. Officer's code and all."

"I think I could make myself available." Despite her tentative speech, Marleigh's gaze was bold and rakish. "But you look a little busy right now."

"I won't be busy this weekend. If I had your phone number, I could call you later about potential fraternization maneuvers."

"You make it sound so sexy." As Zann patted her pockets for a pen, Marleigh produced a business card. "My cell phone is here. Should I bring my notebook, Captain…or will our next chat be off the record?"

There was something deeply erotic about the way she'd uttered the salutation. "Why don't we keep this one classified?"

CHAPTER FOUR

Until this moment in Chief Otis Maubry's office, Zann hadn't realized how much she wanted this job. Police work not only suited her particular skill set, it also appealed to the same core values of discipline and public service that had driven her to join the military. She'd love a job where she got to help people.

The chief liked hiring veterans, he said, ticking off on his fingers the officers at the Colfax Police Department who had served. "There's Joey Crisp, Pete Nelson...and come to think of it, Eileen Edwards was in the Guard unit that went to *Eye-rack*."

Eee-rock. She resisted the impulse to set him straight on the proper pronunciation, as she'd done repeatedly with soldiers under her command. Was he being ignorant or deliberately disrespectful? Marines weren't allowed to be either, but Maubry wasn't a soldier bound to an honor code and he certainly wasn't someone she ought to correct.

After her epiphany at the parade, she'd gone home and downloaded an employment application for the Town of Colfax, meticulously filled it out and hand-delivered it the next morning. Ham had pulled some strings to get her an interview right away. If her skills weren't enough, her experience as team commander should have gotten her hired on the spot. So why was Maubry so obviously unimpressed?

"This injury of yours…is it permanent?"

That was a clue.

"Most likely not, sir. I've kept up my physical therapy and my strength improves a little more every day." When she first sat down in the chair across from his desk, she'd been careful to position both hands in her lap so there wouldn't be any overt sign of immobility. "To be honest I don't know if I'll get to a hundred percent, but I'm confident I'll be able to overcome any deficiencies."

"So could you fire a gun if you had to? Or wrestle a suspect to the ground and get him in handcuffs?"

"Chief, I understand your hesitation, but I wouldn't be here if I didn't think I could do the job." There was a fine line between self-confidence and bluster. What would it take to convince him? "Most Marines I know can do more with one hand than a lot of people can do with two. You give me this chance and I'll prove it."

Clearly skeptical he studied her application again, this time crinkling his nose. "I see you listed our mayor as a reference."

That had seemed like a good idea at the time. She hadn't considered the possibility that the chief might have voted for Ham's opponent. "He and my father are close friends. We all go to the Episcopal church."

After a long silence Maubry squeaked back in his chair and crossed his hands over a bulging belly. "Truth is I don't have any openings right now for patrol officers. And I gotta be honest here, Captain Redeker, if I were to have one, well…I've already got a file drawer full of applicants looking to transfer from other jurisdictions. Sheriff's deputies, state troopers. These are all highly-qualified people with hands-on experience doing this exact kind of job."

It didn't take a genius to know what just happened. He could have told her right away that there weren't any openings, or even had his secretary do it over the phone. Instead he'd granted her a courtesy interview solely because of her relationship with Ham. While that might have been politically prudent for him, it had wasted her time.

He went on, "Now there's a vacancy in the evidence room but it's only part-time. Couple of hours every morning…ten bucks an hour. That's where we catalog what comes in and goes out. Drugs, weapons. Might be some answering phones when things get busy."

In other words, the equivalent of a clerk. A quiet voice in her head said it was perfectly respectable work—her own father had started in the file room at the clerk of courts—and she could prove herself. The louder voice however was howling with insult.

"Not quite what I'm looking for, but thanks for your time."

Walking back to her car, it occurred to her that she'd suffered more rejection in the last two months alone than in all the rest of her life. Her forced separation from the Marine Corps felt like a betrayal. She'd recognized the same self-pity the moment Maubry had deemed her unfit to do the job.

* * *

"Just coffee," Marleigh said, scooting into a diner booth. She barely had time for even that, with the school board meeting in forty minutes to unveil their new bathroom policy for transgender students. It was sure to be a free-for-all and she didn't want to miss a minute. This chat couldn't wait though, because it bugged her to pieces to feel like she was sneaking around.

A dark green Dodge Charger slowed and turned into the parking lot, coming to a stop just yards away from Marleigh's window seat. For a split second, the blue lights mounted across the top flashed a cheeky hello. Michelle Lisper exited the vehicle in her green and khaki uniform, ceremoniously donning the wide-brimmed campaign hat of the Vermont State Police.

Marleigh had always been hot for that uniform, a point "Troop" used to her advantage every chance she got. When they first met four years ago, Troop had boasted of a carousel of semi-steady girlfriends, periodically favoring one over another like a flavor of the month. Now she was down to only two, she said. Which probably meant three. The demands of the VSP took precedence over the expectations of a permanent relationship.

At first Marleigh had been lukewarm about getting involved with someone who wasn't interested in being exclusive. Why spin her wheels on a romance that was going nowhere? Then after a couple of dates she came to appreciate how liberating it was to go out with someone for fun without worrying about the long-term stakes. After all, there weren't that many single lesbians in Colfax, and if she was honest with herself, Troop wasn't someone she'd want to marry anyway.

Tossing her hat into the booth, Troop asked, "To what do I owe this pleasure?"

"What, a girl needs a reason to ask you to lunch?"

"Come on, Marleigh. You know better than to bullshit a bullshitter. You call me at lunchtime, I figure you're looking for the inside scoop on the Conover investigation." She leaned across the table and lowered her voice. "You didn't hear this from me but his blood work came back a two-point-one. That's almost three times the legal limit. Mark my word, somebody's going to to jail."

Quite the juicy tidbit on their state assemblyman, but not at all the reason for her invitation. Still, it was the most newsworthy tip she'd gotten all week and she couldn't ignore her professional duty to ask questions. "And the woman who was with him?"

"Cynthia McIntosh…she's about half his age and works at the Capitol. And that's absolutely all I know about it." She waved their waitress over. "Bacon cheeseburger, fries, Pepsi. And don't bring me that diet crap."

Marleigh's mouth watered. "It's not fair you get to eat all that junk and never gain an ounce."

"Because my high-intensity circuit training burns more than your Pilates." She helped herself to a sip of Marleigh's coffee. "What'd you order? Let me guess. Cottage cheese and carrots."

"Actually I'm just having coffee. I have to be at the—"

"What, you invite me to lunch and don't even eat? Next you'll be telling me you aren't picking up the tab either."

Exasperated, Marleigh rummaged through her bag for her wallet.

"I was kidding! What's so important it couldn't wait till next weekend?"

"About that…I'm afraid I have to cancel."

"Jeez," Troop whined dramatically. "I can't go to this wedding by myself. Last time Gran was so desperate to marry me off, she tried to fix me up with my own cousin." She snorted with mock indignation as the waitress delivered her fries. "So what's up with you next weekend? You have to work or something?"

"No, but I have a feeling something else is going to come up."

"You have a feeling. What's that, some kind of psychic gift?"

It was tempting to carry on with their playful tone, but Marleigh didn't want to minimize the importance of what she needed to say—that she genuinely felt she was on the verge of a significant relationship. "I met somebody and our first date is tomorrow."

Troop paused just long enough for Marleigh to note the earnest wrinkle in her brow. "What's that got to do with next weekend? You renting a U-Haul?"

"Very funny. No, but this one's got a different vibe to it. I want to focus on her without any complications. It might turn into something."

"Fine, but I don't see what that's got to do with us."

"That's the point—it doesn't. It has to do with me." It crossed her mind that Troop understood her perfectly but was being deliberately obtuse. "Why are you making such big deal out of this? We've both dated other people. You see Renate practically every week."

"Yes, but I don't let her come between you and me. All you have is one date. You don't even know if you're going to like her and already you're bailing on me for next weekend. How come you're so serious all of a sudden?"

She decided to let that be a rhetorical question. It was true that Troop had only seen her lighter side, since Marleigh could never be serious about someone with a philosophical aversion to monogamy.

"Is it anybody I know?"

"That depends. Did you happen to catch my story last week about the Marine who got wounded in Afghanistan? She won the Bronze Star for valor, but then they made her retire on account of her injury. She came back to town last month. Malcolm Shively found out about her medal and made her grand marshal at the Fourth of July parade."

"A woman winning the Bronze Star? Are you fucking kidding me? How'd I miss that?"

For some reason Marleigh thought of how Bridget had bristled upon learning Marleigh didn't read her work. It shouldn't have been surprising that Troop didn't read hers.

"So what is it about her? I mean other than the obvious. I always said you liked me better in uniform than naked."

There was more truth to that than she wanted to admit.

"I don't know, it's just a feeling. What she did over there... she's a real honest-to-God hero. She took out four Taliban who were getting ready to attack the Marine base. And she did it all after getting shot." As Zann had done, she made a slicing motion across her arm. "Bullets cut the nerve here and now her arm doesn't work right. So she's out of the Marines and back in Colfax...for good, I hope."

"You always did have kind of a thing for hero-worship," Troop declared, picking at her fries.

"Yeah, I know. I even confessed that I was a little starstruck when I met her. But then I got to know a lot more about her during the interview, like why she enlisted and how she felt about some of the things they asked her to do as a soldier. I thought she was...I guess the word's noble. I saw her again after the parade and got the impression she was flirting with me, so I flirted back."

"And now it's the real deal, huh?"

"You think I'm stupid."

Troop laughed. "I know you're not stupid. But you've definitely got a fetish for the whole 'knight in shining armor' thing. Admit it—your favorite thing about me is the whole state trooper business. I wouldn't want to see you fall in love with an idea and have the real thing turn out to be something completely different."

"Come on, give me more credit than that. I'm not a ten-year-old reading princess books." Her voice took on an edge as a stew of resentment boiled over. She'd been complicit in her own empty future by convincing herself that having Troop as a part-time girlfriend was better than no girlfriend at all. It wasn't, not when what she really needed was a partner. "Can you honestly blame me for wanting something better out of life? All we've done is burn time. Now I'm thirty-four years old and have practically nothing to show for it."

"Whoa! You're totally misreading what I said. I just don't want to see you disappointed. You should do whatever you think will make you happy." She took Marleigh's hand, a gesture that bolstered her sincerity. "All I'm saying is if it doesn't work out, I'll still be around."

Except Marleigh wouldn't be coming back, no matter what happened with Zann Redeker. She'd settled too long for too little.

CHAPTER FIVE

At the ding announcing a new email, Zann scrambled across the bedroom to her laptop. An ad for car insurance, exclusive rates for veterans. She'd gotten dozens of come-ons since her separation was finalized, from which she deduced that her name and email address had been sold to a marketing company for veterans.

She was watching for a response to the application she'd sent electronically the night before, even just a confirmation it had been received. Cerberus was a private contractor that provided security for corporations doing business in the world's hotspots. Their ads were all over the Internet on sites aimed at veterans. They needed scores of ex-soldiers with expertise like hers, and officers especially were encouraged to apply for management positions. Afghanistan, Iraq, Libya…but as a team manager she wouldn't be back on the front lines toting a rifle.

Cerberus looked like a good fit on paper, but she admittedly had reservations about the company's culture. One of her fellow Marines had called them a bunch of cowboys, guys who were itching for an excuse to act aggressively but unbound by the military's ethics and rules of engagement. Their zeal and lack of discipline resulted too often in unnecessary civilian casualties, including some for which the international courts had found them culpable. Joining such a company meant owning the worst of its blunders.

On the other hand, it was a chance to impose her own values, to bring about a better corporate culture from the inside out. An influx of Marines was bound to elevate both standards and judgment.

Sitting on the edge of her bed, she yanked the laces of her new hiking boots to secure the instep. Lightweight and vented, they barely topped her ankle and felt flimsy compared to the rugged ones she'd worn almost daily for the last eight years. Yet another aspect of civilian life she'd have to get used to—at least for now. Cerberus could change all that.

To break the boots in, she'd worn them the day before on a solitary hike through Wright Park north of Middlebury, where she'd happened upon the ideal site for her planned picnic with Marleigh. Not only quiet and scenic, but also somewhat off the beaten path. A good place for them to get to know each other.

Nearly all of her hiking gear was new. The backpack, the water bottle, the poncho in case of rain. Her USMC duffel bag under the bed held the equivalent pieces in camouflage, all purchased from the PX at Camp Lejeune. They were far superior in quality to these, but she'd decided against unpacking them. Vermont wasn't Afghanistan and she didn't want to look like one of those survivalist kooks.

Now standing before the mirror, she felt like a kid on the first day of school. Her shirt and cargo shorts were the latest in breathable microfiber. She hadn't wanted Marleigh to think her a slob. Instead she'd think her a dork.

In the kitchen, she hurriedly scanned the pantry shelves for ideas. The clock was ticking on her promise to pick up Marleigh at ten. "Do we have any peanut butter?"

"Your mother was right." Her father chuckled over his coffee at the kitchen table and yelled through the window to the backyard, "Leeann, you need to get in here and help your daughter get ready for her date."

"Come on, Pops. I've been dating since seventh grade. You'd think I could handle a hike and a picnic."

Her mother stopped in the mudroom to tug off her gardening gloves and dirty shoes. "I've already fixed your lunch, honey. It's in the refrigerator. Turkey and salami, and some of that smoky cheese you like. With grapes and two kinds of crackers. All boxed up and ready to go."

"Jeez, this is Wright Park we're talking about, not the hills of Italy. What's wrong with a peanut butter sandwich?" Nonetheless, she wrapped her mom in an appreciative hug. Both of her parents were excited about her date, especially since all she'd done since coming home was mope around the house. They'd be mortified to know she was looking into a job with Cerberus. "You know this is only a hike, right? Don't go sending out wedding invitations."

"I met her when she came to do the interview. You two make a fine-looking couple. Oh, and your father asked around. She's not a serial killer or anything."

Zann whirled on her dad and smacked his shoulder. "I can't believe this shit. You're actually screening my dates."

He threw up his hands with exaggerated innocence. "Turns out Ham knows her boss, Clay Teele. He said she was a damn good reporter."

"All right then. We'll sit down and pick out the china when I get back." Zann was more excited than she was willing to admit. It was her first date in nearly three years, a fact she didn't want to overthink, since it would fill her head with memories of Whitney Laird.

* * *

Hiking, biking, Pilates and weights. Marleigh prided herself on being fit. She didn't need Zann's help to cross the stream but she wasn't about to refuse the offered hand, especially since it was the one she'd injured. It was hard to resist that kind of gallantry. For today only she'd surrender her Feminist Card.

"I found this place the other day," Zann said, still holding her hand as she led the way through the woods. They reached a small clearing where a sprawling maple tree shaded a well-worn picnic table overlooking a bend of Otter Creek. She dropped her pack on the table and gestured toward the bench.

Marleigh watched with curiosity when Zann eased her left elbow onto the table as she sat. In the car, she'd steered mostly with her right hand while resting her left on the bottom of the wheel, as if to disguise its lack of utility.

"Gorgeous, isn't it?" Zann asked.

"Sweet. I bet you missed this overseas."

"The Helmand Province had its own kind of beauty. Mountain peaks, lakes, big green valleys." She chuckled. "Of course, a lot of those valleys were filled with opium."

"Some of which, believe it or not, makes it all the way here to Vermont. Apparently, while you were off fighting the War on Terror, our state became the heroin capital of the country. Along with meth, coke and prescription pills."

"My mom complains about that. She said the kids trade pills around like candy." She spun on the bench and used her good arm to pull a rectangular container from her backpack, a neat lunch of meat, cheese and fruit. "She packed this for us, by the way. I would have made peanut butter."

"I like peanut butter as much as the next person but cheers to your mom." Marleigh tapped her water bottle to Zann's and helped herself to a cracker. "I did a six-part series for the paper last year on drugs in Vermont. It's definitely an epidemic." As they ate, she shared highlights from interviews with dealers behind bars and recovering addicts, many of whom had started with prescription pills and jumped to heroin because it was cheaper and easier to get. "The drug of choice if you have money is cocaine. You wouldn't believe how much of it runs through here on its way to boardrooms and trendy nightclubs in Canada."

"I read some of your stories. Not like I'm an online stalker or anything, but I Googled you and there was loads of stuff. You write about everything."

"That's how it is at a small-town paper. Hardly anything big ever happens so we have to make hay out of everyday events, play it all like it's the Second Coming. Yesterday, I actually filed a story about this guy they caught stealing lightbulbs off people's front porches on Porter Field Road. How's that for exciting?"

"Hunh, I guess that's why it's big news when a soldier comes home."

"Are you kidding, Zann? You're not just some ordinary soldier. What you did was phenomenal, a real-life macho video game. Do you have any idea how many guys sit on their couches in their underwear fantasizing about doing what you did? And—don't take this the wrong way but it's true—it's an even bigger deal because you're a woman. That makes it a 'man bites dog' story."

A grape Zann had been rolling between her thumb and forefinger escaped her grasp and bounced away. The ordinary act turned momentous when Marleigh realized she'd been doing it with her left hand, probably an exercise recommended by her physical therapist. Going forward, it would be difficult not to notice such endeavors—even minor ones—though she doubted Zann would appreciate her calling attention to it.

"Trust me Marleigh, most of those gamers don't have a clue what war's really like." Zann's voice took on a somber tone as she squinted and gazed off toward the creek. "It's not a hero fantasy. For seven months straight, all you can think about is getting everyone on your team home safe."

Marleigh still knew nothing more about the incident for which Zann was honored than what was published in the commendation. But one thing stood out—a soldier had died. "You lost somebody in your unit. I bet that hurt a lot."

"It did, it really did. Whitney Laird. There's not an hour that goes by that I don't think about it, that I don't wonder what would have happened if I'd gone in first. Or if I'd been two steps behind her instead of four. She was my gunny...my gunnery sergeant." She took a long pull on her water bottle, and with a faraway look, continued, "There were eight of us in the FET that day. We split up in teams of two and went into Dahaneh, this little village not far from our base camp. It was supposed to be a routine sweep, something we did two or three days a week."

The reporter in Marleigh wished she were recording so she could share the story with readers, but this was private, a privileged window into what she suspected were Zann's most protected memories.

"One of our regulars there was a woman named Baheera. She'd give us fresh-baked *noni*—that's what they call the Afghan flatbread—and we'd give her hard candy or chocolate so she could bribe her two boys to behave. Khaled and Gulwan… good kids, made me miss my nephews. They were always running in and out chasing each other." She almost smiled as she remembered aloud. "We suspected her husband Hamza was working with the Taliban but she never outright admitted it. I knew she didn't like whatever he did, that it scared her."

"Because of her kids, I bet."

She nodded. "So that day—you know you can't report any of this, right? I shouldn't even be telling you. It's supposed to be classified."

"I'm not working now, Zann. I'm here as your friend."

"Good, thanks." She inhaled deeply and shook her head as she blew it out. "So that day, we stopped at Baheera's house to check in. It was a small block building with two rooms, hardly any bigger than your average garage or tool shed. Whit went in first, calling out to the boys. I walked in behind her and the first thing I noticed was Baheera acting sort of funny. She kept glancing over at the other room with this terrified look on her face. I yelled at Whit to hold up but it was too late. Guns started going off inside and I…"

As she faltered, Marleigh began stroking the motionless hand that rested on the table. A part of her wanted to say it wasn't necessary to tell her more, but she was gripped to hear it all.

"You know what Marines are trained to do when a gun goes off? You go straight toward the shooter as hard as you can. Put your enemy on defense."

The commendation had spelled out her fearlessness in the face of danger. Still, Marleigh had trouble seeing how someone as calm and steady as Zann could erupt into an aggressive war machine.

"A guy came running at me out of the other room. It was Hamza…he was wild, just spraying bullets all over the place. Even shot his own wife in the leg. I can still see his gun like it was yesterday, one of those old AK74s the Russians left behind. The wooden stock was almost rotted and the barrel was all scratched up. A miracle it still worked. He must've got off…I don't know how many rounds. I remember thinking my vest plates were breaking up, that any second a bullet would get through." She rubbed her wounded arm absently, as though unaware of the gesture. "The whole time I was firing back and he finally dropped. But somebody in the other room was still shooting. I had no idea who was in there or how many."

Marleigh was terrified to think where this awful story might be going. Had Zann also killed the two boys?

"Anyway, by that time I couldn't hold my rifle steady because of my arm, so I grabbed my sidearm. Whit was down just inside the other door, blood all over her face. I couldn't see how bad it was but I knew she didn't have much time. I snuck up next to the doorway and heard this clicking sound. I knew what it was—whoever was in there was changing clips. So I charged in and popped everything that moved. The whole thing—from the time we walked in the house till it was over—lasted less than thirty seconds."

"So…four Taliban?"

Zann nodded. "Yeah, one of them was practically a kid, barely sixteen. Thank God Hamza's kids weren't in there with them."

Thank God indeed. "Where was the rest of your unit?"

"They came running, but it was all over by the time they got there. And Whit…it was too late for her. She took a bullet in the neck"—she gestured with her good hand—"and bled out before we could save her. I can see it like it was yesterday. It was the saddest day of my life."

They sat in silence for over a minute while Marleigh continued to stroke her hand. "I can't imagine how you deal with memories like that. Seeing somebody you know get killed right in front of you. Especially when they won't even let you talk about it."

"They let you talk about it, but only to other people inside the Corps. I've probably told that story a hundred times, what with all the official reports we had to do. Every time, I'd find myself hoping it would be the last."

"I'm sorry, Zann. I didn't mean to—"

"No, it's all right. For better or worse, it's a pretty big part of who I am now. If you're going to know me, you have to know that story too."

"Maybe so, but I'm not going to make you suffer through a bunch of painful memories for my sake. As far as I'm concerned, you can put all that crap in a box if you want to. Lock it up and throw away the key."

"That would be the logical thing to do but apparently I'm not logical." Looking away, Zann grimaced. "Would you believe I just applied for a job with a security contractor? If I get it, odds are they're going to send me back to a place like that."

"You've got to be kidding."

"It's an outfit called Cerberus. Mostly they work with construction companies that are trying to rebuild businesses and bombed-out infrastructure. They need security to go back and forth to the worksite, and then you have to make sure suicide bombers don't get in and blow the place up. And the hotels that cater to Americans are targets too so it's basically a twenty-four-seven job."

It was horrifying to think she could be sent back to such a place. And disappointing that she was considering it, since it meant she didn't feel the same spark as Marleigh. "I don't get it, Zann. Three tours in Afghanistan and now you want to go back? It's one thing to do it for your country, for the good of mankind. But risking your life so a bunch of billionaires can make more money? That doesn't strike me as who you are. You have nothing left to prove to anybody. Let someone else take those risks."

"Maybe it's not me," Zann said, tipping her head thoughtfully. "But the bottom line is I need a job and there's not much else I know how to do."

"Not true. You're obviously a natural-born leader. You can do whatever you want."

"Apparently not. I interviewed yesterday at the Colfax Police Department. The chief wanted to know how I was going to put somebody in handcuffs if I only had one good arm. Talk about a truth bomb."

"That's absurd. Otis Maubry hasn't seen his own feet in ten years, and he's saying you can't do the job because your hand's not perfect? You'd be the most qualified person on the force." Despite her usual enthusiasm for women in uniform, the idea of Zann joining the police force was surprisingly unsettling as well. Covering the crime beat, she'd witnessed firsthand the danger in answering domestic abuse calls, to say nothing of the violence from the growing drug trade. Last year the CPD had lost its first officer ever in the line of duty, a fifteen-year veteran shot in a raid on a meth lab. Just because Zann had proven herself in combat didn't mean she ought to put her life on the line every day. Her hero status was already set in stone. "There's got to be something else. You majored in…"

"Military science. Not exactly a demanding field if you can't serve in the armed forces. But at least it's a bachelor's degree, so I have a few possibilities. To this day my pop wishes he'd finished his degree. Thirty-six years with the Town of Colfax and he can't move up because he doesn't have that piece of paper."

"There you go. Go to work for the town. Friendly people, good values. If we're going to keep it that way, we need more people with integrity like yours."

Zann shrugged. "I guess. Doesn't sound very exciting."

"Exciting doesn't have to mean dangerous." She drew Zann's limp hand into her lap and intertwined their fingers. "Besides, there are lots better ways to get your thrills."

The response was a knowing smile.

Marleigh brought the hand to her cheek and stroked it softly, all the while holding Zann's flirtatious gaze. She planted a gentle kiss in the open palm. "Can you feel this?"

Zann answered by leaning in, her lips parted and her eyes closed.

The kiss wasn't aggressive, but it carried an air of command. At that moment Marleigh learned something about herself. It wasn't the uniform that thrilled her—it was the strength and determination one needed to wear it.

* * *

"Thirty more seconds and we might have been arrested," Marleigh said as they bounced over the rippled dirt road.

Zann laughed nervously, feeling her face grow hot with embarrassment. A couple with four rambunctious children had surprised them by the creek just as Marleigh guided a hand beneath her shirt. For a second, she'd slid back into her military mindset—hide, deflect, deny. The fact that she was no longer a Marine didn't mean she could have sex in a public park.

Turning toward town, she muttered, "You're the person my mother warned me about. Taking advantage of me, attacking my virtue."

"You keep telling yourself that, Captain. One of these days you might even believe it."

Amid all the doubts Zann harbored about being back in Colfax, Marleigh was a breath of fresh air. She was sweet without being slavish, with an unfettered smile and a carefree beauty. But what she found most seductive was Marleigh's deep reverence for her military service. How could she not be drawn to someone who made her feel so worthy?

"Speaking of your mother, tell her I said thanks for lunch. It's my turn now. You'll have to let me make you dinner."

There wasn't a doubt in her mind how dinner at Marleigh's house would end—a single kiss had already sent her passion soaring almost out of control. Behind closed doors there was nothing to hold them in check. Was it really fair to let things go that far when she wasn't even sure she'd stay in Colfax? Marleigh didn't seem like the kind of woman who had sex just for fun. She'd have expectations.

"Okay, this is awkward."

Zann suddenly realized she hadn't answered. "Sorry…I was thinking. I don't think I can make it. There's something else I have to do."

Marleigh's smile faded and she looked away. "Yeah, well…I didn't say when, now did I?"

Just like that Zann had ruined what had been a wonderful day with a woman whose company she genuinely enjoyed. "I'm sorry. Really…I feel like everything's up in the air right now. I don't want to be sending the wrong messages."

"Give me some credit, Zann. It's not my first rodeo. We had a good time, right?"

She nodded.

"So it's fine. If you want to have dinner, give me a call. And if you don't—*c'est la vie*. It was still a good day."

They rode in silence for the last few blocks, with Zann turning over in her head every possible reply. Overthinking had gotten her into this mess—it wasn't going to get her out. She pulled into the gravel driveway and turned off the engine. "Obviously I'm out of practice on the dating front."

"It's not that big a deal. I should have laughed it off like I do everything else."

"I would like very much to have dinner with you."

"Too bad, I've changed my mind." Her exaggerated pout gave way to a grin. "Kidding. Pick a night and let me know." Marleigh bussed her cheek so lightly it could hardly be called a kiss, then hopped out and walked away without looking back.

CHAPTER SIX

Clay Teele, his skinny tie knotted loosely to his chest, stormed from his office to stand with his hands on his hips. "Where's Snyder? It's almost nine o'clock."

Marleigh wondered the same thing but she and Bridget always covered for each other whenever Clay got in one of his irascible moods. His answer to corporate pressure for profits was to micromanage the time clocks of everyone on staff. "I think she's out getting quotes for the school board story. Freeman's been ducking her calls."

"I thought that was your story."

"I asked her to help," she lied. "Something I can do?"

He waved her off and turned to Fran, the paper's secretary, switchboard operator and customer service manager. Sweetening his tone—he knew better than to turn his wrath on Fran—he announced he was leaving for Rotary Club and would be back before lunch.

Another half hour passed before Bridget finally arrived looking unusually disheveled with her wavy blond hair cascading around her face. "Sorry I'm late. Did Clay say anything?"

"He noticed. I covered for you, said you were getting a quote from Freeman. Maybe you should call over there and get him to say something on the record about last week's school board meeting."

Bridget primly situated herself at her desk and removed her oversized sunglasses to reveal a butterfly bandage above her swollen and bruised brow.

"Oh, my God! What the hell happened to you?"

"A little accident in the kitchen. I bent over to pick up a cherry tomato before I stepped on it, and of course forgot that I'd left the cabinet open. I raised up and banged my head on the corner."

Even hearing about it caused Marleigh to shudder. "Did you have to get stitches?"

"Nah, it wasn't that bad. I put a little ice on it and a Band-Aid."

The dismissive clip of her voice—plus the fact that she'd deliberately avoided looking up—made Marleigh uneasy. She knew Rocky Goodson to be a controlling jerk sometimes, but not an abuser.

"Is there coffee?"

Marleigh followed her into the break room, determined to have her say even if Bridget ultimately chose to ignore her. "Look, I know it's none of my business but this is the second time you've come to work with a mark on your face. On your *face*, Bridget."

"Because I'm a klutz." As she reached into the cupboard for a mug, Marleigh grabbed her upper arm. "Ow!"

"Oh, does that hurt? Maybe it's because there's a freaking handprint on your arm. What did he do to you?"

Bridget's eyes filled with tears as she turned her arm over to examine the bruise. "Fine, if you must know we had a fight. But it was just as much my fault as his."

"Don't you dare say that, Bridget. Fighting's one thing— hitting's totally out of bounds. And so is yanking you so hard it leaves a bruise."

"He didn't mean to. It was all a mistake." She held up her left hand, which sported a small diamond solitaire in a silver setting. "See? This is why I was late. He was so sorry that he took me to Rothwell's first thing this morning to pick this out."

"Bridget, that's insane." If Rocky was this bad as her boyfriend, how much worse would he be as her husband? "You don't go marrying somebody after he knocks you around. There's no telling what he'll do next."

With a spiteful sneer, Bridget shot back, "You should talk. I'm not the one worshipping somebody whose claim to fame is killing people. It's morbid if you ask me."

Marleigh recoiled with disbelief, furious with herself for confiding in her about Zann. "You're comparing what she did to Rocky beating you up? For fuck's sake, Bridget! She was a combat soldier. The people she killed were trying to kill her. They'd just shot another American soldier right in front of her eyes. I can't believe you'd name a coward like Rocky Goodson in the same breath."

"Fuck...I'm so sorry. God, I can't believe something so shitty came out of my mouth...it's like I've been eating out of a goddamn toilet." Bridget slumped into a chair and buried her face in her hands. "If you don't forgive me right this fucking minute, I'm walking out of here into traffic."

It wasn't that simple. The vicious words had cut her to the quick.

"Please, Marleigh...I'll give you my lunch. There's a Chocolate Bomb from Mike's."

"Why would you say such a thing?" She realized from her conciliatory tone that she was on her way to forgiveness. "I don't like Zann because she's a badass. I like her because she's a hero. How many people do you know who'd have the courage to do what she did?"

"None. And you're right, Rocky's an asshole. But I told him this was it, that he'd better not ever lay another hand on me. He was really upset about it, said it made him so sick that he'll never do it again. So I'm giving him this one more chance."

Marleigh didn't trust him at all, but attacking him only served to make Bridget defend him that much more. "As long as you know that he only gets one more chance from me too.

I'll call the cops on his ass if you ever come in here looking like this again."

Back at her desk, she toyed with ideas of how somebody like Zann would handle news that a friend of hers was being roughed up by her boyfriend. Easy—Rocky would be eating through a straw. Perhaps it was a little morbid that she relished the thought.

* * *

"…and we're talking state-of-the-art gear, the best on the market. Cerberus pays for everything and you take it with you when you leave. Can't beat that." Gary Laughton, with his buzz cut and black polo shirt, spoke via Skype from a gray-walled office in Fairfax, Virginia. For the last half hour, he'd described the scope of work at Cerberus. Recipients of almost half a billion dollars in corporate security contracts, they were a top destination for former soldiers looking for high wages and guaranteed deployment.

Beneath her desk and out of sight, Zann squeezed a foam ball in her left hand. The simple repetitive exercise was meant to stimulate the synapses so her hand would learn again to grip spontaneously without a deliberate message from her brain.

She'd pored over all the info Gary had sent earlier in a digital file, paying special attention to the specs for Field Coordinator, an overseas job that entailed planning and supervision of security teams, mostly from the comfort of the corporate hotel. Cerberus sought former officers for those positions, especially those experienced in combat command.

"I'll be honest with you, Captain Redeker—"

They were interrupted by her cell phone, which she quickly muted. "Sorry about that."

"No problem. We've got twenty-nine different job sites right now. I could put you on a plane to any one of them tomorrow morning. That's how bad we need somebody with your skills and experience."

His enthusiasm was infectious, and he seemed to know all the buttons to push to evoke her nostalgia for life in the

Marines. He probably did this all day long, selling ex-soldiers on a different kind of military experience, one with the familiar camaraderie of a well-trained team plus all the perks of civilian life—luxury hotel rooms, first-class gear and six-figure pay. Why would anyone say no?

"I assume you looked at my PEB?" she asked. Before saying yes to anything, she had to know they were fully aware of the report from the Marine Corps Physical Evaluation Board. It would crush her to take on the second job of her dreams and have it snatched away again. "I'm still going through therapy but there's no guarantee I'll regain full function of my left hand."

"No worries, Zann. Field Co's an administrative job." He tapped his temple. "Cerberus wants what's up here."

"It all sounds great, Gary…but I don't think I'm quite ready yet to catch that morning flight. Can you give me a few days to think about it?" She'd have to talk it over with her folks and try to get them on board—for their sake. If they were convinced of her safety they'd be more supportive.

"If this were a high-pressure sales pitch, I'd be telling you not to wait too long. But we want the best teams we can get, and that means everybody has to be a hundred percent sure it's where they want to be. So take all the time you need. Next week, next month…hell, next year. We'll still be here."

She thanked him for the interview and signed off. It was a weight off her shoulders to finally feel there was a path for her future. To Marleigh's point, there was honor in working to keep people safe, no matter who got rich.

Marleigh…it was time for their dinner date. They'd decided to go out, since Marleigh got handed a late news assignment and didn't have time to cook.

"I'm going out with Marleigh," she called from the back door, biting her tongue to keep from adding that they shouldn't wait up.

Her mother appeared in the doorway. "Did you get that message from Malcolm Shively?"

"No, what?" She examined her cell phone and saw a new voice mail. Why would the town manager be calling? "Did he say what he wanted?"

"Just that he was going to try to reach you on your cell phone."

"*Captain Redeker, it's Malcolm Shively. I wanted to say thanks again for being our grand marshal last week. Chief Maubry said you stopped in a few days ago to see about a job at the CPD but he didn't have anything. He was impressed by you though and passed your application up the chain to see if we could find something. I can always find something for a bona fide war hero. So give my office a call in the morning and let's get this ball rolling.*"

She shook her head at the irony. It figured she'd go from having no prospects at all to having two. Except Shively's offer probably wasn't even an actual job, but a make-work position of no import meant to check off a quota for veterans or people with disabilities.

Cerberus was the real deal. They respected not only what she'd done, but what she still could do.

* * *

"Cerberus...isn't that the dog that guards the gates of hell?" Marleigh asked. It seemed an apt metaphor considering most of their jobs were in war zones. American efforts were constantly under threat from factions looking to destabilize governments and impede progress.

"Their logo is a three-headed beast with a spiked collar."

"Ooo, scary." She didn't bother to disguise her sarcasm. It was a terrible idea for Zann to take a job so dangerous. "Couldn't you just run away and join the circus like normal people?"

Their waitress interrupted to set a gargantuan pizza between them.

Marleigh topped off their beer mugs from an icy pitcher. "I know what you're thinking—if I really wanted to impress you, I should have taken you for steak and lobster. That's next time. This is the finest pizza you will ever eat."

"Mmm." With cheese dripping down her chin, Zann nodded her agreement. She'd folded a slice over so she could manage it with one hand. "How come you're so down on Cerberus? As much as you admire the military, I thought you'd like it. What gives?"

She had to be kidding. Marleigh's real motives couldn't be more obvious if she spread herself across the table. "Please tell me you're not that clueless, Captain Zann."

A brief flash of confusion was followed by wide eyes and a grin. "D'oh! You're flirting with me again."

"No I'm not. Unless that's what it takes. If I flirt, will you stay?"

"I might stay for this pizza."

Marleigh enjoyed Zann's playfulness but it bugged her how much it reminded her of Troop Lisper. More specifically, it reminded her of herself with Troop. Once again she was hedging, using humor to hide her attraction and keep her emotional distance. And she didn't like it.

"Zann, can I be serious here for a sec? You're a soldier, I'm a reporter. I love what I do but it's not enough by itself. I need other things in my life...namely people. *Special* people. What I'm asking is this—is it enough for you to just be a soldier?"

An eternity ticked by as she waited, long enough to think she might not like the answer.

"I've never been just a soldier. When you're an officer in the Marine Corps, that defines everything about you—the way you look, the way you act...even the way you think. It was my whole life, the one I'd dreamed of since I was a kid. So if you want to know the truth—yeah, that could have been enough. So every morning when I wake up it's like a punch to the gut when I remember that I don't get to be that person anymore."

"That's not what you said in the interview."

"You weren't there to hear my sob story, Marleigh. You came to write about a noble war hero who had it all together, someone who was proud to serve no matter what the sacrifice. Nobody wanted to hear me whine."

Marleigh remembered thinking at the time that Zann was putting up a brave front, that she couldn't possibly be as accepting of her fate as she'd let on. "So what does Cerberus get you? It doesn't make you a Marine again, not by a long shot.

I looked them up, Zann. The Iraqis claim they shot and killed three innocent civilians from a helicopter. And four of them gang-raped a sixteen-year-old in Libya."

Zann took a deep draw on her beer and wiped her mouth on the back of her sleeve. "Don't think I haven't thought about that. But maybe this is their chance for better leadership."

"Sure, but you aren't going to go in there and singlehandedly change a culture like that. There's probably a good reason a lot of those guys aren't in the US military anymore and it's not because they were wounded trying to save somebody."

It was obvious her words were having an impact, though she suspected it had less to do with Zann's own opinion of Cerberus than what others would think. Honor was important to her. She wouldn't do something to degrade her sense of self.

"Do you honestly think I could make the world a better place staying here and doing some lame bureaucrat job for the Town of Colfax? I bet Shively wasn't even being serious."

"I can tell you for a fact that he's serious. I've been covering local politics for twelve years. The whole reason Hammerick got elected in the first place was because people were fed up over all the cronyism at town hall. Contractors were low-balling bids because they knew their pals would okay cost overruns later. Hammerick brought in Shively to clean it up." As she'd done before, she rested a hand on top of Zann's, the injured one that she hoped to bring back to life. "Is it going to make the world a better place for you to stay here in Colfax? I don't know…but it would make *my* world a better place."

CHAPTER SEVEN

From the moment Marleigh invited her back to her place for "dessert," Zann knew exactly what was on the menu. But for now a downpour held them captive in the car a mere thirty feet from Marleigh's apartment on the ground floor of an old two-story house.

"What the hell, right? Don't be a wimp." Marleigh flung the door open and dashed through the rain to the flimsy shelter of an overhang above her back porch.

After a challenge like that, Zann had little choice but to follow. By the time she made it inside, she was soaked to the skin. "This was *so* not necessary. I had a perfectly good poncho under the backseat."

"Where's the fun in that?" She tousled Zann's dripping hair. "How about another beer, Captain?"

"I'm good." She lowered her eyes to Marleigh's chest, where her nipples strained against her wet shirt. "Sure you wouldn't rather have hot chocolate? Looks to me like you need to warm those puppies up a little."

"Oh, very funny. I was going to offer you a dry shirt but forget it." She disappeared around the corner.

Zann followed, discovering an apartment laid out like a nautilus—kitchen to living room to a pair of small bedrooms with a bathroom in between. In the first bedroom, where Marleigh had gone to change her shirt, she could see folded clothes stacked on a twin bed. "Who sleeps in that room?"

"Nobody. I don't even know why I put a bed in there."

"No family?"

"My folks moved to Arizona after Dad retired. We aren't all that close. Mother's a major hypochondriac and Dad just feeds her drama." Marleigh returned wearing a red plaid shirt with the sleeves rolled up. Her short wet hair was combed back, a look Zann found sexy. In her hand was a polo shirt with the *Messenger* logo on the pocket. "Here, this ought to fit. Clay ordered a bunch of them, but all he got were men's sizes."

"Thanks. You call her Mother? Sounds formal."

"Sometimes I tack on 'Superior' under my breath. She can be pretty self-righteous."

Zann slipped into the room and peeled out of her wet shirt, also leaving the door ajar. Her Marine Corps-issued sports bra was damp but not soaked so she left it on. She returned to find Marleigh lounging in the corner of a sectional sofa patting the space next to her. "I don't know if I should. Are you going to try to feel me up?"

"Probably."

"Okay then. I wasn't going to do it if it was just for show." Returning the impish banter was fun. She fell beside her on the sofa and draped her good arm around Marleigh's shoulders.

Marleigh took her other arm and guided it across her waist, holding it beneath her shirt against her skin. "When I was about twelve and started having feelings for girls, I had this damsel in distress fantasy where I'd get rescued by somebody like you. And then you'd fall in love with me. Weird, huh?"

No more fantastical than Zann's own musings in which she saw herself as the savior. "What did you need to be rescued from?"

"A psychiatrist would probably say it was Mother. I always ended up running away with whoever saved me."

"How about we not talk about your mother." Zann closed in for a kiss, and with a mammoth effort from the muscles in her shoulder, let her fingers wander upward, where she discovered Marleigh had shed her bra along with the wet shirt. Her skin was still cold from the dampness, a fact that brought her nipple to attention. "Nice."

Except from where she lay, there was little more she could do. Her fingers lacked the precision to attack the buttons, and if she shifted sides her left arm wouldn't hold her up.

Marleigh seemed to sense her dilemma and loosened her shirt, revealing sumptuous oval breasts, white against her tanned neck and chest. And pink pebbled peaks.

"God, you're gorgeous." She crushed Marleigh with a deep, heated kiss, shuddering as soft hands slid inside her waistband to clutch her hips. This part of her had been dormant too long.

* * *

Marleigh couldn't believe she'd all but confessed her love. Yet from the moment Zann had responded to her flirtations after the parade, she'd known this was a woman who could make her forget everyone else.

Zann's forehead wrinkled with the strain of sliding her left hand across Marleigh's stomach. "I might not be as good at this as I used to be."

"You're with me now. This time was always going to be different." With a heave, she urged Zann onto her back and straddled her waist. "I am of the opinion, Captain Zann, that we both have on far too many clothes."

She pushed the polo shirt over Zann's head and fell forward into a kiss, holding back just enough brain cells to determine if there was a clasp on her sports bra. There was, and when she felt the release, she pulled it away and sat up again to see Zann's firm breasts, rounded like the muscles that curled over her shoulders. *Mesmerizing.*

Before she could move to caress them, Zann yanked at her shirt, snapping the last button that held it closed. She shrugged free, consciously drawing her shoulders back to lift her breasts.

"God, you're gorgeous." Zann hissed with pleasure as she stroked one and squeezed its nipple.

Marleigh collapsed again, fusing their skin as she slid her forearms underneath Zann's back. This time she led their kiss, nuzzling with her cheek and concentrating on the hand that now massaged her hip. Her mind broke down the physical sensations—the texture of their tongues, the warm, purposeful melding of their feminine selves—all while dancing between her own desire and the certainty that Zann wanted her just as much.

Sliding one hand between them, she worked the fasteners on Zann's pants and raised herself as they were pushed away, along with a slim-fitting pair of ladies' boxer briefs. Before she had a chance to explore the naked skin, she felt the tug at her own shorts and hurriedly shook them to the floor.

Continuing their kiss, she caressed Zann with her body, centering her thoughts on the tingling friction caused by thighs that tightened and relaxed as they rocked together. The rhythm was a secret language all their own. With a subtle shift of her weight, she lowered her lips to feast on a nipple, its rubbery stiffness stabbing at her teeth. Such a gorgeous body, sleek and firm with womanly grace.

Zann arched upward, her mouth gaping as her head lolled back. "God, I want you."

Marleigh abandoned all pretense of control as she slid her hand through the slickness and massaged her core. Every surge was answered with a whimper or moan, until the sounds ran together in a cry of release.

* * *

The ceiling fan whipped cool air around the room. Zann hadn't noticed it the night before as they'd tangled atop the sweaty sheets. But then she might not have noticed a four-alarm fire. Three hours of lovemaking, wrestling for control with a woman who seemed bound and determined to make her forget there ever was anyone else. And to make her forget there was any part of her that was less than whole—Marleigh had taken her hand and held it inside her. *"Feel what you did to me."*

Except now she couldn't sense her hand at all…because Marleigh's head rested on her shoulder and had cut off the blood flow. She jiggled her arm until it was free, a move that caused Marleigh to roll away.

"Mmm…what time is it?"

"Your clock says five fifty-six," Zann answered in her croaky morning voice. She spooned against the warm body and made a show of sniffing Marleigh's bare shoulder. "You smell like sex. It's coming out of your pores. Everyone you get close to today will know what you did last night."

Marleigh's shoulders began to shake with silent laughter.

"If I were you I'd call in sick."

"Wish I could but someone has to go speak truth to power."

Zann took a moment to appreciate how comfortable she was. Not just physically, though it was hard to beat being wrapped around a lithe naked body after the kind of night they'd had. The most striking sensation was freedom, so unusual that her subconscious habitually prodded her to check herself, the way she might grope about if she'd suddenly stopped carrying a pack or a wallet. At every impulse she was reassured that no one cared where she was, who she was with or what she'd done. And she was no longer subject to a command structure that ruled her conduct out of bounds.

Marleigh rolled over to face her. A night's rest had rounded her lips and relaxed the lines in her forehead. "What are you thinking about?"

"Life."

"A little more specific."

"I was thinking how long it's been since I felt totally relaxed with a woman. Probably never. There's always been this little voice in my head telling me to watch out, that somebody might catch me and blow my whole career."

"Because you're gay? I thought that was all wiped out when they got rid of Don't Ask, Don't Tell. Or did that not apply to the Marines?"

"It was never as simple as they made it sound. The repeal made it okay to say you were gay, but you still weren't supposed to have gay sex. The Marine Corps considered it *unnatural carnal copulation.*"

"Say that again. I love it when you talk dirty."

Zann murmured it several times until they both were giggling and groping one another under the sheet. Just as their touches turned intimate, the sharp beep of the alarm interrupted their play.

"Damn, time for the real world," Marleigh said, sighing as she extricated her limbs. "By the way, if you think after last night that you're going to sign up with Hell Dog and go back to Afghanistan, I've got news for you. It's not happening, Captain Zann. I'm not letting you go."

There was a weightiness to her voice that Zann couldn't dismiss. "Going to stop me, are you?"

"What would it take?" Her playfulness was gone, in its place a sober plea.

"Marleigh, I…"

"You said you woke up every day thinking about how the Marines had taken away the life you wanted. Did you think about it today?"

She'd thought of only one thing, the woman in her arms. "No."

"Then stay here and give it a chance. Give *us* a chance. I'm willing to bet there's something a whole lot more important than being a soldier." She knelt across the bed and delivered a soft kiss. "Could be this is the life you were meant to live."

CHAPTER EIGHT

Present Day

The gunshots in the outer room were followed by women's screams—Bridget and Fran—and a high-pitched male voice yelling sharply, "Lock the door, David! No one comes, no one leaves." The accent and pronunciation—*Dah-vee*—were French-Canadian like Bridget's boyfriend, but Marleigh knew Luc's voice and that wasn't it.

She instinctively started for the hallway, only to be yanked back. With a finger to her lips, Zann commanded her stillness.

"Ancil? What the hell's going on?" The pleading voice belonged to Bridget. Marleigh recognized the name as one of Luc's Canadian friends, a business associate. She'd met Ancil a couple of weekends ago when he showed up at Bridget's apartment looking for Luc.

"What is going on is that your boyfriend does not have the decency to return my calls. I thought if I came here, I might get his attention."

Still gripping her bicep, Zann steered her abruptly to the counter and checked the cabinets down the line. When she began emptying the contents of the largest one—jumbo packs of hand towels and toilet paper, which she stacked on the counter—it became clear she intended for them to hide inside.

Marleigh went first, scooting all the way back and pulling her knees to her chest to make room. Once Zann got into position beside her, she held the cabinet door with her fingertips so it wouldn't bang as it closed.

The phone on Fran's desk let out a shrill ring.

"Leave it!" Ancil barked. "All of you, move over here and get on the floor! No cell phones." His voice grew loud as he approached the break room, and then faded as he walked away. Only a thin wall separated the cabinet from the lobby, allowing them to hear every word. "And if you know what is good for you, you will keep your hands where my friends here can see them."

Friends…how many were there? Marleigh couldn't believe this was happening. Luc was a nice guy, a businessman. How had he gotten mixed up with a bunch of ruffians?

"That gun isn't necessary." It was Clay, emerging from his office to inject calm. "The man you're looking for obviously isn't here, so it doesn't serve any purpose to threaten us."

"It serves *my* purpose perfectly," Ancil said, his tone sarcastic and sinister. "Luc Michaux has something that belongs to me—something worth a considerable amount of money—and I am here to collect it."

"Do you know those people?" Zann asked, her voice barely audible.

"Ancil somebody…he's one of Luc's friends from Montreal."

A second man shouted, "He said no phones, bitch! Touch it again and you're dead. Now get out here." Unlike Ancil, this man's accent was American.

Marleigh whispered, "He must be yelling at Tammy. She was in her office."

"Shh…let's get the lay of the land and I'll figure out what to do." Zann clung to her still, as though issuing commands through her wrist. She'd slipped seamlessly into what Marleigh thought of as her command mode, honed in the Marines. Cool and collected, confident in her ability to handle whatever obstacle she faced.

Out in the lobby, Clay asserted himself again in his usual no-nonsense style. "This is ridiculous. I'm calling the police. You need to—"

Two more gunshots sparked an eerie echo.

Marleigh flinched in terror, squeezing her eyes tightly to shut out a vision of Clay being shot. The sound of raining debris filled her with relief—the gunman had fired again into the ceiling.

Ancil spoke as calmly as if he were ordering lunch, "You will *not* be calling the police. You will be sitting on the floor with the others, or my next bullet will go into this lovely young lady's head. *Comprenez-vous?*"

"Oh my God, Zann. He's going to kill somebody."

"Shh." Zann touched a finger to her cheek, likely meant for her lips.

There were sounds of scraping chairs and shuffling feet. When the rustling quieted, she pictured her friends now huddled on the floor in front of Fran's tall counter.

The phone sounded again, four rings before it kicked to voice mail.

What would people think if no one answered the phones at their office? Would someone come to help? Marleigh shook off a terrifying vision of one of their customers getting shot as they tried to enter the building.

"While you make yourselves comfortable, Bridget is going to call her boyfriend. She will tell him that stealing from me was a very big mistake." *Stealing?* Luc was a day trader. "And if he does not come to this office immediately and make this right, he will be making a much bigger one."

"He can't come, Ancil. He's in New York meeting with clients. I don't even know when he's supposed to get home. He's been there for the last three days."

Had Luc talked Ancil into a shady investment that didn't pan out? Whatever it was, threatening Bridget and the others wouldn't get him what he wanted as long as Luc was out of reach. And that made the situation dangerous.

With a snide edge to his voice, Ancil replied, "Oh, fair Bridget. I am so sorry to be the one to break this very sad news to you. Your lover lies to you. Let me guess…you believe he is a stockbroker, or some other such thing you find respectable. He is not, though I have observed that he likes to dress the part. I have taken notice of his fine clothes and expensive sports car. And he is not in New York today. For your sake—and for that of your friends, of course—let us hope he is closer. Much closer."

"Get him on the phone!" This was now a third voice, cracking and shrill as though it belonged to a much younger man.

As quietly as she could, Marleigh shifted inside the cabinet to straighten out one of her cramping legs. Zann was hunched across from her with her knees tucked beneath her. The space was so small their breath warmed the air.

"He's not picking up," Bridget said plaintively.

"Leave him a message."

"Luc, it's me. I need you to call me back as soon as you—"

"Tell him what I said," Ancil said icily.

With a shaky voice, she continued. "Luc, Ancil is here at the newspaper office…with two of his friends. He says you stole something from him and he wants you to bring it to him here. Luc, they have guns and they're—"

"Give it to me!" There was a pause as the phone changed hands. "Did you hear that, Luc? You have two choices, both very simple. Either bring my delivery or bring *seven million* in cash to your girlfriend's office. Surely you understand what I would do for that amount of money. You have thirty minutes before bad things begin to happen to these innocent people, these victims of your foolishness. Do not think you can ignore me, Luc. People here will pay the price, and then I will come for you."

Marleigh had a vague idea of street prices from the reporting she'd done on the drug epidemic. Seven million dollars was a lot of meth or heroin, a truckload even. Unless it was heroin laced with fentanyl or carfentanil—trafficked under street names like China White or Serial Killer—considered by some to be the deadliest of street drugs. Luc could easily smuggle seven million in spiked heroin in the trunk of his car. He and Ancil, both of them chic and refined, fit the profile of those who moved drugs but stayed above the fray.

There was a whimper that sounded like Tammy. "This doesn't have anything to do with us. Why can't you just let us go? We won't tell—"

"Shut up!" The younger voice again, accompanied by a flurry of motion.

"Ow!" Tammy shrieked, apparently having suffered a kick or a shove.

"Leave her alone, you animal!" Clay yelled amidst a shuffling of feet.

Another shot rang out, followed by screams and shouts of disbelief. "Oh my God, you shot him!"

"Scotty!" Ancil's voice was sharp and scolding.

"You saw him, Ancil. He took a swing at me," the young man whined. His name and accent suggested he, like David, was American. A couple of hapless locals doing dirty work for a drug dealer from Montreal.

"He's bleeding," Fran said. "We have to call an ambulance."

"No. He was a fool and he paid the price," Ancil said coldly. "There will be no more stupidity, no more heroes. Your only hero today is Luc Michaux—he is the only one who can save you. David, find something to tie these people up so Scotty will not be tempted to shoot them."

Marleigh's heart pounded as footsteps sounded in the break room. Even in the dark, she knew Zann was coiled to attack if David discovered them.

He ransacked the room, banging drawers and cabinets. The drawer above their head slid out, enabling a glimpse of his gloved hands as he rummaged inside and seized a roll of duct tape.

* * *

"This has to be about drugs," Zann whispered. Few things were worth that much money. Plus there was Ancil's lack of concern that Luc would simply pick up the message from Bridget and call the police. Luc was in too deep to implicate himself. He had double-crossed Ancil, absconding with either a shipment of drugs or the money from its sale. Worse, he probably had a three-day head start.

Marleigh spoke softly, "Zann, you have to call the cops. They shot Clay."

"My phone's in my coat pocket." She gently cracked the door, confirming they were alone in the room. By her estimation, it would take about forty seconds to fetch the phone and return safely to the cabinet. She could do that. As long as their captors were busy tying everyone up, they weren't likely to pass by the doorway.

This moment was also their best window for escape, she realized. All they had to do was get to the back exit. Nothing mattered more than getting Marleigh to safety.

"Marleigh, we should sneak over by the door. I'll create some kind of distraction and you run for it. Get out the back and go for help."

"We can't," she whispered. "Fran keeps the back gate locked except on trash days. The keys are in her desk."

The area behind the building was enclosed in a tall chain-link fence that provided added security from break-ins. If someone chased Marleigh out the back, she'd surely be caught before she could clear the fence.

"Okay, I'll go for my phone. But you stay right here if I get caught. Not a sound. I mean it." She closed the cabinet behind her to preserve Marleigh's cover and crept toward where her coat hung on the chair.

"Call him again," Ancil said sharply, sounding dangerously close to the hallway.

Phone in hand, Zann took a quick moment to check a drawer by the sink, hoping to find something she could use as a weapon.

Other than a smattering of plastic utensils, the only item was a manual can opener, its cutting wheel grimy with dried food.

Marleigh tucked her knees again to make room for her return. "Did you hear what Bridget just said? Luc's phone went straight to voice mail this time. That means he probably turned it off."

"It also means he got the message. Maybe he's bringing back whatever he took." Zann knew the odds of that were low, that he'd probably turned off his phone so Bridget couldn't track him. She looked up a text number for the Colfax Police Department and, as calmly as she could, tapped out a series of messages.

911 emergency

3 gunmen at messenger office

1 hostage shot needs doc

i am zann redeker hiding in back room w marleigh anderhall

In only seconds, her phone chimed with a reply, a sound that seemed as loud as a trumpet blast. She fumbled for the mute button and strained to listen for footsteps coming back their way.

"He's going to die if he doesn't get a doctor," Fran said seconds later from the other room, her defiant voice a sign no one had heard the chirping phone.

"Shut up or this tape is going over your mouth," David snapped.

Zann studied the message from the dispatcher, clear and succinct, absent jargon that might be misinterpreted.

Police and ambulance are on the way.

Shelter in place.

Keep this line open if you can.

How many hostages?

She held the phone up so Marleigh could see.

"Five," Marleigh whispered.

"Here, take this and tell them everything you know."

Marleigh responded to the dispatcher, holding up each text for Zann to read.

5 hostages in lobby tied duct tape

fr door prob locked
back gate def locked
gunman is ancil from montreal
prob drug deal
will shoot in 30 min
others r david & scotty
clay teele shot

"It would appear your boyfriend does not love you after all," Ancil said. His perfunctory habit of not using contractions was annoying, as if he were showing off his mastery of English. "That would be extremely bad news for everyone here."

"Whatever you think Luc stole, you're wrong. He isn't like that."

"He *is* like that, you silly twit. And instead of facing me like a man, he has left his woman to clean up after him."

"I have no idea what you're talking about," Bridget said through sniffles.

Another phone rang, but it was silenced immediately and thrown across the room.

"He's talking about our smack!" Scotty shouted. After shooting Clay and throwing the phone, it was clear he was losing all self-control.

With confirmation now that Luc had stolen their heroin, Zann reassessed the situation. The one they called Scotty sounded like an addict in need of a fix. If so, there was no limit to the damage he was capable of inflicting.

"Luc doesn't do drugs. I know him," Bridget whined.

"Pay attention, sweetheart." The warning from Ancil was followed by a quick slap, the kind that was designed more to humiliate than hurt. "Your boyfriend picked up my shipment two days ago in New York. I should have received it yesterday. I am a good guy, right? So naturally, I worried maybe something happened to him. Perhaps he ran into trouble with the locals. Or he was picked up by the police." His voice was cajoling.

"That must have been it. Luc would never—"

Ancil screamed, "It was not! Nothing happened to him except that he stole my shipment. And he made a rather large sale to one of my customers in Albany last night. A sale to *my* customer with *my* product. Except he is not allowed to sell my product. He is allowed only to *deliver* my product to me."

"I don't know anything about that," Bridget wailed. "The Luc I know doesn't have anything to do with drugs. If he does... then he hid that from me, Ancil. You have to believe me."

"Who the fuck cares?" Scotty yelled. Several loud crashes followed as if he were systematically knocking objects off desks. "You know where he is. You said a code word or something... you warned him not to come, you bitch!"

"Look, everybody just calm down." Zann recognized the voice as that of Marleigh's coworker Terry, a forty-something guy who reported on high school sports. "It sounds like Luc screwed you over, but that had nothing to do with any of us. He's obviously not coming back to help Bridget. I'm sorry, Bridget. He's a son of a bitch. But you guys, you need to go find *him* if you want your stuff back. Leave now and let us take care of our friend before something really bad happens. You don't want the cops chasing you for something worse than drugs."

Zann squeezed Marleigh's wrist anxiously as they waited to see if Terry's plea would be considered. What he said was right on the money—if Luc wasn't going to take their bait, there was nothing to gain by staying here and letting one of the hostages die.

David muttered something in French that she didn't understand.

Bridget apparently did, and she replied, "It doesn't matter that we've seen your faces. We don't even know your last names...or anything else about you. We can't tell the cops how to track you down, especially if you leave right now and head to Canada."

"My name is Ancil Leclerc. It seems only fair you should know that."

Marleigh tapped out the new information in another message to the dispatcher.

Meanwhile Zann was startled by his brazen admission— until she processed its likely implication. The men had taken no precautions to protect their faces or identities from the *Messenger* staff, though she'd noticed David had worn gloves so as not to leave fingerprints the authorities could trace. Now with Ancil showing no concern over Clay's injury, no panic about the consequences, it was increasingly clear he had no intention of leaving witnesses behind—whether Luc showed up or not.

That was a game-changer. Feeling an adrenaline surge, she clenched every muscle in her body to hold herself still. Her military training compelled her to confront the enemy rather than wait for an attack. Doing so would put Marleigh in danger, but she couldn't just hide while five defenseless people were slaughtered.

"I have to do something," she whispered.

"Zann, you can't. They have guns."

"Then I'll have to take them away." She eased the door open and crawled out. Before closing it behind her, she pointedly told Marleigh to stay put. "No matter what happens."

"My patience is running out, Bridget. You get one more call to your boyfriend. If he does not respond, your friend here will be the first to pay the price."

"God, Bridget! Tell him where Luc is," Tammy pleaded.

"I don't know!"

Zann peered around the doorjamb and saw the man she presumed to be Ancil. He had Tammy in a chokehold with a pistol to her head. She weighed her odds. He wasn't a large man. The dress shirt and long wool overcoat suggested he relied on others for muscle. The gun however was a problem. She'd have to get close enough to surprise him, to disarm him before he had a chance to hurt someone.

"Call him!"

A few seconds passed while Bridget placed another futile call.

Then Ancil shook his head with disgust and cocked the pistol.

Now or never. Zann took her first step into the hallway.

"Ancil…Ancil, it's the cops! Two cars just pulled up."

He shoved Tammy to the floor and rushed to the window.

Zann heaved a deep sigh of relief and tiptoed back to the cabinet, confident the gunmen wouldn't harm any of the hostages with the police now breathing down their necks. They'd have to surrender. All she and Marleigh had to do was wait it out from the secrecy of their hiding place.

CHAPTER NINE

May, seven months earlier

"…and without regard to personal risk, entered the building to find Mrs. Duckworth overcome by toxic fumes, whereupon she carried her outside to safety. For her quick thinking and heroism, I'm proud to present the Colfax Employee of the Year Award to Zann Redeker."

Marleigh couldn't have been prouder of her wife, now three years removed from the Marine Corps and still every bit the hero. Clapping with glee as Zann accepted the certificate and a handshake from town manager Malcolm Shively, she made a mental note to check with the photographer later so they could get a copy for framing.

As usual when she found herself the center of public attention, Zann glowed red as she returned from the dais to her seat in the small auditorium that hosted town hall meetings.

Chuck Redeker greeted his daughter with a pat on the shoulder. "Proud of you, hon. You'll be running this town before long."

"That would make her your boss," Marleigh whispered, leaning forward to catch his eye. She'd come to love Chuck and Leeann Redeker, as much for their down-to-earth nature as for their unqualified support of Zann's life choices. Like her, they were in awe of the daughter they'd raised, the war hero who approached everything in life with honor and resolve. Plus they'd welcomed Marleigh to the family as if she were their own. Their only disappointment was the intractable news that neither she nor Zann had plans to reproduce.

Zann wafted the certificate and shot her a wink. "Think this should go in the case with the Bronze Star?"

"Give it a rest, Captain. You couldn't stop swashbuckling if you tried." For an instant, she recalled their interview before the Fourth of July parade and Zann's flat assertion that she'd only been doing her job. She'd used those exact words when Joyce Duckworth's family had praised her for rescuing their mom from an industrial leak of Freon gas.

Malcolm concluded the town's annual recognition ceremony with the presentation of pins for those marking various milestones of service. The family cheered again when Chuck went up to collect his forty-year pin, making him the town's longest employee.

"Big day for the Redekers," Marleigh said as they fell in behind the crowd that had pooled at the exit.

"Let's go out this way." With a tip of her head, Zann gestured toward the side door, which would take them directly into the parking lot. "How much longer are you going to work, Pop?"

"Probably till they carry me out in a hearse."

Marleigh bumped his shoulder with hers. "Maybe then you'll show them where all the bodies are buried."

"Don't laugh, kiddo. About six years ago some developer put in for a permit to build a bowling alley on Rutland Road next to the movie theater. I reminded them the old First Baptist Church used to be there before it burned down in 1981. It had a cemetery in the back, but they left all the graves there when they built the new church on Hemlock."

Leeann looped her arm through his elbow to steady herself in her dress shoes. "Chuck knows every single parcel in Addison County like I know my button box."

They'd slowed to a stroll, enjoying one another's company.

"Not just the county," Zann said. "The whole state."

He shrugged. "These days it's all on the web. Nothing's private anymore. You can find out anything about anybody. See Rod Wicker there?" He pointed toward the town's water plant director as he climbed into his pickup. "He lives about a quarter-mile from Malcolm on Branch Road. Same size house, both sitting on an acre. But Rod's in Windsor County. Saves him four thousand a year in property taxes."

"Pop, how do you pack all this stuff in your head?"

"Your father spends all night in front of that computer. I swear he'd bring it to the dinner table if I'd let him."

"Speaking of dinner…" Marleigh tugged Zann toward their SUV as she explained the quick departure. "We need to get going. It's my friend Bridget's birthday. We're meeting her and her husband for dinner tonight."

"Zann!" Malcolm waved her back to the building.

Marleigh climbed into the passenger seat to wait and used the opportunity to study the certificate. Embossed with the town's silver seal, it was perfect for framing…assuming Zann would even let her. To this day, her Marine Corps medals remained at her parents' home in their patriotic exhibit. Zann said she liked how proud they were to show them off. What she didn't seem to grasp was that Marleigh was proud of her too. One of these days they were going to have a talk about bringing those medals home.

* * *

Zann held the steering wheel steady with her left hand as she adjusted the vent control on the dashboard. The plastic knob popped off and fell to the floor. "Damn it! This Jeep's getting to be a piece of shit."

"You're in a foul mood for somebody who just got the Colfax equivalent of an Oscar." Marleigh picked up the knob and snapped it back into place. "What did Malcolm have to tell you that was so important?"

"That I didn't get the Senior Inspector job. He's giving it to Gil Kirby."

"Gil Kirby? How could he do that? Gil doesn't even have a bachelor's degree."

"And I don't have a contractor's license. The job calls for both so neither one of us is qualified."

Gil was probably better suited for the job but she sure could have used the salary bump. Every spare penny went into their house, a bargain fixer-upper they were renovating one project at a time. A new mudroom, a stone fireplace. And in March, a new roof that ate up all their savings. It would take them a year at least to save enough to start work on the master bath.

Their efforts were paying off though. With every upgrade, they were building something that was so much more than a house. A life together, a permanent stake in the ground.

"You were so right about the Robin's Egg," Marleigh said, a reference to the cyan shade of paint they'd chosen for the exterior of their house.

"And you thought I had no taste." It had looked especially pretty against last winter's snow.

After snatching the mail from their roadside box, she pulled around to the back so they could go through the mudroom, where she paused to admire her handiwork. Her contributions to the remodel—laying the tile, spreading insulation, and painting—were relatively simple. The more intricate tasks had proven literally beyond her grasp however. Her recovery had maxed out with decent mobility in her elbow and wrist, but well short of the hand control she needed for tasks like holding a nail in place so she could pound it with a hammer. It even crossed her mind to wonder if her injury had anything to do with Malcolm passing her over for Gil.

"Who's Colonel Leon Grant?" Marleigh asked, waving a business envelope addressed by hand to Zann. The personalized return label, adorned with the silver and blue logo of the US Air Force, was clearly unofficial.

"Beats me." She ripped it open to find a formal-looking letter with a handwritten note at the bottom. "Says here he's Air Force, Operation Desert Storm. Retired a year ago from teaching ROTC at Norwich. Apparently they're starting up a veterans group here in Colfax and he wants me to join."

"A veterans group? You mean like the American Legion?"

"No…says it's an informal group where vets can talk over problems they might be having." She hastily scanned the list of potential topics. "VA benefits, retirement pay, job training, PTSD. 'Who better understands the issues our veterans face than other veterans?' He makes it sound like one of those twelve-step programs. Look, it even meets at the Episcopal church, probably across the hall from Alcoholics Anonymous. Monday nights at seven."

"You should go." Marleigh sorted the rest of the mail and stacked the bills on the antique secretary they'd found at a flea market.

"What would be the point? I don't have all that much to do with the VA anymore, and it's not as if they can do anything to up my retirement pay. I was lucky I qualified at all." Eight years was the minimum threshold of service to be eligible for a portion of her Marine Corps pension. Had she been injured three months sooner, they wouldn't have owed her a dime. "I don't need a job or job training. What would I have to talk about?"

"Uh…maybe the fact that you watched one of your soldiers die right in front of your eyes. I know it still bothers you. Every year when January third rolls around, you beat yourself up about it."

It was true that losing Whitney Laird still haunted her. Remembering the day with a bit of introspection was the least she could do. "What kind of person would I be if I didn't show a little respect for a soldier who gave her life? If you ask me, that's a sign I've got my head together."

Marleigh kissed her temple before starting down the hall toward their bedroom. "I'll give you that much. But it's an even better reason you should go. If one of the other guys—"

"Or women."

"Touché. If one of the other *soldiers* was having problems, you might be just the role model they need. Miss Employee of the Year. Think about it—all that shit you went through and you still managed to get home with your head on straight. It wouldn't hurt for them to see how you've handled all the crap you've had to deal with."

"Sounds a lot like group therapy. They already put me through that at the Naval Hospital at Camp Lejeune. Except we didn't have to drill down to uncover anything. It was staring us in the face…burns, disfigurement, amputations, paralysis. All we talked about was how people were going to cope with life changes. Mine was nothing compared to what the others were going through, but it was mandatory for everybody. Six meetings in all, I think it was." She recalled it with a trace of bitterness, since the medical staff had led her to believe the sessions were a prerequisite for returning her to duty. Instead the Marine Corps separated her as soon as she finished.

In the bedroom, Marleigh peeled off her cable sweater and stood before the closet in her jeans and bra. She had the cutest body from behind, Zann thought, as lean as a teenager. "I have no idea what I'm going to wear tonight. What about you?"

"Something black."

"Is that a commentary on how you feel about the evening?"

Zann feigned an innocent look and decided not to answer. Dinner with Rocky Goodson under any circumstances wasn't her idea of a good time, even though Marleigh said she hadn't seen any signs of abuse in over a year.

"How do you suppose that colonel got your name?"

"No idea. It's not like you guys put me on the front page of the newspaper or anything like that."

"Three years ago, Zann. Who's going to remember that far back?"

She plopped on their bed and gathered all of the pillows behind her, stealing a peek as Marleigh swapped her white bra for a black one. "I could help you with that."

"Yeah, and we'd be two hours late."

"There are worse things." She folded the letter and set it on the bedside table to deal with later, acknowledging that she was intrigued. "It might be kinda cool to meet up with some of the local vets. Gil said there was a guard unit from Colfax that went to Iraq."

"You're serious?"

"What, I shouldn't be? Just a minute ago you were the one saying I should go."

"It would be good for you. Sometimes I think you go out of your way to steer clear of people so you don't have to talk to them. Your mom noticed it too. She says you outgrew all the people here that you went to school with."

There probably was truth to that. She'd come home from college a couple of times to find half of her friends already married and settling into family life and the other half wrapped up in the college sorority scene. Joining the Marines had only exacerbated their differences.

"I guess it wouldn't kill me to give it a try."

Marleigh pulled off her jeans and continued staring into her closet as if waiting for the perfect outfit to shake itself from its hanger. "You make it sound like torture. Does it even occur to you that it might be fun?"

"Does it occur to you that you're flaunting yourself in your underwear?" Zann lunged at her from behind and heaved her to the bed. "I'll show you what fun is."

CHAPTER TEN

If she had it to do over again, Marleigh would have chosen a more casual place for their evening out with Rocky and Bridget, like pizza or wings at a raucous sports bar. The quiet atmosphere of Anthony's, the restaurant of the Crocker Farm Inn where she and Zann had been married a couple of years ago, put the burden of conversation squarely on her shoulders.

Dinner as a foursome had been her idea, a chance for Bridget to enjoy a pleasant night out, something most people took for granted. She needed to see what a healthy relationship looked like. Rocky had grown increasingly possessive and domineering, she said, especially after cutbacks at the paper had saddled the whole staff with longer hours. That's all Marleigh could get from her, but the subtle signs of physical abuse had resurfaced— long sleeves on a hot day and more makeup than usual.

Eyeing him now across the cloth-draped table, she thought him a textbook example of a man who bullied women because he lacked self-esteem. He was the classic wannabe, a short, skinny guy who never quite grew into manhood. What he couldn't do against the guys in the gym, he made up for by dominating his wife.

They were seated at a square table on the covered deck alongside several other parties, all of them well-dressed and in polite conversation. New age piano music hummed from hidden speakers.

"Rocky, tell them what you found in the yard the other day. You guys aren't going to believe this."

"A timber rattler over two feet long. He was curled up in the rocks by the mailbox. I'm lucky I didn't step on him when I went to get the mail." He withdrew his phone to show them the photo.

Marleigh had done a feature several years ago about snakes in Vermont. The one in Rocky's photo was very obviously a milk snake, an utterly harmless creature with markings that were somewhat similar to those of a timber rattler. The distinction was its solid black tail.

"What did you do with it?"

"Blew its head off with a Glock 18," he said smugly. "One shot. Motherfucker never knew what hit him."

A deep chill shook her as he confirmed one of her worst fears, that her best friend's controlling and abusive husband owned a handgun. She could easily picture him waving it in Bridget's face, telling her what he'd do if he ever caught her talking to another guy or lying to him about where she'd been. Why hadn't Bridget ever mentioned it? Probably because she was too ashamed for anyone to know how he treated her.

The waiter appeared at their table to announce the night's specials. "Would anyone care for something from the bar?"

Rocky ordered a double Jack and Coke, evidently unaware of the gentlemanly custom of "ladies first."

As Zann studied the menu in silence, she shifted her chair and crossed a leg, a posture that made her look almost disengaged, as if she might stand at any moment and leave. She'd been on edge ever since they left the house, right after Marleigh had shared her suspicions that Rocky had returned to his old ways. "Are you having anything, babe?"

They'd made a pact about drinking alcohol whenever they drove somewhere together. A single beer or glass of wine was fine, but only one of them could exceed that limit. That left the other sober enough to drive home. Considering the prices at Anthony's—twelve bucks for a glass of their house zinfandel—Marleigh was willing to skip a cocktail altogether. "I think I'll just stick with sparkling water tonight."

"Okay then, make mine a Johnnie Walker Black on the rocks."

It was rare for Zann to drink hard liquor, and Marleigh wondered if it was her way of showing Rocky she was just as tough as he was. The last thing she or Bridget needed tonight was for their spouses to get into a drunken pissing match, especially one that could turn Rocky violent by the time they got home.

Bridget clutched his hand on the table in what looked like an exaggerated display of affection. "So here's a question: Am I a bad person for hoping the Memorial Day picnic gets rained out next week?"

"That would make me a bad person too," Marleigh said. "If it rains, we get a holiday like everybody else. Otherwise we're stuck working all day in the hot sun."

It was a canned response, staged to ease Rocky's skepticism about whether Bridget was telling the truth about having to work on the holiday. Clay Teele would scratch her from the schedule if he had any idea the extra assignments were causing this kind of strife in her home life. There was no roundabout way she could ask him for special considerations without confessing she had a husband who went ballistic every time she worked late. She'd practically begged Marleigh not to tell anyone on the *Messenger* staff. Rocky would calm down again eventually, she said, once he realized he could trust her. If it got too bad, she promised to leave him.

For Bridget's sake, Marleigh hoped it wouldn't take another dangerous episode of violence to make her see the light. Rocky had always been volatile. And while he'd been tolerant of their friendship, that would change in a hurry if he found out she'd been putting the bug in Bridget's ear to start planning her exit strategy.

"Hey Zann," he said, "what kind of firepower did you guys have in the Marine Corps?"

"I carried an M16 and an M9 Beretta."

"M16, huh…I'd take the Bushmaster over that any day. It's easier to modify. You can get a conversion kit for a hundred bucks that'll make the AR-15 fully auto."

Zann scoffed as she took a sip of her drink. "So you can waste a bunch of bullets trying to get close to the target? The only reason anybody needs an auto is if they don't know how to aim."

His ears turned red and Marleigh braced for an angry eruption. Guys like Rocky weren't used to being on the butt end of a putdown.

With a sneer, he replied, "Just saying it's more fun, that's all."

"I wouldn't know about that. I didn't use my rifle for fun."

"Bridget said you smoked a bunch of Tally-ban over there. And fuck, you got shot and lived to tell about it. That's badass."

Zann raised her glass toward the waiter to indicate she was ready for another. It might have interested her to talk about her time in the Marine Corps with someone she respected, real soldiers like the group that Air Force colonel was putting together. She'd shown nothing but disdain for guys who thought toting guns into Hannaford's supermarket made them heroes.

"I want to hear more about that rattlesnake," Marleigh interjected to break the tension. Surely Rocky would rather talk about himself than Zann's military exploits. "Aren't you worried you'll find more?"

He ignored her, his eyes riveted on Zann. "Come on, you blew a bunch of rag heads to smithereens. You can't tell me that wasn't fun."

"There's nothing fun about killing people. The only people who think there is have some kind of mental defect. I shot them because they were the enemy and that's what I was trained to do. It's called kill or be killed. War isn't some video game where Rambo wannabes can hit the reset button after they get their heads blown off because they weren't quick enough on the joystick."

A cold silence hung over the table while the waiter delivered Zann and Rocky's second round. Marleigh knew from Bridget that he never let anyone else get the last word.

"You still shoot?"

Zann shook her head.

"You ought to come out to Horse Trail Road sometime. We got us a range out there at Jeb Hickman's farm. First dirt road on the left past Otter Creek. There's a bunch of targets set up out there in the field...everything you'd want all the way up to about five hundred yards."

"Is it backstopped?"

Marleigh was stunned to hear Zann express curiosity. She didn't even own a gun.

"Yeah, Jeb used to let construction companies come in there to get fill dirt off the hillside, so now there's this big dirt wall at the far end. It's real safe. Nothing's leaking out of there." Rocky's croaky voice rose with excitement as he sensed her interest. "I always go early in the morning 'cause there's hardly anybody else out there. Jeb leaves the gate unlocked and he's put this box out there with a padlock on it so shooters can put money in it. Everything's on the honor system...supposed to be twenty bucks a trip, but nobody knows if you don't put it in every time."

"Pistol range too?"

"Fuck yeah, with a big ol' bullet box."

It was frightening that Bridget had never mentioned his guns before. Given the way she tried to hide her cuts and bruises, it made sense she wouldn't want anyone to know her home life was actually worse than it appeared.

What didn't make sense was Zann asking all these questions. She'd never expressed any interest in guns, not once in all the time Marleigh had known her.

"That sucks about your hand," Rocky said, crassly pointing to her injured arm. "There's a couple of rifle stands though. You might could do it that way...some of the targets are pretty close."

A flicker of anger flashed in Zann's eyes as she tipped her head back. Looking down her nose at Rocky, she practically growled, "I guarantee you I could do it if I decided that's how I wanted to waste my time."

* * *

"I wasn't serious," Zann grumbled as she tugged the scratchy seat belt from her bare neck. No wonder Marleigh complained so much when she rode in the passenger seat of the Cherokee. "I just thought it was better to let him talk about shooting targets than people. Rocky would shit his pants if he ever had to look down the barrel of an enemy rifle. It's all a macho game to guys like that. The best they'll ever do is popping paper targets that stand still and don't shoot back."

She'd had only two drinks at dinner, but rules were rules. A license check could put her in jail if they caught her driving over the limit.

Considering the kind of day she'd had, she should have been in a better mood. An award at work, making love in the afternoon. But coming on top of her doubts about why she hadn't gotten the Senior Inspector job, Rocky had pushed her button with his crack about her not being able to shoot because of her hand. "Can you possibly tell me why Bridget hasn't left that dickwad already? I don't care if he's hung like a horse. He's one of the biggest assholes I've ever met."

Marleigh sighed. "Who knows? She swears she loves him, that he can be the sweetest guy in the world. I get a scary vibe about it sometimes. I was at their apartment one day right after Christmas and he came in all mad about something. I heard him yelling at her that she couldn't do better than him, that nobody else would put up with somebody so lazy and stupid. Then when he realized I was in the kitchen, he tried to make like he was joking. It was creepy as hell. I think she's a lot more afraid of him than she lets on."

"That's what I mean, so why doesn't she just leave?"

"Obviously he holds some kind of power over her. Or she's afraid he'll track her down, and now that I know he worships his guns, I can understand why. Sometimes I just want to scream at her to stand up to him. But if she does and he beats the crap out of her, it would be my fault."

"Hunh…promise me you'll be careful about getting in the middle of that." Marleigh was exactly the kind of friend who would try to come to the rescue without regard for her own safety. "Tell her she can call me if she's in trouble. I wouldn't need any hands at all to kick his scrawny ass."

"That's what I love about you, Captain Zann. You're ready to be everybody's hero." They met over the console for a quick peck on the lips. "But I don't want you in the middle of their fights either, especially with his guns."

She doubted a guy like Rocky could keep his head if he ever really felt threatened. A highly trained combat veteran would take his gun away and shoot him with it. That's what she'd do.

"I need to practice doing more stuff with my left hand. I've gotten kind of lazy about my exercises. You know what they say—use it or lose it."

Marleigh surprised her with a snicker. "I have to admit, there was a second there where I wanted to see you rare back with it and punch Rocky in the face."

For the most part she'd made peace with her limitations. Likely the injury wasn't obvious to casual observers, since she'd trained other muscles to bend her elbow and wrist, and to swing her arm when she walked. They wouldn't notice how she compensated for her weakened grip, or that she usually avoided in public any activities that required both hands.

They pulled into the driveway where the headlights illuminated their cozy house, its white shutters gleaming against the pale blue siding. Again Zann felt a surge of pride at all the work they'd done to make it home. "We're so lucky, Marleigh. We have such a nice life."

As they came to a stop, Marleigh grabbed her hand and threaded their fingers. "I'm never letting you go. You got that?"

"Got it, babe. Trapped forever. And loving every minute of it." Their doting declarations shattered the melancholy she'd been fighting all evening, its effects made worse by alcohol.

As they walked up the stairs to the front porch, she pushed her hand into Marleigh's hip pocket and squeezed her butt through the denim. There were plenty of things worse than being a prisoner of the woman she loved.

CHAPTER ELEVEN

Zann cringed to see a couple of dozen chairs arranged in a wide circle. Exactly as she feared, like a group therapy session. She'd hoped to hide in the back row where she could get up and sneak out if she didn't like it.

"Captain Redeker, glad you could make it." Air Force Colonel Leon Grant, an African-American whose temples were tinged with silver, wore creased gray slacks and a white shirt.

For a second she was embarrassed not to have taken more care with her own appearance. Officers were trained to conduct themselves with excellence at all times. In her jeans and T-shirt, she looked like the others, who she guessed were enlisted. Some of the names and faces were vaguely familiar, people who'd been a couple of years ahead or behind her in high school.

"Sounds weird to be called a captain again. I've gotten used to just being Zann." She shook his hand and allowed herself to be led to a table with coffee and donuts.

"Force of habit," he said. "Thirty years in the Air Force will do that. But we don't stand on ceremony here, so feel free to be yourself. What we all have in common is the belief that serving our country is fundamental to who we are…the good and sometimes the not-so-good. So now we're here to help each other get through this thing called life."

Yep, that sounded like group therapy. As a courtesy to Colonel Grant, she was willing to give it one meeting but couldn't imagine she'd come back for support she didn't need.

The group had met twice already, and it was apparent from the various clusters that friendships had already formed. She was pleased not to be the only woman present. Two were seated already and chatting with a handful of men.

"Welcome," the colonel announced. "We have some new faces joining us tonight, so why don't we start with introductions?"

The oldest of the group was in his eighties, a Korean War veteran who admitted he'd joined because those "sons of bitches over at Legion Hall" cheated at poker and he wanted nothing to do with them. Two others had served in Vietnam, and another three in Desert Storm in the early 1990s. Everyone else was around Zann's age, including the two women. They and several of the men were from a local National Guard unit that had been called up to provide support services for Operation Iraqi Freedom.

The man sitting next to her was a first-timer too, rugged-looking with his barrel chest and full beard. He introduced himself as Staff Sergeant Wesley Jackson of the 82nd Airborne. Wes, he called himself. A Georgia native, he'd joined the army right out of high school two years prior to 9/11, and had spent four tours training Iraqi troops and Afghani police before joining an outfit called Black Slate. It was obvious from the wave of approval that the other veterans respected his service, and he acknowledged it with a small wave. "Back atcha."

All eyes turned to Zann, the last to introduce herself.

"Zann Redeker, Marine Corps, assigned to the Three-Two." Anyone who knew military jargon would recognize that as the Third Battalion, Second Division, an infantry unit based out of Camp Lejeune. "I did three tours in the Helmand Province."

Jackson cast a look of disbelief and drawled, "I don't think so, missy. That's a combat unit."

She bristled with anger, more for him calling her "missy" than questioning her service. His already crooked nose suggested he made a habit of shooting off his mouth.

"Uh, soldier…" Colonel Grant interrupted calmly, just in time to keep her forearm from connecting with Jackson's chin. "You might want to check yourself. We agreed we weren't going to get into rank and seniority here, but I can assure you Captain Redeker has the goods. She also has a Bronze-V to back it up."

His incredulous expression gave way to a broad grin. "Well, ho-o-ly shit! Why didn't you say so, Cap'n?"

She reluctantly grinned at his mock salute and shook his other hand. "At ease, Sergeant. And call me Zann."

The colonel continued, "All right, we have a few items up for discussion. First is an update from Kenny, who followed up with Senator Sanders's office on the status of the bill to…"

Zann chided herself for not paying more attention to issues that affected her and other veterans. In addition to her modest pension, there were plenty of programs that provided benefits she might have used had she not landed a job so quickly with the town, such as business and home loans, continuing education and employment opportunities. Marleigh was right—the fact that she'd landed on her feet meant she might be able to help others who weren't so fortunate.

That sentiment grew even more apparent once they got through the business meeting and started sharing war experiences.

"I was standing there like a zombie trying to figure out how bad I was hit. I was scared to reach up…scared the whole side of my head would be gone. It just about was." The speaker was TJ Harding, a guardsman whose checkpoint was hit by a suicide bomber. His injury was starkly visible as a deep red gouge running from his jaw to his hairline, and it had cost him both sight and hearing on one side.

Zann knew his feeling exactly, the surreal moment during which her brain sorted threat from relief. Adrenaline still surging and no one left to shoot, blood gushing painlessly from her mangled arm. And her gunnery sergeant sprawled on the dirt floor with eyes eerily fixed.

"Now I'm stuck between a rock and a hard place. I can't draw enough disability to live on, but I can't get hired if I'm standing there next to somebody with two good eyes and ears. I worked construction for six years...had all the contracts I could handle. Now I'm lucky if I can get day labor."

Since losing out on the Senior Inspector's job to Gil Kirby, she'd admittedly been feeling sorry for herself for the modest struggles with her left hand. Now TJ's injuries, plainly disfiguring and limiting in his line of work, put hers in perspective.

When they took a break for more donuts, she pulled him aside and handed him a business card. "Hey, I work for the town in the planning department. Nothing fancy, just a building code inspector. I can't promise anything, but if you're interested in getting on with maintenance or at the water treatment plant, I might be able to put in a good word. I know pretty much everybody."

"Are you kidding! That'd be fantastic."

When TJ left to call his wife with the hopeful news, she was approached again by Wes. "You still mad at me? I've been known to step in dog shit a time or two."

"It's all right. I learned not to expect much from army."

"Come on, Airborne's not just army."

"True...it takes a special kind of crazy to jump out of airplanes." She couldn't help but like him. "So how did a guy that talks as slow as you do end up in Vermont?"

"Damn, you're cold, Cap'n. The company I work for bought the quarry in Ripton. Made me a site foreman. 'Course, I didn't know y'all were gonna dump ten feet of snow on me my first winter. Not very neighborly."

"It's definitely not Baghdad."

"You're telling me. So what'd you do in the Three-Two? I know them jarheads wouldn't let soldiers of the female persuasion work the front lines."

"I was the OIC for a Female Engagement Team." He'd get her abbreviation for the officer in charge.

"Man, that took some chops. My hat's off to you." He literally removed his cap and ruffled his own shaggy hair. It was a compliment coming from a guy whose work to train security forces was the centerpiece of the whole Afghan operation. Arguably, his job was more dangerous than going on patrol, since local forces working with Americans were targeted daily by suicide bombers determined to wipe out dozens of recruits at a time.

Despite their bungled introduction, she owed him a compliment. "Without what you guys were doing in Airborne, we wouldn't have made a difference at all. What's this Black Slate you were talking about?"

"Private security in Baghdad…making sure diplomats and CEOs didn't get their asses blown off by some innocent-looking kid begging for candy. I only worked there a few months. You know how it is when you first get out—gotta save up some dough."

"Like Cerberus?"

"Not *like* Cerberus. It *was* Cerberus. Except they used to be called Black Slate. They had to change their name after a couple of low-level State Department officials they were supposed to be protecting went missing along with three millions dollars in cash. It was all hush-hush. The Pentagon yanked their funding and they had to regroup."

"I considered a job with them. I never could figure out if they were on the up and up."

"I don't know about the up and up but some of those boys are goddamn crazy. If I were a betting fool, I'd lay odds they took that money and those officials ended up in a shallow grave somewhere in the desert."

She shuddered to realize how close she'd come to signing on with an outfit so corrupt. "Sounds like I dodged a bullet."

"If I can get you all back to your seats," the colonel said.

They spent the next hour sharing more personal stories, some of the moments during deployment that were forever burned into their DNA. Fears of ambush, harrowing brushes with the enemy. The guard unit had lost a soldier, a young man several of them had known all their lives.

"It's not something you forget." The speaker had introduced himself earlier as Eugene, who worked as a butcher at Hannaford's. "His name was Will Maynard...we all called him Maynard. He hated that."

A round of soft chuckles followed as the others remembered and nodded along.

"Not the brightest bulb in the pack, if you know what I mean."

"But he had a good heart," one of the women added. This was Angie, a mother of two who now sorted donated goods at a local thrift store. She'd described her stint with the Guard as a weekend gig meant to bring the family a few extra bucks. Never had she dreamed their unit would end up being deployed. "He got picked on a lot but he was good-natured about it, never got mad over anything."

Maynard's story unfolded bit by bit as Guardsmen recalled their unique perspective of his tragic death. Their unit was transporting supplies in a convoy and stopped to inspect a suspicious segment of the road for IEDs. As Maynard stood guard in front of the column, the unattended fuel truck behind him slipped its gear and crushed him.

"It was horrible," Angie said. "One minute we were all laughing in the back of the APC over who had the worst BO. Then just like that Maynard was dead. I'll never forget what it felt like having to ride four hours back to Baghdad with his body zipped up in a bag right under my seat. I still get nightmares about it, like it's a big joke and all I have to do is unzip him and let him out."

A shattering vision pierced Zann's consciousness, triggering the dusty odor of gunpowder and sweat. Dazed by a loss of blood and the disorienting horizontal perspective, she was trying to make sense of the lumbering gait as they evacuated her from Dahaneh. At one point her fellow Marines brought her stretcher even with the black body bag and wrapped her good hand around one of the grips so that she could share in the honor of carrying a fallen solder on the first leg of her final journey home.

How on earth had she managed to bury a memory so vivid and profound?

Wes leaned toward her ear and whispered, "You all right, Cap'n?"

Zann suddenly felt her tears and hurriedly wiped her cheeks with her sleeve. "Just thinking how hard that must've been on their unit."

"Yeah, the Guard doesn't exactly prepare you for shit like that."

It didn't matter what branch of service you were in. There was no preparation for losing someone in war and having to live with knowing it could just as easily have been you. Far from feeling supported by this circle of fellow veterans, she wanted to bury her pain even deeper. As the meeting broke up, she told herself she wouldn't be back.

"Hey, Zann." Angie caught up to her at the door. Up close the corporal was painfully thin with a tattoo that crept from her hand and disappeared under her sleeve. Her eyes were ringed in dark mascara, an odd look for someone with her fair coloring.

"Angie, right? How's it going?"

"I was just talking to Reese and we wanted to ask you something." She buried her hands in the pockets of her ragged jeans and swiveled from side to side without making eye contact. "Colonel Grant keeps telling us we should talk about our feelings now that we're home, how being over there affected us. If me and Reese tell what happened to us all hell's going to break loose. You know what I'm saying?"

It took a few seconds for Zann to realize what she was talking about—women who'd been sexually assaulted during deployment. As the OIC of an all-female unit, she'd laid down strict rules to limit their vulnerability, rules that held everyone responsible for the safety of the others. "There wasn't anything like that in our unit. We always hung together during down time. Buddies, teams…nobody went anywhere alone."

"Okay, never mind."

Zann caught her arm as she started to walk away. "That doesn't mean you shouldn't talk about it. We all took an oath to serve with honor under the law. Anyone who didn't live up to that deserves to be called out. And that also goes for whoever stood by and let it happen."

Angie tipped her head in a gesture to have Reese join them. "So you'll back us up if we say something?"

"Of course."

Reese added, "Like she said, it could get messy." Unlike Angie, Reese was heavyset, but she too wore an abundance of black eye makeup. Obviously, it was the fashion of the day, one that had escaped Zann's notice until now. "Nothing like having your rapist sitting two chairs down and pretending he didn't do anything wrong. Maybe you can sit with us next time. You're a captain, plus you got that valor medal. They'll have to take us serious."

Walking back to her Jeep Zann acknowledged that her promise to Angie and Reese meant she had to return. No matter that she'd already convinced herself this fraternity of soldiers could stir more harm than good, especially when it came to her own memories of what happened to Whit. But when faced with adversity, Marines were programmed to run toward it—never away. And she would always be a Marine.

CHAPTER TWELVE

Bridget hissed as the icepack made contact with the cut above her brow. "Easy…fucking hell, that hurts like a son of a bitch."

"I know. You just need to lie back and let it work. It'll keep the swelling down and numb the pain." Marleigh switched off the bedside lamp, glad she no longer had to look at the swollen, purple eye. "The doctor said for you to rest. That means no TV, no texting…nothing that uses your brain."

"That should be a piece of cake for me, huh?" Bridget was settled into the bottom bunk of Zann and Marleigh's guest room, the one they'd set up for when Zann's nephews stayed over. "At least now I have an excuse every time I screw up the copy. I can honestly tell Clay I may have brain damage."

Not to mention a broken wrist, twenty stitches and a raw patch on her scalp from where her hair had been pulled out. Rocky had yanked her out of the bathroom after breaking down the locked door, causing her to hit her head against the vanity. Because of all the blood, she'd been forced to go to the hospital this time, and in a rare moment of courage and candor, had called Marleigh to pick her up and drive her there. Maybe this time she'd finally had enough.

"I don't feel like joking around about this, Bridget. He's gone too far this time."

"I know," she said, all traces of humor gone. "He had a bee up his ass because I bought those Audrey Brookes without asking him. Do you realize I haven't had a new pair of shoes in over a year? It's fine for him to spend eight hundred dollars a month on ammo and cigarettes, but I can't have one goddamned pair of shoes without him going fucking ballistic."

Marleigh couldn't bear to think what it would be like to live with someone so selfish, so controlling. She and Zann shared everything, and there was nothing they couldn't talk about.

"So I thought if I stayed in the bathroom awhile, he'd eventually cool off. It might've worked if he hadn't come around and jiggled the door. I shouldn't have locked it. He went apeshit and tore it off with a crowbar."

It was at least a blessing he hadn't taken the crowbar to her. "So how come you didn't tell the cops any of this? They can help, you know."

"They haven't helped Kayla Matthews. She called them twice on Mick and all they did was talk to him. By the time they left, he was even more pissed off than before."

Kayla was a woman from their Pilates class. She'd confided in Bridget that their fights had turned physical, that the neighbors had called the police because they were making so much noise.

"Forget Kayla. She's not my best friend—you are. Rocky broke your wrist and nearly put your eye out. If you'd told the cops that, you know as well as I do they'd have picked him up and thrown his ass in jail." There was still time to change her mind, but Bridget had taken a huge step tonight by having Marleigh call him from the hospital to say she wasn't coming home. "Tonight needs to be the beginning of the end, Bridget. This is your life we're talking about. You don't have to go back ever again. Stay here with us for as long as you need to."

Bridget scoffed. "I bet you a thousand dollars he'll be over here tomorrow telling me it's time to come home."

"If he gets any closer than the curb, he'll be trespassing. And you know I won't hesitate to call the cops. Zann already said she'd take off a couple of hours on Monday while he's at work. You guys can go over there with the Jeep and bring all your stuff back here."

She groaned but didn't otherwise put up a fight. It was a good sign.

Marleigh opened the window to let the June breeze filter in. Their house didn't have central air-conditioning. "Want me to turn the fan on? You won't get much of a cross breeze with the door closed."

"The window should be enough." She'd peeled back all but the cotton sheet. "Rocky runs his mouth all the time about heading out to North Dakota where his brother is. Says he'd make good money working the oil fields. I wish he'd just shut up and go already."

That would be the ideal solution, since Rocky wasn't going to learn all of a sudden how to manage his temper or curb his controlling impulses.

Marleigh sat by the bed on a trunk filled with linens until Bridget grew quiet and began to breathe evenly. Then she tiptoed out to find Zann hunched over her laptop at the kitchen table.

"She's finally asleep. I gotta say, this one really threw me. I had a feeling he'd started smacking her around again, but I had no idea it was this bad. Thank God she called me this time."

"She needs to file for divorce first thing Monday morning."

"He's never going to agree to that. I can predict exactly what he'll do next. Flowers, dinner. He'll say he's sorry and swear it'll never happen again. Then she'll start making excuses for him… him being under pressure, her pushing his buttons, whatever. And she'll probably end up going back."

"Come look at this," she said, waving Marleigh over to the table. "This is all you need to file for divorce in Vermont. They don't have kids, don't own a house. All it takes is one simple form. If Rocky signs it—boom—divorce is final in six months. And if he doesn't, she can still put it through by herself but it takes a year. The only catch is they have to live apart for six months before she can file."

"You're preaching to the choir. The problem is that Bridget's singing out of a different book. Nothing changes until she decides to stand up for herself." She couldn't count the number of times she and Zann had talked about Bridget this way, always ending with the same conclusions. "For the life of me, I can't understand why someone as sweet as her thinks she can't do better than an asshole like Rocky Goodson. She's got so much to offer."

"Maybe this time it'll be different. It already is—she called you."

"I wish you'd been there to talk some sense into her. The ER doctor took one look at her and called the cops, but when they got there she wouldn't even tell them what happened."

"I wouldn't read too much into that." Zann closed her laptop and stretched her arms high above her head. "She might just want to handle it her own way where it's not out there for everybody to see. I wouldn't want people to know I'd put up with crap like that."

Abusers counted on that. In fact, Marleigh had argued with Clay about his policy of listing all the domestic disputes in the crime section, thinking it might keep some women from speaking up.

"She thinks Rocky will show up here tomorrow. I guess we have to be ready for that."

Zann pushed her chair back from the table and tugged Marleigh into her lap. "I guarantee that's not going to happen."

* * *

Wes Jackson sat beside her in the front seat of the Jeep, fidgeting with the scratchy seat belt but apparently too polite to complain. Atop his head was a deep red beret, the official cover of the 82nd Airborne. "What'd you say this scumbag's name was?"

"Rocky Goodson."

"You'll recognize him when you see him," Kenny Wales interjected from the backseat. "He's here every weekend. Drives that black Ford pickup with one of those idiot bumper stickers that says this truck's insured by Smith and Wesson, or some such bullshit."

Moe Morgan was the third passenger. Behind them in another vehicle were Leon, TJ and Brandon. It was a show of force, all recruited the night before with a mass email sent to everyone in the veterans group.

Zann turned onto Horse Trail Road. At the end they spotted Rocky's truck, the only vehicle in sight. "I appreciate you guys doing this for me. Sorry to get you up so early on a Saturday. This is when he likes to come."

Wes answered, "We got each other's back, right? That was cool what you did for TJ. I never saw anybody so happy to be working in a shit factory."

Technically, it was a water treatment plant. Malcolm Shively hadn't hesitated over her recommendation, giving TJ his first full-time job with benefits since returning from Iraq with his National Guard unit.

Though there was ample space at the end of the road, they parked directly behind Rocky's truck in a show of dominance, even going so far as to graze his bumper. One by one, the men retrieved their weapons from the trunk of Leon's car. Zann no longer owned one and had declined Wes's offer to use one of his. Her left hand wouldn't cooperate and she was too much of a perfectionist to show up with a bunch of trained shooters and flail around like a fool.

The gun range at Jeb Hickman's farm was far more elaborate than Rocky had described at dinner a month ago, nice enough to turn a tidy profit if Hickman decided to advertise and take the enterprise commercial. For now he still relied on the donation box, clearly marked beneath a sign absolving him of legal liability. The field was deeper than the five hundred yards Rocky had estimated—by her guess it was almost half a mile to the carved-out side of a hill. As wide as a football field and buffered on each side by thick trees, it could easily accommodate eight shooters at the rifle benches and four more at the pistol range, where the covered shooting bays were separated by sheets of lattice.

When the crew gathered at the open gate, she took a visual inventory of their collective firepower. Leon's rifle was a semiauto Armalite like the M16 and Moe's was a bolt action Remington. Both were outfitted with scopes for long-range targeting. The other four men carried sidearms similar to the M9 Beretta they'd all handled in the military. Wes showed off an especially fine SIG Sauer that reportedly cost him north of three thousand bucks.

The shooting benches, used to help steady a long-range rifle shot, were staggered. Downrange at varying distances all the way to the hillside, someone had hung several aluminum pans and skillets from posts. A shooter would know he'd hit the target by the sound and sway. It really was quite an impressive range for amateurs.

Rocky was at the far end, all alone at the pistol range. He'd tacked a paper target—the characteristic silhouette of a man's head and torso—against a stack of hay bales situated twenty-five yards away. Behind the bales was a bullet box, a high bunker filled with sand to trap the errant shots.

With Zann leading the way, they walked single file to meet him. There was no mistaking his nervousness as he stepped out of the bay and lowered his pistol.

Leon and Moe stopped with their rifles a few yards away at the shooting bench nearest the pistol range. The colonel wasted no time lining up his first shot, which pinged a skillet over a hundred yards out. Clearly, he still put in time at the range.

"How're you doing, Rocky?" As she sauntered toward him, the other four men slipped behind him into the pistol bays and began firing at his paper target.

Rocky glanced toward the range when Leon struck another pan that clanged like a bell.

"I figure you know why I'm here, right? We need to talk about Bridget's accident last night."

As she spoke, she studied his demeanor for any signs he might try to do something extraordinarily stupid. Though his eyes darted all around and his hands shook, she was confident the show of force would keep him in check.

"It must be hard on you being married to a woman who's so clumsy...how she's always running into things with her face. I don't know how you stand it, man."

After a handful of shots from the rifle stand, the farthest pan was left spinning. Moe yelled, "No way! Okay, my turn."

"These guys...they're so crazy," she said with a sardonic laugh. "By the way, I see why you like it out here. It's fixed up really good."

"I don't have a rifle no more," Rocky mumbled, as if to suggest it was unfair to threaten him with one. "I sold it."

"This business with Bridget...what with her breaking her wrist and getting that nasty cut over her eye. You know how rumors fly around. Some people say it's you doing that...but then Bridget talks about falling down, bumping her eye on the door...that kind of shit. I don't know what to believe." She paused as the men at the pistol range emptied their clips in unison, creating a racket that reverberated throughout the open field. "The way I figure is *real* tough guys—not the fake ones— they don't need to practice on women, you know what I mean? Take my friends here for instance...they're tough, all right. But they don't go home and beat on their wives and girlfriends. And they don't like men who do."

"I didn't mean for her to get hurt. It was just an argument and I accidentally made her fall. I felt so bad about it." His whining was pathetic. "I was going to call her later...tell her how sorry I am. She knows I'll make it up to her. And I'll be really careful from now on. It won't happen again."

It was exactly the response she'd expected, probably the same one Bridget had heard over and over. "That's right, Rocky. Never again. It's important you understand that this time."

His cheeks had turned as red as a schoolboy's.

"Tell me you do."

"I do." He nodded stiffly.

"Good, good. Now about you calling her to apologize...that won't be necessary this time. In fact, starting right now you're going to leave her alone. No more seeing her, no talking to her, no texting her…not ever again. Are we clear? She's finished with you for good."

His jaw twitched with unconcealed rage. What galled him most—losing control of his wife or being pushed around by a woman?

"Bridget says you've been talking about moving to North Dakota."

"I got a brother who works out there in the oil field. Makes in a week what I make in a month."

"That's just great." She rubbed her hands together. "So what do you say we make this your going-away party? People around here are going to find out what you did—my friends will make sure of that, starting today. Who wants to hang out with a guy who beats up on his wife? So this would be a good time for you to go home and pack up all your stuff in that shiny truck of yours and start driving west. I bet you could be in North Dakota by Tuesday."

After a small wave to indicate she was finished, her friends holstered their guns and began heading back to the parking area.

She took a folded document from inside her jacket. "Oh, and I need for you to sign this. It's a petition for divorce. Bridget's already filled out her part and signed it. She's going to file it at the courthouse first thing Monday morning."

He studied it only briefly before accepting her shoulder so he could scratch his name on the line.

Wes stopped to hand Rocky the ragged remains of his paper target, which he and the others had shot to bits. In his deep Southern drawl, he said, "Whatever the cap'n just told you, it goes double for the rest of us. If I was you, I'd be hightailing it outta here"—he pointed to the emblem on his beret—"'cause I didn't buy this on the Internet."

"One more thing, Rocky. I know you'll be gone and all, but if Bridget should ever fall down the stairs or run into a door again…my friends will take that personally. And you'll never see it coming."

On her way back to the car, she stopped to shove a couple of twenties into Hickman's donation box. Money well spent.

* * *

If what she and her friends had just done wasn't blatantly illegal, it was as close to the line as they could get. There wasn't one among them who'd actually shoot Rocky, but they'd be happy to make his life a living hell—just as they'd done to Daryl Phillips when Reese shared her story about what he'd done to her in Iraq. While Daryl had managed to hold on to a friend or two, his girlfriend had dumped him and he was no longer welcome at any of Colfax's watering holes. It was only a matter of time before he moved away to start over, out of Reese's life forever.

Marleigh had been right to encourage her to join the veterans group. She'd missed the camaraderie of the Marine Corps more than she realized, and not just the companionship. The events their group had planned—volunteer outings, toy drives for Christmas—gave her a chance to recapture a feeling of togetherness and common purpose she'd taken for granted as a Marine. She liked walking into that basement room at the church and knowing everyone there had shared the experience of being shipped off far from home and asked to put their life on the line for a military operation. After today, she also knew she had loyal friends she could call on if she ever needed anything.

Pulling into the driveway alongside Marleigh's Subaru, it occurred to her they ought to pick up Bridget's car today in case Rocky decided to trash it. The screen door banged behind her as she entered. "Marleigh?"

"We're back here in the kitchen." Marleigh handed her a fresh cup of coffee. "We've been going over the joint property list you downloaded last night. I can't believe how easy it is. Way easier than getting married."

Bridget looked up anxiously from the breakfast nook. "What happened? I need to know everything he said."

She laid out the paper with Rocky's signature. "I don't think you'll be seeing him anymore. I'll go over to the apartment with you on Monday to check it out, but I expect all his stuff to be gone."

"Oh, my God!" Bridget put her hands to her cheeks as tears flooded her eyes. "Please tell me you're serious."

"I suggested North Dakota like you said. I'm pretty sure it won't be Vermont." She snagged a strip of bacon from a plate on the stove and paced the kitchen as Bridget and Marleigh peppered her with questions.

"You really are a hero—just like Marleigh always said," Bridget gushed.

"I wouldn't go that far," Zann said sheepishly. "All I did was make a few suggestions. It was the other guys who convinced him."

"She's always been *my* hero." Marleigh wrapped her in a hug, still addressing Bridget. "Remember back when I first met Zann and interviewed her for the paper, how excited I was? How could I not fall for somebody like this? She's so amazing."

"Oh, please." Zann had gotten her fill of their fawning and headed down the hall to the living room. Several envelopes were stacked on a side table near the front door. "The mail came already?"

Marleigh shouted from the kitchen, "It's yesterday's. I forgot about it, what with everything else going on."

The stack was mostly junk. On the bottom was a letter addressed to her, handwritten in a flowing script she didn't recognize, with no return address. The faded gray postmark was hard to read in the dim light of the living room lamp. A creative solicitation probably, made to look like a personal letter.

She turned it over to rip through the seal and discovered it did indeed have a return address, written in the same hand as the script on the front. No name, just a street address in a city that sent a shudder up her spine. Zanesville, Ohio.

"Anything important?" Marleigh called.

"No…nothing." She knew only one person from Zanesville— Staff Sergeant Whitney Laird. Her former lover.

CHAPTER THIRTEEN

"I'm going to need a cold shower," Marleigh said, fanning herself at the sight of Zann in her Marine Corps uniform. It still fit her beautifully, the iconic blue pants with the distinctive Blood Stripe and an open-collared khaki shirt. Her chest was adorned with a rack of ribbons three rows high and a silver marksman medal. "What's a girl gotta do to get you to wear that to bed sometime?"

Zann cracked a vague smile that was too grim to be considered playful. Something was bothering her, no matter how much she insisted otherwise. She'd been sulking for the past four days, ever since she got back from her showdown with Rocky.

"I can't get over them giving you all of three days to get down there for a checkup. And why Bethesda? Couldn't you have gone to the VA over at Whitewater Junction?"

"I told you, they sent another letter but it must have gotten lost or something. I wouldn't even have known about it if she hadn't called Monday to confirm. Miss something like this and I'm considered AWOL."

"Yeah, I know. It's just too bad we didn't have more notice. I probably could have gotten time off too. It would have been nice to hang out for a few days in DC. See the monuments, the museums." She persisted with her wish list despite the fact that nothing in Zann's demeanor even remotely suggested she wanted company. "And frankly, it just seems like a waste to go all the way down there and back on the same day."

Zann rolled her eyes and let out a dramatic sigh. "I get it, you're annoyed. Did it occur to you that I might not like DC, that I might resent having to go back there because that's where I had three surgeries? We're not going to fix all that by gawking at monuments. Now can we just drop it?"

"Fine! I didn't realize my wanting to go with you was so intolerable." She spun in the doorway and marched indignantly to the kitchen. It was bad enough that Zann wouldn't tell her what she was brooding about. She didn't seem to care about her feelings either.

Moments later Zann came in and embraced her from behind, dropping a kiss on her neck. "I'm sorry, sweetheart. Obviously I'm the one annoyed about them springing this on me at the last minute. I wish we could have planned it out for you to come with me. As it is, I've got so much to do at work that I barely have time to get down there and back, so it wouldn't have worked out anyway."

It was unusual for them to fight, especially over trivial things. But when they did, it always ended exactly like this. Nothing was so important that it couldn't be smoothed over with a kiss.

"I probably couldn't have gone anyway. Clay wants me ready to go to Montpelier whenever they start the hearings on the runoff in Otter Creek. That could be any day."

"We'll do something fun soon. I promise."

"Something involving you in that uniform, I hope."

* * *

Zann had a window seat in the cramped regional jet. Any minute they'd start tacking along the Potomac past the

Washington Monument and Capitol Building, but the majestic sights were no solace for her guilt. Not once since they'd met had she lied to Marleigh, certainly not on a scale like this. A compulsory assessment at Bethesda Naval Hospital to ensure future benefits? Not only was it an elaborate lie, it had rolled easily off her tongue with uncommon conviction. She'd even piled it on thicker by claiming an aversion to the whole city caused by the time she'd spent there in treatment.

"Ladies and gentlemen, the captain has begun our descent..."

If her guilt weren't enough, she also had to worry about getting caught in her deception. As a reporter, Marleigh had easy access to regulations and statutes that would debunk her excuse.

The reason for the visit had nothing to do with military benefits, or for that matter with the hospital at Bethesda. After receiving the letter on Saturday, she'd done a frantic online search for military records but reached a dead end. The soldier archives she needed were kept in St. Louis and accessible only by family of service members. That left her only one option—the Marine Corps Office of the Commandant in DC. It held records of every Marine who'd died in action. Unless those records were protected by secret classification, they were subject to release through a request under the Freedom of Information Act. The problem was that processing one of those could take months if not years. Zann couldn't bear to wait that long for answers. She'd used a Camp Lejeune connection to get her to the front of the line if she presented herself in person.

Her only luggage was a zipped leather binder in which she carried a blank tablet and the letter from Vanessa Laird, Whit's younger sister whose social media profile showed her living in Zanesville and teaching history at the local high school. Whit had bragged endlessly about Vanessa, the first in their family to graduate from college. However, it was Vanessa who had the bigger case of hero worship, evidenced by the letters from home that Whit read aloud to her fellow soldiers.

Zann knew as well as anyone the prideful effect military service had on family members. Marleigh's sweet words of respect and admiration echoed in her ear all the time, but today they brought an almost unbearable shame. *My hero. My shining warrior.*

After an unusually bumpy landing in crosswinds, they taxied to the gate and filed out.

"Thank you for your service," the flight attendant said, offering a handshake. It had been a while since Zann had heard that—and today was the first time it didn't fill her with pride.

Stopping in the ladies' room, she took stock of the soldier staring back at her in the mirror. Her pride in having worn this uniform was a defining characteristic of her life, as an honorable Marine who'd served her country with integrity and valor. But if Vanessa Laird was right, she'd never see herself the same way again.

* * *

Marleigh cleared a space at the break table and sat down with her lunch of microwaved leftovers. Reporting on an accident with minor injuries involving a school bus had kept her out of the office most of the morning. Bridget usually got the traffic-related assignments, but she'd been in Rutland all morning covering the county's annual quilt show, an important story for a loyal segment of their readers. Marleigh admitted to herself that she didn't mind the occasional spot news assignment, as it kept her reporting skills sharpened.

Bridget clomped into the break room in platform sandals that made her nearly six feet tall. "Who wants to look at quilts when it's ninety frickin' degrees in the shade? Thought I'd never get out of there. They were handing out the ribbons and got down to the last two. The judges couldn't agree, and I swear I thought there was going to be a rumble about it. Now *that's* a story everybody would read."

"So did you get it filed?" Their deadline was thirty minutes ago.

"Yeah, I had it all typed up on my laptop while they were bickering back and forth. All I had to do was write in the winner.

Somebody found an extra blue ribbon in a box and they called it a tie. But their Wi-Fi was down at the rec center so I had to do one of those hotspots on my phone like Terry showed us."

It may have been Marleigh's imagination, but Bridget seemed to have blossomed into a whole new person in just the last four days.

"Marleigh, you'll never guess who called me last night. Maxine Goodson, Rocky's mother."

"Uh-oh, that can't be good."

"It was fan-frickin-tastic!" she declared, slapping the table emphatically. "Rocky told her we were getting a divorce, that I'd been running around on him like a whore."

"That's awful." She should have known Rocky wouldn't just disappear without getting in a scathing parting shot. "Right when I think he can't be a bigger asshole, he goes and proves me wrong."

Bridget huffed and waved her off. "Who gives a shit? I don't care if he told her I blew the Pope as long as he's out of here."

Zann also would be glad to hear Rocky had mentioned the divorce as if it were a done deal. Though Marleigh thought it best not to tell her about the rumors he was trying to spread through his mother. The more she thought about Zann and her friends confronting him at the gun range, the more relieved she was that it hadn't gone off the rails. Someone as volatile as Rocky could have done something foolish and tragic.

"What are you guys doing later tonight? I got this coupon for free dessert with dinner at the Storm Café. I want to take you and Zann out...my way of saying thanks for saving my ass last weekend. But it has to be tonight because it's only good for Wednesdays."

"Can't—Zann had to go to DC and won't get back till late tonight."

"What did she go for?"

"Something about getting her arm checked out at Bethesda."

Bridget opened a salad she'd picked up at Subway, wafting the awful smell of processed turkey and honey mustard dressing. "Did she hurt it again? Please don't tell me something happened at the gun range. I'll feel like crap."

"No, no…she said it was just routine. They needed to evaluate it so they could keep her active in the system."

"Weird. I didn't know they made them go all the way back. Daddy only had to go to the VA over at Whitewater Junction when his foot flared up. He broke it doing one of those fake parachute jumps on the obstacle course when he first joined the army. Thirty-five years later, guess where he gets a bone spur? His regular insurance wouldn't cover it—they made him go back to the VA. But I remember him complaining about having to wait like forever to get an appointment. Hey, maybe they'll have some kind of new technology so Zann can get her hand working right again."

Marleigh didn't notice the injury much anymore and wondered if that was because she was used to it. "Can you tell her arm's still hurt?"

"Well…yeah. Everybody can, I guess." Bridget covered her mouth as though she'd made a gaffe. "It's not that bad though. Just when she walks, she doesn't swing that one the same way. And if you watch her for a minute, you can see she tries not to use that hand. Like I noticed she puts her fork down to pick up a glass…that kind of stuff."

Zann had worked so hard on improving her strength and muscle control. She'd be mortified to know people still noticed her injury. But she wouldn't hear it from Marleigh.

* * *

Zann slid her butt back on the bench and straightened her shoulders against the wall, ever mindful that she was in the official headquarters of the US Marine Corps. It was strange being surrounded again by so many others in uniform.

The higher-ranking officers who walked by triggered an unexpected wave of nostalgia for the career she'd always assumed she'd have. In all probability, she'd have been a major by now—perhaps even working in this building or at the Pentagon.

Instead she was back in Colfax checking construction sites for compliance with the building code. Quite a difference. And yet, there wasn't a moment of her time with Marleigh that she'd trade for an oak leaf on her shoulder.

"Captain Redeker?"

She rocketed to her feet, scanning the busy hallway for who had called her name. A female staff sergeant beckoned her from an office three doors down.

"I'm Captain Suzann Redeker," she said smartly.

"Good afternoon, Captain. I hope you had a pleasant trip." Though Zann held the higher rank, the sergeant wasn't required to salute indoors.

"I did. Thank you."

She was led to an inner office barely large enough for the massive steel desk.

"Please have a seat. The major will be right in."

Major Jorge Rodriguez, according to the placard on his desk, a friend of a friend at Camp Lejeune. The folder on his desk was marked "Restricted," meaning its release might cause undesirable effects. But then the War on Terror had rendered virtually all military information classified at some level, from troop movements all the way down to dental records.

She'd been in offices exactly like this one hundreds of times. Major Rodriguez's desk was free of clutter and his walls decorated with framed creeds and Marine Corps emblems. The visitor chairs were more cushioned than she'd expected, a welcome change from the marble bench in the hall.

At the sound of footsteps, she rose and issued a smart salute, a requirement at the start of a meeting with a superior.

"Captain, at ease." The major was dressed similarly to her, though in a long-sleeved shirt with a matching tie. His graying hair looked as though it had been parted with a straightedge, and his posture was ramrod straight.

"Thank you for seeing me so quickly, sir."

"You should thank Lieutenant Colonel McCombs at Camp Lejeune. He's the one who suggested I fit you in right away. You indicated to him that resolution of this matter was urgent." He drummed his fingers on the folder without opening it. "Could you elaborate on exactly what it is about your request that warrants such urgency?"

She was taken aback by the question, though his tone struck her as official rather than challenging, as if he were required to submit a report and needed this detail to complete it.

"Of course, sir. I recently received a piece of personal correspondence from a family member regarding the death of a soldier under my command. I hoped to avoid a delay in my response."

"I see." He fingered the corner of the file and twirled it slowly, almost absently. "You've requested information on the death of Gunnery Sergeant Whitney Laird."

"Yes, sir. The correspondence came from Sergeant Laird's sister, a Vanessa Laird, of Zanesville, Ohio. In her letter, she suggested the details of the sergeant's death were different from my own personal recollection of events."

"Captain, you are aware that as inactive reserve, you are no longer required by the Marine Corps to address requests from family members regarding service members who are deceased, even those who perished under your command. In fact, it may not be advisable for you to do so, since you no longer have access to such classified information as might be needed to provide a proper reply."

She held his gaze, trying to hear what he wasn't saying. He clearly wasn't eager to share whatever was in the file on his desk. "Sir, as Sergeant Laird's commanding officer, I was the one responsible for getting her home. I failed to do that and I need to understand why."

He leaned back in his squeaky chair and tapped the file against his hand. "There could be circumstances noted in this file that the Marine Corps would prefer to keep confidential for various concerns, which is why they've been classified as Restricted. I'm willing to make an exception in this extraordinary situation but I'd like your assurance as an officer that the information won't leave this room. Understood?"

"Yes, sir."

"Gunnery Sergeant Whitney Jane Laird, Third Battalion-Second Marine Division, was killed in action as she engaged enemy combatants in the village of Dahaneh in the Helmand

Province of Afghanistan on three January, 2012. At the time of her death she was on patrol with her Female Engagement Team..."

As he read through the incident report, Zann realized her heart was pounding, that she couldn't breathe without drawing deep gulps of air.

"...and within minutes, Gunnery Sergeant Laird succumbed to her injuries, which included six bullet wounds to her thighs, shoulders and neck. The fatal wound in her neck was found to have resulted from a five-point-five-six by forty-five millimeter round..."

The words thundered in her head. She and Whit were the only two people in the house that day who were firing ammunition that matched that caliber. Vanessa Laird had gotten her hands on a copy of the report in the major's hands and learned that her sister's fatal bullet had come from Zann's M16.

* * *

Zann closed her window to shield the setting sun and stretched her legs as far as the seat in front of her would allow. The ninety-minute flight would put her in Burlington at ten thirty, meaning she wouldn't get home until midnight. That would spare her having to talk, though Marleigh would have questions in the morning about her supposed doctor visit.

Major Rodriguez had done his best to quiet her distress, but there was nothing he could say to change the fact that she was directly responsible for the death of a fellow soldier. Not just a soldier—a soldier under her command, a friend. Someone who'd once been her lover. So why had she been given a medal for that?

"You weren't, Captain. You were given a medal for showing extraordinary bravery. You charged into a hostile dwelling and dispatched four Taliban combatants who had ambushed your unit. Four combatants who at that very moment were assembling explosives that almost certainly would have resulted in innumerable casualties

of fellow Marines if not for your actions. There's no way of knowing how many lives you saved that day, how many families you saved from having to hear the dreaded words that their Marine was lost."

She gripped her biceps and flexed her arm just to prove she could. The report made special mention of her injury. Hamza's bullet had rendered her momentarily incapacitated, that moment being the milliseconds before she realized she could no longer hold her rifle steady with her left arm. It was in that fleeting window that an errant shot had found Whit—who was undeniably the true hero that day.

For her sacrifice, Whit was posthumously awarded the Marine Corps Commendation Medal, a fine honor but nowhere near as prestigious as the Bronze Star with the Combat-V they'd presented to Zann. It was already a sticking point with enlisted personnel throughout the military that officers typically received higher honors for lesser actions. What would they say if they knew her medal of valor had come through even after officials had learned of her mistake?

If she were honest with herself, Whit's death had always held her back from celebrating the honors others wanted to bestow. From the medal ceremony at Camp Lejeune to Marleigh's newspaper article to being honored at the Fourth of July parade, she'd always felt a solemn remorse that Whit had made the greater sacrifice and gotten less recognition.

Despite Major Rodriguez's assurances, the pride in knowing her actions that day had saved Marines at Camp Leatherneck did nothing to erase the horror. The question now was whether or not she could bring herself to tell the people who loved her that she didn't deserve their lofty esteem. She'd always said she hadn't done anything special, that her actions that day were the result of the hard-nosed training all Marines went through to prepare for moments like that. *Just doing my job.*

From the moment they met, Marleigh had worshipped her as a hero. What would she say if she learned that in the one moment where training and instincts truly mattered, Zann had failed and it had cost a soldier her life?

CHAPTER FOURTEEN

With her eyes still closed, Marleigh swung her arm across the cool sheets to find the bed empty. Meanwhile the aroma of coffee teased her nostrils and guaranteed she wouldn't be going back to sleep.

Zann was sitting at the breakfast table watching the sunrise through the bay window. It had been yet another restless night, another early morning.

"You're up early for a Saturday," she said, sliding her arms around Zann's shoulders from behind. "Everything okay?"

"Yeah, sure." Zann patted her hand and shrugged out of the embrace as she stood. "Guess my body had all the sleep it needed. I didn't want to wake you."

A couple of weeks ago, that might have been an ordinary reply. Now it was just another in a growing string of denials and diversions, whatever it took to avoid talking about what had her so on edge. Though Marleigh could pinpoint *when* it started, she was no closer to knowing *why*.

It must have something to do with Rocky because that's when she started brooding. Zann had yet to come totally clean about what she and her friends had done that day to scare him into leaving town. It must have been intimidating as hell, since Bridget hadn't heard from him since. She hated to think Zann had crossed a line, that she'd allowed her friends to beat Rocky to a pulp or humiliate him in some way that was beyond the pale. Zann didn't have it in her to bully someone that way, but had she stood by while it happened? That would certainly explain her behavior over the last couple of weeks, her withdrawal and obvious remorse, like she was wrestling every day with feelings of dishonor that ran counter to her identity.

She winced at the bitterness of the coffee, which probably had been brewed hours ago. "Hey, why don't we go out for breakfast? We haven't done that in ages."

"I ate already…just some cereal."

"Come on, couldn't you go for some French toast at Rosie's? Great way to fuel up for spreading that truckload of gravel."

Their supplier had dumped a pile in the side yard the day before while they were at work. That meant hauling it one wheelbarrow load at a time to the driveway and smoothing it out.

Zann retrieved a cap from a hook in the hallway and pulled her ponytail through the back. "I need to go meet somebody from the veterans group. I'll take care of the gravel when I get home."

"Seriously?" Marleigh blocked her path to the back door. "What kind of veterans meeting gets scheduled for seven o'clock on a Saturday morning?"

"I didn't say it was a meeting."

"No, you really didn't say what it was. Or who it was or what it's about. You've gotten so you don't tell me anything at all." The deliberate evasiveness wasn't only concerning—it was infuriating. "Can you not see that whatever's in your head is affecting me too?"

"For Christ's sake, Marleigh. What we do is private for a reason. People talk about things they did, things they feel.

When they tell people stuff, they need to know it's not going to get blabbed all over town."

"Right, because blabbing all over town is what I do for a living. Is that what you're saying? I at least have a right to know where you're going at the crack of dawn on a Saturday morning. Giving me that courtesy isn't what I'd call spilling state secrets."

Zann shimmied by her and out to the back steps. "I'll be home before lunchtime. If you still want to go out, we can go then. Leave the gravel for me when I get back."

In those very few moments, something fundamental had shifted between them—a stubborn acknowledgment from Zann that for the first time since they'd known each other, she was keeping a secret. What could she possibly…a sickening shudder made her want to throw up. No, Zann wouldn't do something like that. They'd made love only two days ago. If anything, it was deeper, more intense than usual of late. It was only their communication that was off.

* * *

Wes's red pickup truck boasted oversized tires, chrome running boards and cab-mounted fog lights. The sight triggered a mild sense of panic, and Zann braked before she reached the end of the dirt road. This was her last chance to turn around. Once Wes saw her, she'd feel obligated to follow through.

A stabbing pain in her stomach, probably indigestion or acid from the coffee, might as well have been Marleigh punching her in the gut. Zann could rationalize all she wanted, but there was no denying she'd lied again. The truth about where she was going and why would have set off an argument even worse than the one they'd just had.

Wes was leaning against the tailgate as she pulled into a space beside him. With his head tipped back, he peered at her beneath the bill of his cap. "Wasn't sure you'd make it."

"Neither was I." She still had time to change her mind. "I'm not sure I want to do this."

"Don't have to if you don't want to. S'pose we just have a little fun today and see how you feel about it?" He dropped the tailgate and dragged a small padlocked trunk closer to him. "I'm a SIG guy, you know. Got a sweet Legion here you can try…double-action, three-fifty-seven, fifteen round. Retails for thirteen but it's got a few rounds on it. 'Cause it's you, I'll let it go for a grand."

He definitely had champagne tastes when it came to handguns, but she had only a beer budget to work with. Marleigh would miss a thousand bucks from their joint checking account, especially after what they'd laid out for the new roof. "I was thinking something in the five hundred range, more like the Beretta nine millimeter."

"You want the one good ol' Uncle Sam gave you." His nod was so exaggerated there was no mistaking his condescension. "Great gun for beginners, but that's not you, now is it?"

"Maybe it is. If I'd still been able to shoot, they probably wouldn't have kicked me out of the Marines."

He rummaged in the trunk and drew out an aluminum case painted over in a camouflage design. "Fine, here's a brand spanking new 92FS if that's what you gotta have. Six hundred retail right off the shelf. But I promise if you shoot this Legion, you'll want to walk it down the aisle and marry it. I'm serious. Go ahead, try 'em both."

There was no one else on the range at the early hour, a fact that made her wonder briefly what Rocky was up to these days, if he'd made it to North Dakota and gone to work in the oil fields like he said. Jeb Hickman wouldn't miss his paltry donations, especially since he'd picked up at least a dozen new shooters now that the guys in her veterans group knew about the range.

"You load up and I'll stick up a couple of targets," he said as they reached the pistol range.

While stocking the spare clips for the Beretta, she noted the differential in price for cartridges. "See, here's another thing. This ammo for the SIG runs ten bucks higher."

"You're gonna pay more to hit the target, Cap'n. It's just a fact. Now if all you want is to get close, maybe pop Paper Man in the chest once every five or ten shots and get all excited about it, get the Beretta." He opened a sleek black case holding the SIG and a pair of clips. It was indeed a sweet-looking gun, a brushed gray finish on the frame and slide, with a checkered grip. "They don't make a better sight on a semiauto. Oh, and the trigger's adjustable."

She felt its weight in her hand, compact and balanced, not as clunky as the M9. "I'll give it a try but I'm not promising anything."

"Then do me a favor. Shoot the Beretta first." He pressed the grip into her hand, not bothering with the showman's presentation. "Clip's already loaded. Gimme three body shots."

She hadn't fired a gun since Dahaneh, but that didn't matter. Her Marine Corps training came back instantly as she assumed the stance, placing her left foot forward and bending slightly at the waist. There was a stark difference in which muscles came into play as she raised her left arm to steady her grip, an unnatural feel. With her head cocked, she closed one eye and lined the sights at the chest of the paper target Wes had hung on a hook against a hay bale. Focusing only on the front sight, she squeezed off three shots in rapid succession.

"Congratulations, Redeker. You managed to hit the bullet box."

As she lowered her gun, she peered ahead and saw the target untouched. "Damn."

"S'okay. You went high and left. What does that tell you?"

Basically it meant her wrist had probably cocked on ejection because her left hand wasn't strong enough to hold the right one firm. "Let me try again." This time she concentrated on locking her right wrist so it wouldn't flail. Three more shots.

"That's better. You caught him in the shoulder, but in combat we still call that a dead Marine."

His words were jarring, prompting an unwelcome vision of Whitney Laird lying just inside the doorway of the small hut, bleeding out. As a wave of rage overtook her, Zann raised the gun again and emptied the clip.

"Pair of deuces," he said drolly, an apparent reference to two shots that managed to hit the edge of the silhouette.

She knew better than to come out to a pistol range and fire without discipline. That's what guys like Rocky did, all the while imagining they were Dirty Harry. "This is ridiculous. I've got no business out here if I can't even hold a damn gun."

"Nah, you're all right. Just a little rusty is all. You're gonna love it when you get back into it."

She wasn't looking to love it. What mattered was reclaiming what Hamza had taken from her and making sure she never gave up on herself again. From the moment his bullet ripped through her arm, she'd accepted her weakness as if it were a proud memento of heroism. How sick was that? She'd made it her excuse for all the things she couldn't be—a Marine, a police officer, a lousy senior inspector. In the eyes of the Marine Corps, it even absolved her from killing Whit. But not for Vanessa... and not for Zann either now that she knew what her weakness had cost. A real hero fought through pain and weakness. A real hero triumphed.

"Yo." Wes waved his hand in front of her eyes, breaking her stare. "How about you humor me now and give this Legion a try? Swear to God, if it doesn't make you want to take it home and make love to it all night, I'll shut the fuck up and sell you the Beretta for five hundred bucks."

She studied the weight and balance again, even transferring it to her left hand to feel its stubbly grip with the three fingers that still produced sensation. "That's a pretty good deal, Wes. I might have to fake it for that."

"You won't be able to. I'm telling you, the SIG's gonna steal your heart. Seventeen-rounder. Now gimme three."

The sight gave her a sharper view of the target, and its bright green color made it easier to focus. Concentrating again on holding her right wrist firm and the rest of her body in a state of fixed calm, she pulled back on the trigger once...twice...a third time, with a steady beat in between.

"Now that's what I call shooting, Cap'n. See what I mean about marrying this gun?"

All three shots had landed inside the body, with one finding dead center in the chest.

"That was luck." She aimed again and rang out three more, all of which belted the target with a thump. A smile she couldn't control spread across her face.

"I accept cash or personal check."

"Jesus, I honestly didn't know a gun could make that much difference." What if she'd been carrying one of these when Hamza came through the door? He never would have gotten off a shot.

"The SIG's no ordinary gun. I wouldn't carry anything else."

She gestured toward his truck, shaking off her thoughts of Dahaneh. "So how come you have all these? What are you, an arms dealer or something?"

"Call me a collector. One of the reasons I jumped on this transfer was how easy it is to buy and sell in Vermont." The state had virtually no restrictions on gun ownership, and actually prohibited government entities from interfering with a sale or requiring registration. Practically anyone who wanted to carry a gun could do so with no permit required.

She took a long, last look at the SIG and handed it back. "I can't afford it, at least not today. But I'll give you five hundred right now and another five at the first of the month when I get my check. You keep the gun till it's paid for."

"Aw, no way. I know you're good for it. Pay me when you see me."

It was way more than she'd planned to spend, not just for the gun but for the ammo. If she came out here a couple of times a week and got off a hundred rounds of practice, that was two hundred a month in cartridges, and one-sixty in range fees. An expensive hobby, money she and Marleigh would miss in their renovation fund. It wasn't fair to spend that much without talking it over.

Except Marleigh would say no, not because it was expensive but because she hated guns. And that wasn't fair either. Zann had every right to hold back some of her own money for things she wanted to do. Her Marine Corps pension was all hers, eight hundred a month. She'd earned that before she and Marleigh ever met. Spending it now to learn how to shoot again felt like a reasonable expense…even as she knew keeping secrets from her wife wasn't reasonable at all.

* * *

Marleigh drew a deep relaxing breath and centered her attention on the fingertips and lips that gently teased her breast. This was Zann's signature lovemaking style, easing her back down as their passion ebbed as if she couldn't bring herself to let go. Precious moments like this defined their love.

There was no better bookend to a day that had gotten off to a difficult start. Though Zann still hadn't opened up about where she'd gone that morning or with whom, at least she'd come home in a lighter mood. After spreading the gravel, she'd playfully pushed Marleigh around the yard in the wheelbarrow and even labored in the kitchen over an Internet recipe for French toast. An odd dinner choice, but a clear sign she was feeling guilty about storming off at breakfast.

"I love you so much, Captain Zann," she murmured, feeling her eyes grow heavy with sleep.

"I'm sorry, sweetheart," Zann continued her tender caress. "About this morning, I mean. I met up with Wes, no big deal. I was a jerk not to tell you where I was going. There was no good reason other than me being stubborn. It's just...I've been thinking you were right, that I ought to do more stuff with my friends. I let myself get in a rut, going to work every day and coming home. You and Bridget hang out all the time. It would be good for me to have my own friends too."

"Of course it would if that's what you want." She struggled against the weight to sit up. "But I never meant for you to feel like I was pushing you out of the house or making you do things you didn't want to do. I only encouraged you about the veterans group because I thought you might like meeting some other people around here who went through some of the same stuff you did."

"I know and you were right. And now that I've made some friends..." She let the thought dangle so long, it became obvious she was struggling to justify her secrecy and irritation. "It's really stupid that I got so agitated this morning because it's nothing. It's hard sometimes to figure out what I'm allowed to say to other people, even you. Take Wes Jackson, for instance. He's a good guy, Eighty-Second Airborne. Like me, he's seen a lot of action, so we hit it off pretty good. But I shouldn't be the one telling his stories, just like I don't want him telling mine to his friends."

"That's fine. Maybe you'll bring him around one of these days and he can tell me himself." As soon as she said it, she worried Zann would get annoyed again that she was asking to be let inside their inner circle. "But only if you want me to meet him. I'm not saying you need to."

"Hmm...he's kind of an acquired taste. Rubbed me the wrong way at first, but I like him now. I might even go so far as to call him my best friend."

"Honey, that's great." It was an understatement to say she felt inadequate to fully engage with Zann over her time in Afghanistan. Obviously there were things Zann held back to protect her from the brutality of war, from the horror of how it felt to see people killed or to take another life. "I always thought it would be good if you could talk to somebody who could relate to what you went through."

Zann relaxed and rested her head across Marleigh's chest as she lay back down. "Would it be all right if I hung out with him on the weekends? Not all the time. Just maybe like today, a few hours on Saturday morning. Then you and I would have the rest of the day to ourselves."

"Of course." Even as she agreed, she admitted to herself the disappointment of losing a lazy morning in bed or a possible breakfast run to Rosie's. They'd have to make up for it on Sundays. "Can I ask you something?"

"Anything," Zann whispered, once again nuzzling her breast.

"Don't get mad, please. I'm just trying to understand what's going on. Okay?"

Zann responded with the slightest tension, one Marleigh might not have even noticed had she not been looking for it. "You want to know why I've been such a jerk lately."

"Kinda. Not really about you being a jerk, but it's obvious something's been eating at you for a while. I was wondering if maybe it had to do with Rocky. You never told me what you did, how you got him to leave. Did you get some of your friends to beat him up?"

"No! Jesus, people go to jail for that kind of stuff, Marleigh. Do you really think I'd risk something like that?"

Part of her felt guilty even for asking, but it bothered her more that she was uncertain. Zann's secrecy had done that. "I didn't want to think that, but I thought it was weird you never told me exactly what happened. We've always been able to talk about everything before. I figured whatever it was, it bothered you enough that you couldn't tell me."

Zann sighed deeply and rolled onto her back with her hands behind her head. "Marleigh, I'm not going to come home and brag about bullying a guy till he nearly wet his pants. That's what I did and it's not something I'm proud of. But guys like Rocky, they think it makes them tough that they keep their woman in line. Real men though, men like my vet friends…they stand up for women who need it. And that's what I told him, that the guys in Colfax weren't going to put up with him beating on Bridget like that. I said some friends of mine were already spreading the word around town, that he'd better not show his face anymore or somebody was going to call him out."

It made sense that having people find out would be humiliating for a cocky prick like Rocky, especially if it meant someone bigger and stronger might rearrange his face. As far as Marleigh was concerned, there was nothing dishonorable about Zann putting an abusive husband in his place, no matter how she did it. She hadn't crossed a line and therefore had done nothing that ought to keep her up at night.

The problem then…if her angst and restlessness had nothing to do with Rocky, what else could it be? She wasn't sleeping well, and she'd been moodier, quicker to rile. There was the trip to Bethesda about that time. They'd examined her arm and certified her for whatever care might be necessary down the road. Nothing unusual, nothing unexpected.

That left only the veterans group. The timing made it plausible as a source of concern, and the people and their stories obviously meant a lot to her. It would be just like Zann to take on their problems as if they were her own. That's what the officer in charge would do, especially if that officer was someone as noble and self-sacrificing as Zann.

The more she thought about it, the more sense it made. Hearing about other soldiers' difficulties adjusting to life after the military had triggered this uneasiness, and it would probably have to run its course. In the meantime, she was in no position to help.

CHAPTER FIFTEEN

"Zann, you need to calm down. What did you think you were going to do to that kid? Punch him in the face?" Marleigh barreled through the front door and threw her shoulder bag on the dining table. She'd never seen Zann so angry, so out of control. "It was just a stupid prank."

She'd been pulling up to the house from work when a carload of teenage boys drove by and threw a brick at their mailbox, smashing it and knocking it off its post. Zann peeled out after them in her Jeep and yanked the boy from the driver's seat at a stoplight. Thankfully, Marleigh had gotten there just in time to pull her off, and then stood defiantly in the road until Zann got back in her car and turned for home.

"What in the world has gotten into you? Since when do you go off on somebody like that? A kid, for Christ's sake!"

Zann pushed by her into the bedroom without a word, clearly absorbed in her anger and unconcerned over a near disastrous incident. It was more than just the kids that had gotten under her skin lately. She'd been agitated for a couple of days for reasons Marleigh couldn't fathom.

Ten minutes of cold silence followed, enough time for both of them to cool off, Marleigh thought. "I'm still out here if you want to talk. Come on…whatever this is, we can deal with it."

Not even a grunt.

Resigned to make the first move, she slapped the sofa as she stood and pushed open the door to the bedroom. Zann was rolling up a T-shirt to stuff in her backpack. "What the hell do you think you're doing?"

Zann froze but didn't look up. "There's something I need to do."

"I'll say. You need to tell me what's going on. You've been moping around here since Wednesday with a fuse the size of a hangnail. No matter what I say, you either ignore me or act like you're going to bite my head off. So I'll ask you again, what the hell is going on?"

"It's nothing to do with you."

"Oh, that's a relief!" She made no effort to cover her sarcasm. "I feel all better now. You know, for a minute there I finally understood what Bridget must have felt like, always tiptoeing around on eggshells because she was afraid of doing something to piss Rocky off."

"Jesus, Marleigh. You know I'd never hurt you like that."

"You mean because you haven't knocked me around? I've got news for you—there's such a thing as emotional abuse too."

She slammed the door and stormed back to the other room. This was the same tired bullshit they went through a month ago when Zann had sulked around and gone off with her veteran friends without telling her where or why. Her own wife didn't trust her enough to let her in.

Fuming as she paced the hall, she was tempted to get in her car and drive off, giving Zann a taste of her own medicine. That would accomplish exactly nothing except to make a bad situation worse. She couldn't stand another show of indifference. There had to be a way to crack this iron shell.

Zann emerged from the bedroom jangling her keys and carrying a backpack.

"Please don't go back out again. Talk to me. Help me understand what's gotten you so riled up. This isn't the Zann Redeker I know."

"Marleigh, there's something I have to do. You have every right to be upset. It's just…I'm in a bad place right now. I fucked something up and I have to fix it." Her manner had shifted from sullen to methodical, and her unfaltering march to the door made it clear her mind was made up.

"What did you do?"

Zann groaned with undisguised impatience. For a second it looked as if she might come clean, but then she shook her head. "I'm really sorry."

"Great, at least you're sorry." She bit her lip, frustrated that she too was losing patience. "Any idea what time you'll be back?"

"I'm not sure. Two days…maybe three. I don't have to be back at work till Monday."

"*Days?*" Barely conscious of how her feet got her there, she positioned herself between Zann and the door. "You're leaving for *days* and I don't even get to know where or why?"

"I can't talk about this. Not now. I just know I have to take care of it or it'll eat me up from the inside out."

"So you're going to let it eat *me* up instead. See, the way I look at it is you *can* talk about it—you just won't. And I'm supposed to be okay with that?" She deserved better than this, and it was clear she wouldn't get an answer unless she demanded it. "For all I know you're running off to meet another woman. Is that it? You've got a girlfriend on the side who snaps her fingers and you—"

"That's a load of shit and you know it! I've never cheated on you. Hell, I've never even looked at anybody else. How could you even say something like that?"

Marleigh replied through gritted teeth, "How can you walk out of here and think I don't deserve to know where you're going? It's like you've totally forgotten we're married. That means *I'm* the person you're supposed to talk to when you're in a bad place."

Zann sighed and dropped her backpack on the hardwood floor with a thud. "Marleigh, for God's sake. This has nothing to do with you." An air of frustration overtook her face, and she scooped the backpack onto her shoulder and sidestepped her to the door. "I'll call you from the road."

"You know what? Don't fucking bother." She knew she'd regret those words. And yet, it felt better to say them than to stand there feeling utterly disgraced and humiliated while Zann walked out the door.

* * *

Keeping her head down and her hands in her pockets, Zann walked briskly across the rest area. According to the sign, this was Conneaut, Ohio. The coffee thermos she'd topped off four hundred miles ago in Saratoga Springs, New York, was empty and she still had three hours to go. One small paper cup at a time, she methodically refilled it from the vending machine and headed back to her Jeep, careful to stay in the path of the streetlamp. Anything could happen in a strange place at three in the morning.

Several semi trucks were lined up behind the welcome center, their engines humming to keep the cabs cool while the drivers took a mandatory break. The only other car in the lot was a beat-up sedan parked at the end of the ramp, its occupants probably asleep. What she wouldn't give to close her eyes for just an hour or two. But her best chance of catching Vanessa was to get to her house first thing in the morning before she left for the day.

Inside her vehicle with the doors locked, she turned on the dome light and pulled out the letter that had arrived on Wednesday, the second from Vanessa Laird. It was mailed four days earlier on what would have been Whit's thirty-third birthday. Did Zann ever think of her, it asked, or had she found a way to forget? Vanessa would never forget. Missing her sister made these birthdays unbearable now that she knew the truth about how she died. Would she be alive today if they hadn't once been lovers?

As she pulled back onto the interstate, she turned her thoughts from Whit to Marleigh, whose angry words still echoed in her mind. Of course she would call home, of course she would apologize. But could she ever explain? There was no good way to tell Marleigh that the woman she'd fallen in love with—the woman she'd married—was a fraud. Captain Zann, her shining warrior. Marleigh put too much stock in her supposed heroism to wipe it all away and expect her to keep feeling the same way.

* * *

The road to the quarry was paved but littered with gravel from passing trucks. Marleigh wasn't sure they'd be open for business on Saturday, so she was glad to see a handful of pickup trucks parked next to an office trailer.

A bearded man in a henley shirt and ball cap looked up from a desk as she entered the dusty building. "Can I help you, ma'am?" His accent was decidedly Southern, and she recalled Zann saying Wes had moved up from Georgia.

"I'm looking for Wes Jackson."

"You found him. What can I do for you?"

She introduced herself by name and paused for a sign of recognition. When he didn't respond, she continued, "I'm Zann Redeker's wife."

"Oh, oh…Marleigh! Yeah, I know who you are." He grinned broadly and hurried around the desk to shake her hand. His pinky and ring finger were taped together in a splint. "Zann talks about you all the time, said you were the best thing about coming home to Colfax. What's she been up to?"

The question took her by surprise. Zann had gone off early three times in the past week, ostensibly to hang out with this guy, her best friend. "You haven't seen her?"

"Not for a couple of weeks." He held up his injured hand. "Got this caught in my tailgate like an idiot. It'll probably be a month or more till I can get back out to the range."

The range.

Suddenly it all made sense. The timing, the secrecy. Marleigh recalled vividly the dinner with Bridget and Rocky, how he'd bragged about going out to some farm on the weekends to shoot. At the time, Zann had denied her interest rather emphatically. Then when Rocky had beaten Bridget, she'd gone to the gun range to issue her threat. Something about it had appealed to her—and she must have known Marleigh would disapprove.

"So that's where you guys usually get together...that gun range up by Otter Creek?"

He looked at her warily, and under his breath muttered a curse. "Son of a bitch...I had no idea she didn't tell you. She's gonna kick my pink ass black and blue."

"No, it's okay. I'm not even going to tell her I came out here. Maybe you shouldn't either." She strolled around the trailer taking in the scant decorations...a dusty painting of a hunter with his dogs and an outdated girlie calendar. "She took off last night. Said she'd be gone a couple of days, that she'd screwed up something and had to go make it right. Any idea what she might be talking about?"

"Beats the hell outta me."

"Would you tell me if you knew?"

He scratched his ear absently as he contemplated how to reply. "I guess...maybe."

"I've been worried about her, is all. She knows I'm not a big fan of guns so that's probably why she didn't say anything. But it's fine...I'll deal with it."

"Yeah, I'd say that cat's officially out of the bag. We've been meeting out there on the weekends and I think she goes by herself before work sometimes. At first she couldn't hit the broad side of a barn on account of her hand and all, but she keeps working at it. It's like she won't be satisfied till she gets it back the way it used to be, you know?"

Zann rarely talked about her injury anymore. She'd started her exercises again after Gil got the promotion, but Marleigh figured she'd mostly made peace with her limitations. After encouraging her to join the veterans group, she could hardly complain if going out to the gun range was how they bonded. It made sense, given it was something they all had in common.

She recalled Zann saying she didn't like Wes at first. He definitely had a rakish air about him, but also a charm. "Wes, could I ask you something? I don't want to put you on the spot or anything...it's about your group. I know it's private and all, but do you ever notice Zann getting upset about anything?"

"Maybe a couple of times," he hedged, stroking his beard thoughtfully. "All of us got riled up over a guy there who took some liberties with one of the ladies while they was in Iraq. Some of us got together for beers one night and straightened him out...same as with that dipshit who whupped up on his wife. You know about that, right?"

"You mean running Rocky Goodson out of town. You guys did Colfax a favor."

"Yeah, Zann read him the riot act and a bunch of us went out there to back her up." A twinkle in his eye suggested he'd enjoyed it. "And there was one other time I saw her get kind of emotional. Hell, we all did. Angie told us about a guy in her unit getting run over by a truck."

"Did Zann ever talk about losing one of her soldiers?"

He shook his head. "Nope, not that I remember. About Zann...I noticed a while back that she kinda fades in the background when we talk about shit that still keeps us up at night, you know? She listens but she don't have much to say."

Interesting that she wouldn't have mentioned her sergeant, since she'd always said it was the toughest thing she'd ever faced. The emotional toll must have been too much.

"See, the way our group works, people tell their stories and then we go around the room to let everybody put in their two cents...or their quarter, if it's a big mouth like mine. She used to speak up every now and then, but the last couple of times I was there, I noticed she was taking a pass."

"Was there anybody in the group who maybe rubbed her the wrong way?"

"You mean besides the first time we met and I called her missy?" Laughing, he added, "In case you can't tell, I have a habit of running my mouth before my brain gets to working. She got over it though. She gets along with everybody. Sometimes us enlisted bastards like to rag on the officers, but I could tell right away she was one of the good ones. Give me a cap'n who's willing to take a bullet for his team—or *her* team. Hell, I'd follow 'em anywhere."

"Okay…I appreciate your help. Like I said, it might be best if she doesn't hear about me coming out here. I don't want to make things worse than they are. I was just worried, thought maybe you could help."

As she spoke, he walked her out onto the small porch. "Everybody needs somebody to worry about them. You might be right about something getting under her skin. I can see it now that you mention it. You lemme know if there's anything I can do to help."

Though she was no closer to uncovering the mystery of why Zann had shut her out, at least she'd crossed some potential issues off the list. What worried her now was that she was eliminating every possible source but herself.

* * *

The Lairds' neighborhood reminded Zann of Colfax east of Rutland Road where a smattering of new homes sat among some that had been remodeled and others in need of repair. Military records confirmed this was the address Whit had supplied for her next of kin. It had been renovated at least three times, Zann guessed, given the roof lines and siding materials. A bungalow style, deeper than it was wide, probably with three bedrooms and two baths, one of which wasn't part of the original structure.

The lights had been on inside since six a.m. when she parked at the curb across the street. Vanessa most likely lived there with her parents, since she'd used it as her return address.

So what was keeping Zann from marching onto the porch and ringing the doorbell?

"Nothing, except being terrified," she answered aloud. The whole family might want to hear what she had to say but the longer she sat there the more she thought it was best to talk only with Vanessa. It was possible Whit had confided in her sister that she was gay but not her parents. They certainly didn't need to hear that from a stranger on their porch.

For that matter, Vanessa may not have told them of her correspondence with the Marine Corps, of her newfound knowledge that Whit had been killed by friendly fire. Zann couldn't go charging in and destroy their memories just to cleanse her soul of this awful stain.

Clifton and Kathy Laird. She remembered Whit saying he was a city bus driver and she, a school cafeteria worker. Working class, just like the Redekers. No wonder they were so proud of Vanessa getting through college. At an age when most were striking out on their own, she still lived at home. Perhaps it was to help fill the void they all suffered when Whit was killed.

The front door opened but it was several seconds before a young woman appeared on the porch, apparently shouting her goodbyes and confirming what time she'd return. She wore a summer frock and sandals, and carried a delicate purse on a thin strap. Long blond hair—exactly like her sister's—flowed from beneath a straw sunhat.

Zann couldn't stall another moment. She left her Jeep and crossed the empty street. "Vanessa? Vanessa Laird?"

The young woman stopped abruptly on the sidewalk. That she was Whit's sister was irrefutable—they had the same blue eyes, oval face and slender nose.

"I'm Suzann Redeker."

"I know who you are." She clutched her purse defensively, as though girding herself. "Why did you come here?"

"You know why, Vanessa. I have to talk to you."

"I don't have to listen." Her face contorted with pain and she pushed on toward her car.

"Whitney would want you to. I'm sure you know that." She'd practiced all night what she'd say, how she'd tell of Whit's courage and final moments as a hero. "Your sister was the one who saved us all. She went in first, Vanessa. She found the Taliban. She bought me the time I needed to defend myself… the time we all needed."

"You should have told them that." Her voice rose with hurt and anger. "You shot her and then stood there like a hero while they pinned a medal on your chest."

"I told them exactly what happened, how fearless she was. I didn't know it was my bullet that killed her until I got your letter." She slowly closed the distance between them, encouraged that Vanessa at least was hearing her out. "I'm so sorry. I can't imagine how much it hurts. But they never told me what really happened, I swear. I didn't want to believe it but I went all the way to the Commandant's Office to hear it myself."

The wrath in her youthful face gave way to unmistakable anguish. Her shoulders sagged and the purse dropped to the driveway with a thud.

"If it weren't for what she did...going into the house like that...hundreds of Marines could have died."

Vanessa sniffed loudly as her chin quivered.

"She was more than brave, Vanessa. She was an outstanding Marine and she loved every minute of what she did. I can promise you that. I can still remember how we'd all sit there in camp trying to get psyched about going out on patrol. Not Whit though. She was always pumped up, telling everybody to get off their asses because we needed to go change hearts and minds. That's all she cared about."

"She cared about you," Vanessa managed to choke out as she leaned against her car. "She told me that, and that you tossed her aside when you were finished with her."

"It wasn't like that. The first time we met I thought she was an officer too." It was an honest mistake on Zann's part, since they both were out of uniform at a bar in Wrightsville Beach and Whit had deliberately lied to her after learning she was a first lieutenant. "As soon as I found out she was enlisted, that was it. We couldn't see each other anymore. The Marine Corps has regulations against fraternization. Both of us could have been kicked out."

"She told me you busted her chops every day after that."

"Because she transferred into my unit and I was her CO. I busted everybody's chops—that's what made us good Marines."

She remembered being furious that Whit had put in for the transfer knowing she was in charge of the FET. More than once, she'd been forced to shut down romantic advances with threats of getting her demoted or even discharged. Despite their dubious history, there was nothing to be gained from telling Vanessa that her sister had practically stalked her, that she'd broken policy over and over. None of that had anything to do with her death.

"Did you ever love her?"

The temptation to placate a grieving woman was mighty, but Zann hadn't driven seven hundred miles to lie. "No...no, I didn't. But I respected her more than you'll ever know for the kind of Marine she was. If I could go back in time, I'd give my life for her just like she did for me."

The front door opened and a middle-aged man stepped out onto the porch to investigate.

"Take this, Vanessa," Zann said, drawing the Bronze Star from her pocket and holding it out. "I didn't deserve it. Your sister did."

Vanessa held the medal in her hand as she finally released her tears in a heart-wrenching sob. Then her eyes went cold and she flung it to the ground. "Don't come here thinking you're going to wash all this off by giving me that. Why would I want to look at it every day and remember what you did?"

CHAPTER SIXTEEN

Fuming, Marleigh paced the break room as Bridget cleaned up the powdery residue from a box of sugar donuts. "And that's not all. This morning I turned my face at the last second and made her kiss me on the cheek. It's going to take a lot more than bringing me coffee in bed to get over her being gone all last weekend and not telling where she went."

After almost a week, the pressure of holding everything inside had finally cracked. She could barely speak to Zann at home. The quiet was killing her.

"That's so weird, Marleigh. It doesn't sound like the Zann I know."

"Tell me about it. And get this—she's hiding a rifle in the garage on the top shelf behind some boxes. I had to get the ladder to reach it."

"Now you're scaring me."

"No, not like that." She should have realized Bridget would overreact. "I'm not afraid of her hurting me. She's never threatened me or anything."

"Neither had Rocky until he did."

"Zann doesn't have a mean bone in her body. But it's driving me crazy that she's gotten so secretive all of a sudden." And that she was obsessed with guns. "I'm starting to wonder if she feels threatened about something. I can't figure out what she had to go fix."

"You don't think she's gotten mixed up with some of those militia nuts? Don't they go off on the weekends and play army in the woods?"

Marleigh grunted and shook her head. As outlandish as that sounded, the pieces fit better than anything else she'd come up with. Except Zann wasn't the paranoid type and she hardly ever talked about politics. For that matter, she no longer talked much about her military life either except for the recent trip to Bethesda.

Assuming of course she'd actually gone to Bethesda... No, Marleigh wasn't going down that rabbit hole.

"I went over to her parents' house last Sunday to see if they knew anything. I didn't want to come right out and ask them, but Chuck Redeker's one of those guys everybody wants to play poker with because his face gives him away every time." Except she'd gotten nothing from him, not even a vibe. "I barely got through the door before he asked me what was up with Zann. Apparently she went by there last week and took her Bronze Star medal out of the display case. No idea what she did with it. It's not anywhere in our house...unless she's hidden it with more guns."

"Why would she do that?"

"That's what I want to know. Nothing she does makes sense anymore."

"Bridget, Marleigh?" Fran appeared in the doorway, chastising both with a scowl. "In case you're planning to work today, I've got a twofer. Scanner says they're busting a meth lab on Snake Mountain Road. And somebody from Maubry's office called to say Jimmy Finch is about to be arraigned on two counts of vehicular manslaughter."

Bridget sighed and rolled her eyes. "I better take Jimmy Finch. A meth lab on Snake Mountain Road might be one of my cousins."

* * *

Miles Blake was possibly the most obnoxious homeowner Zann had ever worked with on a building permit. If he treated his contractors with as much disdain as he treated the town's code inspectors, it was a wonder any of them ever finished the job.

"Carter's boys have no idea what they're doing. If they didn't already have so much of my money, I'd send them all packing." Blake gestured toward the small building erected in his backyard, a two-room structure meant to house a workshop for him and a craft room for his wife. A carpenter crew was inside repairing the sheetrock they'd damaged when they put up the vinyl siding. "Can you believe those idiots? If I hadn't walked in when I did, they'd have ruined the whole damn thing."

The chief problem was Blake's micromanagement of the project, including his insistence on buying all the materials himself so he wouldn't have to pay the standard contractor's fee of ten percent. He was a builder's nightmare, and right this minute he was Zann's nightmare too. "Mr. Blake, you're the one who purchased two-inch nails. That's too long for vinyl siding. Town code calls for an inch and three-quarters. I was standing right here last week when Mr. Carter tried to tell you that."

"Then the town code is bullshit," he barked, his ruddy face growing even redder. "My cousin built his whole house from the ground up so you can't tell me he doesn't know what he's doing. He told me to get two-inch nails or they wouldn't hold in the summertime when it got hot. Vinyl expands, or didn't you know that?"

That meant his cousin was an idiot too, since he obviously hadn't bothered to specify they be galvanized, the standard for outdoor construction. Regular nails would start to rust after the first rain. Still, she didn't belong in a dispute between Blake and his contractor. It was past time to finish here and get on to the next job site.

She was dead on her feet, having spent the night before tossing and turning. The trip to Zanesville was supposed to have exorcised her demons. Instead they were getting worse. Night after night when she closed her eyes, she fought helplessly to warn Whit away from the house, waking herself with strained squeals that wouldn't leave her throat. The worst was when she reached Whit's body and rolled her over to find Marleigh's face.

Marleigh was losing patience, not with her restless nights but with her continued refusal to come clean about the nature of her horrid dreams. That was the biggest demon she faced—a confession to the person she loved most that she wasn't the hero everyone believed her to be.

Her guilt was piling up. She'd lied to Marleigh just this morning, saying she'd gotten behind at work and was going in early to catch up. Instead she'd gone out to the shooting range to blow off steam, something she now did at least two mornings a week on top of her regular stint on Saturdays with the guys from her veterans group. There weren't enough hours in the week for practice, especially now that she'd also acquired a Colt semiauto rifle—a civilian model made to emulate the M16.

Unlike the others, she wasn't shooting for the thrill of hearing a skillet clang or a pop on a paper target. She was shooting not to miss. Never to miss.

Her intensive training should have prepared her for Dahaneh. Even injured, she should never have lost control of her rifle, should never have pulled the trigger without knowing where her bullet would go. Her battle instincts had failed her when it mattered most.

"Zann?" Alan Carter, a contractor she knew from his work on dozens of permits, waved to her from the arch of the building's entry. "We upgraded the junction box for Mrs. Blake's pottery kiln like you asked. If I could get your John Hancock on that, we can finish up with the sheetrock in the back room."

Blake led the way inside, where his wife stood over her still-crated kiln reading the operator's manual. Carter's crew was in the craft room repairing the sheetrock. As Blake veered toward the room that would be his workshop, someone moved behind him in the doorway, a blurry figure that caused Zann's spine to ripple.

From the other room came a flurry of sharp bursts. *Pop! Pop! Pop!* For a millisecond, she saw Whit casually wandering through Baheera's humble dwelling. "No!" she yelled to Blake. Then with a mighty shove, she sent him sprawling.

"Son of a bitch," he groaned, clutching his shoulder as he rolled from side to side on the concrete floor.

One of the carpenters rushed from the other room, still holding a nail gun. "What happened?"

Blake glared at her. "That crazy woman just knocked me down."

"I'm so sorry. I thought…" Her lie materialized almost instantly. "That nail gun…it sounded so close. I was worried you might get hit through the sheetrock."

He lumbered to his feet and continued to rub his shoulder. "Donna, come over here and feel my collarbone. I think she broke it."

Zann's hope that he was being overly dramatic was dashed when he unbuttoned his shirt and tugged it aside. Sure enough, his clavicle showed an obvious reddening bump, a clear indication the fall had caused a break.

"We should get you to a doctor right away," she said. He could have torn a blood vessel under the skin or even severed a nerve. Someone needed to stabilize the bone immediately.

"I'm not going anywhere till the police get here and take my statement. Call them right now, Donna. I need to report an assault."

"The police?" Carter sounded incredulous. "Jesus, it's not like she was fighting with you, Miles. Shit happens, man."

Zann spun and walked outside to gather her wits. It took all her courage not to get in her car and drive away from the chaotic flashbacks. The cops were on the way and she'd have to give them a statement. But first she needed to tell her boss what she'd done.

"You stay right where you are and don't say another word," Malcolm Shively told her sharply over the phone. "I'll be right there."

The police arrived first, two officers she recognized from their comings and goings at town hall. They bypassed her on their way into the building as she leaned on her city vehicle.

Malcolm arrived in a luxury sedan belonging to Jackie Patterson, the town council's attorney. Unlike the town manager, who was rotund and usually cheery, Patterson was thin and severe-looking, with graying hair drawn into a bun, and bold, black spectacles. She demanded to know if Zann had given a statement.

Zann shook her head and gave them the lay of the land. "Everything happened so fast. I know this is going to sound crazy, but I thought one of those guys was about to pop him with a nail gun so I pushed him out of the way."

"Do *not* say that word again," Patterson told her, shaking a finger in her face. "It was not crazy. It was a simple misunderstanding. Do you hear what I'm saying? Nod your head. That is exactly what you will tell the police."

The officer who eventually took her statement was Joey Crisp, a veteran of the force whose easygoing demeanor injected a much-needed sense of calm in the chaos. As he jotted down her side of events, Malcolm and Patterson stood by, the latter giving nonverbal cues and interjecting whenever she feared Zann would convict herself with her own words. The situation went from bad to worse when a pair of emergency medical technicians arrived in an ambulance and went inside to administer to Blake.

Crisp pursed his lips as he tucked his notepad back into his shirt pocket and removed his handcuffs from a clip on his belt. "I'm really sorry I have to do this but it's policy. No exceptions."

"You're *arresting* me?"

"It's just procedure. Mr. Blake is filing assault charges so we need to take you down to the station and get you booked."

"Don't worry, Suzann," Patterson assured her. "I'll take this to Judge Dougherty within the hour and get him to set bail. We'll have you out of there this afternoon."

Malcolm held out his hand. "I'm going to need the keys to your city vehicle, Zann. I'll drive it back to the lot and you can have Marleigh drop you off later for your car."

A second wave of panic consumed her. "I'll get the keys back this afternoon though, right?"

Patterson shook her head. "It's best for all parties for you to remain on suspension until we get all of the details about what happened and determine what charges Mr. Blake is planning to file. Paid suspension, of course…unless it's determined there was wrongdoing. If we come to some kind of understanding and get him to drop the charges, you should be free to return to work."

"So sorry," the officer murmured again as he clicked the cuffs into place behind her back. Though he hadn't wrenched them tight, the uneven pull of her left arm rendered them uncomfortable.

A growing panic pounded in her chest. "Wait. Malcolm, I…I have some things in the trunk, underneath the spare tire… my pistol's there. It's not loaded but there's a box of ammo too. I went out to the shooting range this morning before work."

He took a menacing step close enough that his belly brushed against hers. "You carried a handgun in a city vehicle while you were on duty? What in the name of Jesus Holy Christ were you thinking, Zann?" After a sidelong glance at Patterson, he marched to the car, popped the trunk and removed her gun case.

"It was never accessible while I was working," she argued.

Dropping the case in the backseat of the vehicle, he gestured toward the second officer coming out of the building. "I'm done talking to my employee. She's all yours now."

CHAPTER SEVENTEEN

With almost fifteen years of news reporting under her belt, Marleigh had visited the jail more times than she could count. That did nothing to normalize the eerie feeling of why she was there—to pick up her wife, who'd been arrested for assault.

She'd gotten only scant details about the initial altercation from Ham, who'd been good enough to call her once word reached the mayor's office. According to him, it was all one big misunderstanding. Zann was trying to prevent an accident and ended up causing one instead. But the business about her having a gun in the trunk of her city car…that was unfortunate, he said. The town council would not be pleased.

Zann appeared in the hallway on the other side of a glass door, where she stopped and collected her belongings. Apparently in no hurry, she slid her belt through its loops and tucked her wallet into her back pocket, saving her wedding ring for last.

The tension as they walked to the car was electric. It was bad enough they were barely speaking because of her disappearance last weekend. Zann had lied again this morning about where she was going at a quarter to seven, saying she was behind at work and needed to catch up. Now with every step, Marleigh grew more furious at the lies and at her stubborn refusal to speak. Surely Zann realized it was up to her to explain herself.

"What the hell were you thinking?" she finally blurted once they pulled out of the parking lot. "A gun in your city car?"

After a deep sigh, Zann turned away to stare out the window. "Malcolm already chewed my ass out. I'd appreciate it if you'd cut me some slack."

"Cut you some slack." Marleigh lurched forward after stopping at an intersection, enough that her back wheels squealed against the pavement. Given how much her knees were shaking, it was a miracle she could drive at all. "I'll cut you some slack when you start telling me the truth for a change. I want to know where you go, who you've been with and what you were doing."

"What's left to tell? You already heard I had a gun in the car. The reason was because I went to the range this morning."

"This morning...when you lied to me and said you had to go to work early because you were behind." The lies bothered her more than the guns.

"I didn't want to lie but..." She sighed dramatically, a gesture that riled Marleigh even more. "Remember that night we went out with Bridget and Rocky? You practically went ballistic when I started asking him about the gun range, so I knew you'd get on my case about it. Did you forget that I'm a trained marksman? I happen to enjoy target shooting. What's the big deal?"

"The big deal is you've been sneaking around behind my back like I'm stupid. Did you think I wouldn't notice that you took sixteen hundred dollars out of our house account, and you haven't been putting your check in? Don't even think about denying it."

"I'm not denying anything. Saturdays I usually meet up with some of the guys from the vets group, but during the week I go out there by myself. Sneaking around...there you go again, making it sound like I was cheating on you." Zann's defensive tone was way more hostile than it needed to be, especially since she should have been showing at least a hint of shame and remorse. "Not that any of it matters now because Malcolm confiscated my gun. And he suspended me from work because that douchebag made a federal case out of a broken collarbone. It was an accident."

"You know what, Zann? I don't give a shit about your stupid guns—including the rifle you're hiding in the garage. You can drive around with a rocket launcher on top of your car for all I care, okay?" She angrily pounded the steering wheel. "Just tell me why every goddamn thing you do has to be such a big fucking secret. Huh? Can you at least tell me that?"

It shamed her to hear the harshness in her voice and language. This wasn't the way they talked to each other, but no amount of patient cajoling and concern had cracked the wall Zann had put up all around herself. Anger and frustration were all she had left.

"Look, if you aren't going to talk to me, then at least talk to somebody. A therapist, not those guys at your veterans group. I don't know what's going on down there, but they're making it worse instead of better."

When they reached the city lot at town hall, Zann exited without a word and trudged toward her vehicle. Marleigh drove off slowly, peeking in her rearview mirror to see if Zann was following her home. It wouldn't have surprised her if she'd turned the other way in another effort to avoid more pointed questions about her behavior.

The day's events should have been a breaking point, forcing Zann to finally come clean about the secrets she was hoarding, about the nightmares that awakened them both with her panting and agitation. Instead, she was digging in even deeper, her stubborn silence now turned to open hostility.

And confrontation had only made matters worse, Marleigh admitted dismally. Whatever the cause of her turmoil, she needed love and encouragement, not harping and blame. Hard as it might be, it was time for Marleigh to suck up her pride and try to treat Zann the way she'd want to be treated.

She waited in the driveway until the Jeep pulled alongside, willing herself to behave like the supportive partner she wanted to be. "Zann, I'm sorry. I shouldn't have yelled at you. What happened today, with the police and Malcolm and all...I know it's been hard on you. I can see that. It's not fair what Miles Blake's putting you through." She held out her hand and led them up the stairs to the porch. "Let's forget about this for now and you go chill. Stretch out on the couch or take a soak in the tub if you want. I'll throw something together for dinner and we'll just hang out tonight. No more fighting."

Sadness overwhelmed her as she caught Zann wiping tears from her cheek with the back of her hand. It wasn't at all like her to cry.

"Sweetheart, please don't cry. We're going to get through this. I love you with all my heart. And whatever it is, I'm here for you."

Zann shook her head, making only fleeting eye contact as she slogged through the door. "I'm not who you think I am, Marleigh."

There it was, the first clue to her confession, so cryptic it cast even more confusion. "Who are you then?"

"I don't even know anymore. But I'm sorry for everything. I promise I'll make this up to you." She fell onto the couch and stabbed at the TV remote, signaling her intent to disengage.

Marleigh couldn't quit now, not after Zann had shown a crack in her facade. For days she'd been sitting on the knowledge that Zann was meeting her friends at the gun range in hopes she'd voluntarily confess when the time was right. That secret was out in the open now, meaning the one she continued to protect had to be even darker.

"Okay...okay, Zann. But there's one thing I have to know. Promise you'll tell me the truth." Until that moment, Marleigh had mostly pushed the horrible thoughts from her head, but her resolve was crumbling. With tears building, she asked the question that gnawed at her day and night. "Do you still love me?"

"God, are you serious?" Zann leapt up and pulled her into a crushing hug. "Of course I love you. I can't believe you're even asking me that. You're the most important thing in my life. Don't you ever, *ever* forget that."

There was an anguish in her voice Marleigh hadn't heard before, a desperation that made her ashamed for asking. Yet it was exactly the assurance she needed most, to know that whatever Zann was fighting, it wasn't rooted in a desire to throw their life away.

* * *

Her body still pulsing with the aftershocks of her climax, Zann pushed herself up on her elbows so she could look into Marleigh's eyes. "I truly am sorry for today. I screwed up royally. But hearing you doubt me…that was the worst feeling in the world. I don't ever want you to think that again."

"I know, I won't." Marleigh raised her lips for a light kiss. "We've been together for four years, Zann. I never saw you cry about your feelings before. I know there's something that's tearing you up inside. It kills me to watch you suffer and not be able to help."

The tears were because it shamed her to hear Marleigh apologize when she'd been the one causing all the pain. And then Marleigh questioning her love had been devastating. That's what her secrets had done.

"It's Afghanistan, isn't it?" Marleigh murmured, her voice so low it was if she hadn't intended Zann to hear.

The question shocked her, even if it shouldn't have. She'd always worried Marleigh would become frustrated with her silence and find a way to investigate her, especially given all the resources she could access through her work at the newspaper. "What makes you ask?"

"You were talking about Hamza in your sleep the other night. He's the man you killed, right?"

"What did I say?"

Marleigh shook her head. "Just his name. I couldn't make out the rest. That's when you woke up."

Zann remembered it vividly. She was trying to warn Whit that Hamza was inside. "It was just a bad dream...probably because of something we talked about at one of our meetings. I think about that stuff a lot more than I used to." A superficial explanation, to be sure, but maybe enough to quiet the concern.

"I wish I'd never encouraged you to go. You were in such a good place before." She urged Zann onto her back and began tickling her chest with obvious intent. "You were wrong, what you said earlier...that I didn't know you. I think I do. I know it still bothers you that you lost somebody in your unit, and you probably replay that in your head every day trying to figure out how you could have saved her. That's who you are. You don't give yourself credit for what you did, how you saved all the others. That's the woman I fell in love with...she's a hero. So no matter what you think of yourself, you'll always be my shining warrior."

The words cut her like a knife. "Don't call me that. I don't like it."

"Zann?"

Surging with shame, she turned away and drew her knees to her chest. This was exactly why she couldn't tell Marleigh the truth. She'd pretend to understand, offer some condescending bullshit.

The truth would change everything.

CHAPTER EIGHTEEN

Present day

Thank God the police had arrived!

Marleigh shook with fear anyway as Zann scooted back into their hiding place.

"Everybody's okay for now," she whispered. "The cops are here."

The thought that Zann could have been killed trying to save Tammy made Marleigh physically ill. In that instant, she'd gotten a terrifying glimpse of what life must have been like for her every day in Afghanistan. No matter what happened next, she wouldn't let her go out there alone again. If they were meant to die today, they'd go down fighting—together.

Zann found her hand and intertwined their fingers. "We just need to stay cool while they negotiate an end to this. Everyone will be all right."

David called out what he saw through the glass door. "Three police cars, an ambulance...shit, there's even a fire truck." That was practically the entirety of Colfax's emergency response team.

"There goes one around the back. They're taking up positions."

Marleigh knew most of the town's officers from her work on the crime beat. Which ones had come to their rescue? Pete Nelson, the senior patrolman who weighed over two-fifty? Or maybe Rance Fuller, all of twenty years old. Joey Crisp. Eileen Edwards. They wrote traffic citations and ran kids with skateboards off church property. Was there anyone on the Colfax force with the mettle to negotiate with a gun-waving drug gang for the lives of seven hostages?

"Goddamn it! *Goddamn it!*" The one they called Scotty was coming apart. "You fucking bitch. You called the cops."

"No, I didn't," Tammy cried. "Please don't shoot."

"Scotty! Keep your head, my friend." Ancil sounded calm for a guy who was surrounded by police.

From the front of the building came the muffled sound of a bullhorn, instructions for the gunmen that Marleigh couldn't decipher.

"Then how the fuck did they know we were here?" Scotty asked, clearly panicked. "They said your name, Ancil. Shit, they probably know all of us."

Ancil replied grimly, "It appears I was wrong about Luc Michaux. He does care for you, Bridget. Or perhaps he believes the police will capture us and that he will get away free."

Marleigh tensed as footsteps grew close. Someone was pacing the break room, probably to check out the situation through the back window. The clicks of a touchpad signaled he was making a call on a smartphone.

"Bobby." The voice belonged to Ancil. "We are blown, my friend. You must come for us… Okay, fifteen minutes. We will be ready."

Fifteen minutes. Fifteen minutes and this nightmare would be over.

Surely Ancil and his friends didn't expect to waltz out of the building and into their friend's waiting car. The only way the cops would let them out was if they took someone hostage. Bridget was the logical choice since she was bait for Luc.

As Ancil returned to the lobby, Zann's smartphone lit with a string of messages from the dispatcher.

Law enforcement has arrived on scene.

Please hold your position.

Do you have an update on the condition of Mr. Teele?

"What should I say?" Marleigh whispered.

"Tell her no change. It's probably good that nobody's yelling about it. Maybe they got the bleeding stopped."

A second bullhorn message was followed by the main phone ringing in the lobby. Ancil calmly instructed Bridget to pick it up.

"This is Bridget Snyder…yes…he's standing right here."

It was maddening not to know what the authorities were saying over the phone. Marleigh could only surmise they were verifying the information she'd sent, buying time before beginning the negotiations that would end this.

"They want to talk to you, Ancil…"

"Give it to me," he stated curtly. Then in a loud voice, he said, "One of the hostages is shot and bleeding. If you want to save him, you will do exactly as I say. I will negotiate only with a federal agent, someone with the authority to guarantee our safe passage out of this building. You will immediately withdraw from this side of the street and wait for one to arrive, or we will shoot someone else and it will be your fault. You have exactly thirty seconds to move before someone else gets hurt. Do I make myself clear?"

After a chilling silence, Scotty spoke again in his agitated state, "What the fuck are we gonna do, Ancil? You said Luc wouldn't call the police."

"Relax, my friend. See? They are moving back, just as I instructed. That is because of you, Scotty…because you had the courage to shoot this man. Now they know we mean what we say. They understand there will be dire consequences if anyone causes unnecessary trouble. So it is up to you to keep an eye on them, Scotty. Do you understand?" After a short pause, he said, "David, come with me."

Moments later, two sets of footsteps entered the break room.

"Your cousin is an idiot. I will not allow him to get us shot by a band of glorified security guards." Ancil's angry voice was so close, he could have been standing at the counter not six inches from where they hid.

"All he needs is a bump, man. You holding anything? Doesn't matter what…just something to take the edge off."

A bump. So Scotty needed a snort of something because he was coming down from a high. Marleigh had met drug addicts in jail and read their police reports. They were extremely volatile when they reached the point of physical withdrawal, capable of anything.

"So I am expected to carry heroin in my pocket to dole out to imbeciles?"

"I told you he was dumber than shit. There's half a point in my coat. That ought to be enough to calm him down. But it's in the bag they took to Chimney Point. We just have to get there."

Chimney Point was where Highway 17 crossed Lake Champlain into New York. Either someone was picking them up there or they'd stashed a getaway vehicle near the state line. And they were counting on Bobby to get them there. It made sense. There were more routes on the New York side of the lake, untraveled back roads that would take them north to the Canadian border without being seen.

Ancil snapped, "We are in a pressure cooker with a lunatic who cannot function without drugs." He paced across the floor and spun around, his shoes squeaking on the tile floor. "I will take care of Scotty. Bobby will be here soon. Be ready to leave. We will take Bridget with us."

"Why? Luc doesn't give a shit about her."

"But she knows where his father lives. That will get his attention."

These men were ruthless. If they took Bridget, they probably would kill her once she outlived her usefulness. Marleigh messaged the dispatcher again, warning them not to let that happen.

* * *

Zann tried to make sense of their plan. Under the circumstances, the gunmen didn't seem overly concerned.

The one called David returned to the outer room, while Ancil remained behind in the break room, still close to the counter where she and Marleigh hid. By the sound of pings, he was placing another call.

"Everett...this is Ancil. I am afraid we have encountered unexpected difficulty in our effort to draw Monsieur Michaux out of hiding. The woman is not—"

The man on the other end of the call erupted so loudly that Zann could hear his yell even through the cabinet. She wasn't able to make out the words, but there was no mistaking his fury toward Ancil.

"He is not picking up his phone, and I am reasonably convinced she does not know his whereabouts at the moment. But we have another way to make her help us."

Apparently Ancil wasn't the big shot he made himself out to be, a revelation Zann found interesting. Perhaps he'd been the one responsible for recruiting Luc as a drug mule, and now he was on the hook for Luc's brazen theft. That was the emerging picture—Ancil had been ordered by someone higher up in the distribution chain to recover whatever Luc had stolen by squeezing Bridget for his location.

His pacing gave away his anxiousness over staying in Everett's good graces. "No, she will help, I am sure. She has been to the house in Montreal. It is my understanding Luc's father is in declining health. That should be sufficient leverage to lure him out."

Ancil seemed dead certain of his escape plan, but he clearly was intimidated by this Everett person, too afraid to confess that his hostage scenario had gone south and the police were waiting at the curb. He also didn't bother to tell Everett that Bobby was picking them up.

"Very well, Everett. We will be there tonight...give us three hours...yes, seven o'clock."

Three hours…exactly how long it took to drive across the Canadian border to Montreal, assuming Bobby arrived soon.

The muscles in Zann's hips and legs screamed for want of a change in position, but she couldn't risk even the smallest movement as long as Ancil chose to bide his time in the break room. The stillness was almost unbearable.

The loudspeaker outside called again, this time more clearly, imploring him to answer the ringing phone.

When his footsteps faded, Zann peered through a crack in the cabinet and shifted her legs so they pushed into Marleigh's scant space. "They're headed to Chimney Point. Be sure you text them that."

"And that he's planning to take Bridget hostage," Marleigh whispered.

"It doesn't make any sense. The cops aren't going to let them just march out the door with a hostage and not chase them all the way to the Canadian border."

"They have nothing to lose, Zann. They already shot Clay."

And they might in fact shoot someone else to demonstrate the veracity of their threats. That's the only way the cops would back off—if they showed no qualms about killing hostages.

Their situation reminded her of an incident in Girishk, one of the hairier clashes of her first Afghanistan tour. She and three other members of the FET under her command were pinned behind a pair of burned-out vehicles at the end of an alley while the weapons platoon fired on militants who were unaware of their position. Their only path to escape would have meant revealing themselves to the enemy, something they were ordered not to do. After several hours of crossfire, she and the platoon leader devised a plan to corral the militants in the alley and have Zann's team close in from behind. It was high risk—the FETs had standing orders to avoid direct hostilities because they lacked the tactical and weapons training of their male counterparts in the infantry. But left with no options, her team executed the plan to perfection, resulting in the killing of four militants and the capture of three.

Could something like that work here? It would be simple enough to coordinate with the officers outside—have them charge through the front door and push Ancil and his friends into the break room, where Zann would be waiting. All she had to do was disarm the first one through the door, something made easier because she'd have the element of surprise.

Scotty was the wild card. In his agitated state, he could start shooting hostages at the first sign of trouble. But if Ancil's new plan to get out with his friend Bobby still depended on leaving no witnesses behind, they might be forced to take that risk.

No matter what she ultimately decided, she was determined Marleigh would stay safely hidden.

* * *

"No way," Marleigh whispered. "Our chances will be better if it's both of us."

"Negative. You'd just be giving them another target to shoot at. Besides, only one of us is actually trained for this stuff and it isn't you."

It was Zann's commando voice, and Marleigh had teased her for years about the seductive power of authority. Her Captain Zann. But there was no teasing on a day when the stakes were so high.

This was the only time she'd ever witnessed the extent of Zann's high-level training. It had kicked in the instant the first shots were fired with a move that so far had saved their lives… whereas her own first instinct had been to walk right out there and do whatever she could to help the others. The problem was that Zann seemed to be forgetting that she no longer had two good hands. She didn't stand a chance against three men with guns.

"I need to set up this plan with the cops outside," Zann whispered. "Let me see my phone."

Marleigh snatched it away. "Forget it. I'm not going to hide back here by myself while those bastards are shooting at my wife and trying to kill my best friend."

"I won't let that happen, Marleigh. I promise you I'll do everything I can to save Bridget. But I care a helluva lot more about protecting you. How could you not know that?" She was speaking so forcefully, anyone who happened to be in the break room would have heard.

Marleigh groped for her lips in the dark and pressed a finger against them. "I do know. So we'll both stay right where we are and save each other. You don't get to be a hero today."

Zann released an exasperated sigh, her usual response to being on the losing end of an argument. Marleigh didn't care how annoyed she was. Either they were going out there together or not at all.

And if they made it through this day, she never wanted to think about the commando inside Zann again.

CHAPTER NINETEEN

November, one month earlier

Zann bagged the last of the season's leaves from their beech tree in the backyard. Before long, she'd be shoveling snow from the driveway again. At least it gave her something to do.

Her suspension from work was now at four months—the last three unpaid—with no end in sight. Malcolm said his hands were tied by the council…liability concerns. Miles Blake was still holding criminal assault charges over her head as he negotiated with the town for a financial settlement big enough to buy a private island. Meanwhile, she and Marleigh had blown through the last of their savings and were already two months behind on their mortgage. It hadn't helped that she'd spent thousands on guns and ammo.

As if their financial problems weren't enough, the solitude of her typical day was maddening. She couldn't recall a time in her life when she wasn't surrounded by people, often in close quarters. Now she was lucky to see anyone at all besides

Marleigh, who'd taken on freelance work for the Burlington paper to bring in extra cash. She left early for work most days and returned home exhausted and ready for bed.

The lonely routine left lots of time for soul searching, much of it still toward making peace with herself over the revelations about Whitney Laird. Some days she managed to convince herself she'd done the best she could under the circumstances. Had she doubted herself and hesitated, Hamza would have killed her too and probably escaped with the explosives meant for the Marine base. If only they hadn't given her that medal, she wouldn't feel like such a fraud. No wonder Vanessa and her family had felt disrespected.

None of this new clarity meant she was ready to share the real story with Marleigh, or her parents either. After all the attention her military service record had garnered in Colfax— people still called her a war hero—she couldn't bear to have her loved ones share her humiliation. It was bad enough they had to defend her over this crap with Miles Blake.

As she climbed the stairs to the porch, her cell phone sounded with a techno trill, the ringtone she and Marleigh used when they called each other. "Hey, babe. I just finished the yard. You on your way home?" No matter how glum she felt, she always tried to be chipper when Marleigh called.

"That's what I'm calling about. Bridget wants me to go with her for a drink at The Lobby so I can meet her new boyfriend. It's that day trader from Montreal…Luc somebody."

Zann played the statement back in her head to see if it contained an invitation to join them. It did not. "I can hold dinner. Any idea when you'll be home?"

"Go ahead without me. We'll probably just grab some bar food." There was nothing subtle about her casual dismissal. Whether deliberate or not, she seemed to have torn a page out of Zann's avoidance manual, making plans of her own and expecting Zann to carry on as usual. And all the while pretending nothing was wrong.

* * *

"Okay honey, we'll see you when you get here." Bridget ended the call and laid her phone on the bar. "Luc's running a little late. Said he had to drop off some papers for a client. He works so hard."

It was good to see her so excited over a new boyfriend, Marleigh thought. Lord knows she deserved it after Rocky. "I thought day traders worked at home in their pajamas. He meets with clients too?"

"I don't know about the others but Luc certainly does. Maybe it's a Canadian thing. I guess here we'd call him a stockbroker."

Too bad he was running late. Marleigh unexpectedly found herself anxious to get home. Zann had sounded so disappointed about her missing dinner. These days they hardly saw each other, since she was out half the night covering police scanner activity, anything she might sell to the papers in Burlington or Montpelier.

"How come you're so down in the dumps lately?" Bridget asked. "And don't give me that shrug. I know it's something. You and Zann still fighting? I mean other than the fact that you're working your ass off while she's…what? Sitting on the couch playing video games all day?"

"Zann doesn't play video games," she replied, noting a faint streak of defensiveness. Just because she'd shared her frustrations with Bridget didn't mean it was all right for her to pile on. "And besides, she's been catching up on a lot of stuff that needed doing around the house. She sanded the floors, painted the garage. I get to walk in the door every night and put my feet up. No cooking, no laundry. Nothing."

"Like having your own hausfrau."

Zann would be humiliated to hear someone talk about her that way. The public guilt and shame of her suspension was enough, since practically everyone in town had heard about the incident with Miles Blake. Instead of seeing her as an honorable war hero, they saw a veteran with PTSD issues or just a garden-variety hothead who couldn't control her aggressions.

"Be honest, Marleigh. It has to be getting to you. The least she could do is go out there and find a job—slinging hamburgers, picking up trash. Anything to help."

Marleigh nursed her warming beer, needing to make it last. After months of venting her exasperation, it was her own fault Bridget had turned against Zann. "It's more complicated than that. If she takes another job, the town will drop all her benefits. She loses her health insurance, her seniority and whatever she's got vested in her pension. Once they settle this mess and call her back to work—assuming that's what happens—she'd have to start over again at the bottom of the pay scale."

"I'm just saying it's not fair to you. Especially with all her lies. Did she ever 'fess up about where she went last summer?" Bridget had raised this issue repeatedly, making Marleigh wish she hadn't told her about it.

"No, but I'm pretty sure it had to do with somebody she knew in Afghanistan. She still won't talk about it."

Using the tiny mirror of her compact, Bridget freshened her lipstick as she talked. "If you ask me, that's just plain weird. I mean, you're married. Who runs off like that and thinks they have the right not to say anything? Sounds like she needs to talk to a psychiatrist or something."

Marleigh had suggested that only once. Zann's reaction was over the top, mocking her for days by pretending to be deranged. "Things are a little better. At least we aren't fighting anymore. It's mostly the mortgage that's stressing us out. The bank won't even talk about refinancing as long as she's out of work."

"What about her parents? Can't they help you out till this blows over?"

"Her dad retired in September after he got that blood clot. They're living on his city pension and what little bit of Social Security her mom gets. Besides, we're too old to be running to our parents to fix our problems."

"Well, you can't hold on forever. You need a plan." If anyone knew that, it was Bridget. Rocky had left her with all the bills and an apartment lease she couldn't afford.

"I know. If this drags on for another month, we could be looking at foreclosure." All that said, commiserating over their debts wasn't the relaxing time Marleigh had in mind when she'd agreed to stop in for a drink after work. If Luc didn't show up soon, she was calling it a night.

"It's only going to get worse, Marleigh. You need to call Pete back and tell him to put your house on the market now—like today. Get out from under it before they totally fuck you over. And you need to do something about Zann too. They don't give prizes for going down with the ship."

Do something about Zann. There was nothing to do as long as she refused to help herself. They didn't talk about their problems anymore. Marleigh feared letting loose her frustrations, and Zann...who knew what secrets she still was hiding? Her one fleeting admission—that she wasn't the woman Marleigh thought she was—had vanished into the ether, never explained.

"There's Luc!"

Finally, the elusive Luc Michaux. Wearing a slate-gray business suit with a crisp white shirt and yellow tie, he cut a handsome figure. His face lit up in a shimmering smile when he saw Bridget, a gesture Marleigh found encouraging given Bridget's past luck with men.

Before he reached them, Bridget gripped her forearm and squeezed it almost hard enough to hurt. In a voice barely above a whisper, she hastily added, "I mean it, Marleigh. You can't let Zann drag you down into the toilet too. You have to save yourself."

She didn't even know what that meant. Her emotions vacillated every hour between sorrow and anger, with each pointing her in a different direction. She ached over whatever had caused Zann to draw up into a knot, and her inclination as a wife was to try to help fix it. But then her fury over a months-long deception made her question if Zann was even the same woman she'd married. If she wasn't, why should Marleigh lose everything to hold on to her?

* * *

The sound of crunching gravel signaled Marleigh's car in the driveway, and Zann looked around the living room to make sure everything was in its place. Her guilt at work again. She'd become meticulous about taking care of the house so Marleigh wouldn't have to lift a finger at home.

When, after several minutes, Marleigh hadn't come inside, she peeked out the front window to find her sitting in the rocker on the porch going through the mail. How long had it been since they'd sat out there together laughing and talking about their day? Deep conversation was a thing of the past. Now Marleigh was the one keeping her feelings bottled up inside.

"Did you have a good time with Bridget?" She took her usual place on the porch swing, following Marleigh's gaze to see if she was looking at anything in particular in the distance or just avoiding eye contact. The air was brisk, the edge of a cold front moving through overnight.

Marleigh bundled the mail in a neat stack and laid it aside. "It was okay, I guess. Luc seems like a nice guy, but anyone would be an improvement over Rocky." Her faraway voice matched her overall demeanor.

"Good for Bridget. I'm happy for her. Tell her I said that, would you?" Her feeble efforts failed to spur additional conversation. Marleigh seemed to prefer the quiet. "You look like you want me to go back inside and leave you alone."

After a measured silence, Marleigh heaved what sounded like a reluctant sigh but still wouldn't even meet her eye.

"Hey, my check comes next week. That'll help." Though admittedly, her military pension was a pittance compared to the salary she'd lost, and a drop in the bucket to what they needed. She'd already sold everything of value, including her guns. To scrape together a house payment this month, they'd have to skip the utilities, or vice versa. "I'll call Malcolm again on Monday and see where things stand. Last I heard, Miles Blake was still being a dick."

She didn't know what to make of Marleigh's continued refusal to talk. It wasn't like her to pout, but anything was possible given the stress they were under.

"Come on, Marleigh. Don't keep shutting me out."

"Sucks, doesn't it?" She abruptly pushed herself up and began pacing the porch, leaving her chair to rock hauntingly against the rippled boards. "You finally know how it feels."

"Is that what this is about? You don't think I've been punished enough?"

"For taking a gun to work? Yeah, but not for how you've been treating me since July. You're all, 'Hey, no big deal. I worked it out by myself.' Never mind that I still get up every single day wondering what was so awful you couldn't even tell me what it was. Now you know what it feels like to be talking to brick wall. So if you're wondering why we hardly talk at all anymore, there's your answer."

Zann had noticed a string of little things ever since the day Marleigh picked her up at the jail. They'd talked it out for a day or two, both promising their love was strong enough to get through anything. Then gradually, Marleigh had started working late, hanging out with Bridget instead of coming home. They'd have superficial chats about nothing of consequence, as if afraid of where a serious conversation might lead. It was only now she realized these were deliberate paybacks. Bitterness boiling over.

"Marleigh, I know this is hard, but it's just a rough patch. Everybody goes through it at one time or another." They wouldn't even be in this mess if she hadn't been suspended. "Maybe I should see about taking on a part-time job or something. That would take some of the pressure off. So what if they cancel my health insurance? I can't afford the copay anyway."

"Did you even hear what I said? It's not just the money. It's all the lies and secrets. I can't get over the fact that you don't trust me anymore. That your secrets are so important you're ready to throw our life away over it. Do you have any idea how that makes me feel?"

"I do trust you. It's me...I don't like myself very much right now. I haven't for a long time. I'm still working on it, but there's no point in dragging you down into my sewer." It was perhaps the most revealing response she'd given, confirming that something was troubling her. "If it makes you feel better, I'll apologize again for not telling you about the guns. I knew you wouldn't like it but I needed to do it...to prove to myself that I still could."

"The guns were just a symptom. I could live with you going out there with your friends. But this blowing me off every time

I try to talk to you…do you seriously think what you do is none of my business?" Her voice had taken on a sharpness Zann had never heard before. She turned her back on Zann and stood at the rail, her voice rising. "Do you ever stop to wonder why I quit asking about it? I've stood by you through all this crap with your job, gave you all the time in the world to 'fess up on your own terms. You didn't even try. Now every day that goes by is a day I have to tell myself that my wife doesn't give a shit how it makes me feel."

"Being married doesn't entitle you to know everything in my head, Marleigh. What you call secret, I call private. Do you honestly think I need to confess all the mistakes I've ever made? All the bad thoughts I've ever had? You want me on my knees begging forgiveness?"

Marleigh whirled to face her, jabbing a finger in the air defiantly. "At least now I know you've done something that needs forgiving."

"Good God! Do you hear yourself?" She slumped against the back of the swing, shaking her head. "I've been tried and convicted and you don't even know if what I did was a crime."

"I'm sick of this," Marleigh snapped, her tone cold. She snatched an envelope from the stack on the floor and waved it in the air. "This just came from the bank. We're going to lose the house—it's just a matter of time. Everything we worked for down the drain. Years of busting our asses at work and nothing to show for it."

"We can hold on. It won't be much longer."

Marleigh leaned against the banister and pinched the bridge of her nose. "There's nothing to hold on to. The only money we have is what I've put in my IRA. That's a huge tax penalty if I draw it out and it leaves me absolutely nothing for retirement. We need to sell the house now or the bank's going to foreclose and it'll ruin our credit forever."

Zann had gamed out the possibilities too and knew they were running out of options. But losing the house…that was all they had.

"There's no other way out of this, Zann. It's only going to get worse."

"What if we rented it out for a year or two while we got back on our feet? Where could we live in the meantime?"

Marleigh let several seconds pass before even attempting to speak, her reply interrupted with a brush of tears from her cheek. "I don't want to deal with it anymore. Bridget said I could stay with her. You could move back in with your folks."

The words hit her like a sledgehammer. "Oh, my God. Marleigh...you're not serious."

"I'm tired, Zann. All this time I've been trying to figure out what I could do to help you. How come you haven't been trying to help me, huh?"

That they would actually separate...it was incomprehensible. "God, Marleigh...listen to yourself. This is insane."

"You know what's insane? The fact that I even let you back in the house after you ran off last summer. I should have had the locks changed. But no, I rolled over and let you get away with it. All this time I've been trying to be patient while you got your shit together, and you've been coasting along like you don't have a care in the world."

"Marleigh, I can't—"

"You know what? If a million dollars fell out of the sky right now, it wouldn't fix what's broken between us." She pounded her chest with her fist. "You broke it when you shut me out."

Marleigh didn't linger for a response.

And why should she? Zann had squandered her chance to explain herself last summer, and with each passing day the lie about who she really was grew bigger. It was an impossible ultimatum—continue her silence and see their home torn apart, or admit the truth and watch Marleigh's respect for her crumble. Either way, she stood to lose everything that mattered.

CHAPTER TWENTY

Connie Wagstaff typed with one hand while the other fanned her face. Hot flashes, probably, since her pale cheeks had gone up in flames three times while Zann sat waiting in her office at town hall. The scheduled meeting to determine her return to work was forty minutes overdue. Why were they dragging this out?

Today marked the beginning of the end of her long nightmare. Or so she hoped. For five months, she'd twisted in the wind while the town negotiated her fate. Whatever they decided—even if they fired her—at least it wouldn't be hanging over her head anymore. When she walked out of here, she could get on with her life.

"Zann?" Ham Hammerick passed through the lobby and stopped. "You doing all right?"

She jumped to her feet and took his offered hand. As he squeezed it in a fatherly way, it struck her that he'd always stood by her with warmth and kindness. That was basically true for all the folks who worked at town hall, with the exception of the two that mattered most—Malcolm Shively and Jackie Patterson.

"I ran into your mom and dad the other day. They said you're living back home again." A pained look crossed his face. "I can't tell you how sorry I was to hear that. You and Marleigh...I hope you work it out."

"We'll be okay, Ham. There's been a lot of stress, what with me being out of work so long."

"I'm sure that's been tough on both of you." He shook his head grimly. "I went over this situation with Malcolm and the council the other night at our meeting. Just so you know, that business with Miles Blake...nobody believes you did that on purpose."

"I know. It was the gun...probably the stupidest thing I've ever done. I didn't think it through. I thought it would be safer locked up in the trunk than sitting in my car on the lot where some kid could have broken in." Even to her own ear, the words sounded like an excuse. "I'm not blaming anyone but myself. If I had it to do over again, I'd have dropped it off at home before coming in to work."

"I think they'll come around, Zann...once they get all this righteous indignation out of their system. We all slip up now and then. You keep your chin up, and give Marleigh my best."

She hoped he was right about the council coming around. And sooner rather than later, before her whole life went all to hell. But as for Marleigh...that was more than a simple mistake. They'd barely talked since she moved out, just a few emails to plead her case. Once she'd thought she was making headway only to have Marleigh abruptly retreat, shutting down any possibility of seeing her until she'd followed through with getting help. What would "help" accomplish? It wouldn't change what had happened.

"Zann..." Holding up a finger, Connie signaled a message coming through her headset. "They're ready for you now. Second door on the left."

She proceeded down the hallway to the conference room, where Malcolm and Jackie were seated alone at the end of a long table. Jackie gathered several papers into a neat pile and pointed to an empty seat.

Malcolm's chair squeaked in protest as he rocked back. "Zann, we met yesterday with Mr. Blake and his attorney. The council has agreed on a settlement that we hope will put this unfortunate incident behind us."

Jackie twirled a sheet of paper and slid it across the table. "The town—our insurance company, that is—will cover his medical fees and pay him an additional twenty-five thousand dollars in damages for pain and suffering. His acceptance of these terms is contingent on a written apology from you, to be delivered in person along with the check. Malcolm and I have taken the liberty of drafting your statement. All you have to do is copy it by hand and present it to him."

Zann had no problem at all with issuing a formal apology. In fact, she looked forward to the chance to accept responsibility for her actions. Blake's over-the-top reaction notwithstanding, she was genuinely sorry for causing his injury.

There was a certain irony in the settlement figure though, which she estimated would fully cover the cost of construction for the new building in his backyard. Who wouldn't take a broken collarbone for that?

"I'm sure what you've written is fine," Zann said, "but he wants the apology from me, right? Seems like I should write it in my own words."

"No chance of that." Jackie shoved her glasses onto her forehead and rubbed her eyes. "This is a very sensitive matter, Zann. Speaking as the town's attorney, we simply cannot allow you to admit to anything that might leave us vulnerable in future litigation. This settlement is an official record, meaning anyone who sues the city for years to come has the right to use its terms as evidence or argument. It's imperative you confine your remarks to our legal position."

"Fine, whatever you need." Putting the issue to rest was really all that mattered. Besides, a quick scan assured her there was nothing objectionable in their version of the written apology. "What's the timetable on this?"

"End of this week."

Zann nodded. "Okay, I'll go home and write the note today. Does this mean I can finally come back to work?" She eyed Malcolm hopefully.

He pursed his lips and looked down. "There's one other outstanding issue, I'm afraid."

The cynic in her wasn't surprised to hear they were moving the goalpost. If they fired her now, they were assholes for stringing her along.

"Certain members of the town council have expressed liability concerns with regard to your continued employment. To put it simply, we can't afford to have something like this happen again."

"It won't. I sold my guns, and I—"

Jackie interjected, "Hear us out, Zann. I don't mean to understate the disappointment in you for carrying a firearm in your city vehicle, but the council's reservations actually have more to do with the incident involving Mr. Blake. To be honest, there were several calling for your termination, but Malcolm and I were able to persuade them to accept another solution, one we believe is fair to all parties."

It turned her stomach to think of men and women she'd known for years—people who'd gushed over her service in the Marines—sitting around this very table discussing whether or not to fire her. "This will never happen again, Malcolm. I swear it on a stack of Bibles."

"I believe you really mean that," he said, his voice achingly patronizing. "But it isn't that simple. We spoke with everyone who was present when this incident occurred, and we still have concerns about why you behaved the way you did. It was unsettling. Until we fully understand, we can't be assured it won't happen again."

She'd given her statement several times already, always citing her fear that Blake would be injured by the nail gun. The missing piece was how she'd suddenly found herself back in a two-room house in Afghanistan. To confess that was to admit she was compromised and every bit the liability the council feared.

"What do you want me to say, Malcolm?"

He cleared his throat and folded his stubby fingers meekly on the table. "We'd like you to submit to a psychological evaluation."

"A shrink? Are you kidding me?" She was a combat-tested Marine. Her panic over Blake walking into a nail gun was a trained response, not something she'd done because she'd lost her mind.

"It's for your own good, Zann…and ours, of course," he said. "We need assurances from a professional that you're unlikely to repeat this behavior. We just can't have you going off on somebody like this again."

Jackie eyed her squarely. "Zann, this is part of our legal due diligence. We'd be negligent if we didn't insist. I'm afraid it isn't negotiable."

Zann managed not to groan, replacing the urge with a grim nod.

Everything she'd done since the day Vanessa's letter arrived was aimed at getting her life back in balance. Face the truth and make it right with the Lairds. Reclaim her confidence and instinct. Become again the "shining warrior" Marleigh thought she was, all while hiding the horror of what she'd done. But in the eyes of virtually everyone, she'd gone from respected hero to crazed lunatic.

Now forced to dig inside this awful secret, she faced a new fear—being told she was too messed up to recover.

* * *

Marleigh dragged the cardboard box across the floor. Books and magazines they'd already read, DVDs they'd watched and filed away. Maybe Zann would drop them off at the senior center on her way to the landfill.

On the advice of the real estate agent handling their sale, she'd spent every spare minute of the last three weeks stripping the house of all but its most basic furnishings. Get the clutter out and open up the floor space, Pete had said. It'll make the house look bigger. Their personal items—from photos to decorative knickknacks—Zann had agreed to store in the shed behind her parents' house.

The sorting process was excruciating, as she was constantly confronted with memories of happier times. Wedding gifts, goofy snapshots, souvenirs from places they'd visited. These she set aside in a stack they'd have to go through together. If this separation became permanent, someone would get "custody" of these mementos.

The thought of such a painful reckoning brought a fresh flow of tears, a common response now that she spent most of her time alone. Moments of joy from remembering brighter days withered with the knowledge that Zann still valued her secrecy even more than their marriage. Given one last chance to come clean, she'd chosen to pack up and leave.

She straightened and clutched her aching back just as sunlight glinted off Zann's SUV pulling into the driveway. Today was their first face-to-face meeting since the bitter fight two weeks ago that had exposed her pent-up resentment and their mutual lack of trust. While they'd exchanged tersely worded texts and emails to resolve the necessary decisions related to selling the house, they hadn't spoken, not even on the phone. She had no idea of Zann's state of mind. Indeed, she hardly knew her own.

An uncontrollable thrill surged through her when Zann stepped from her vehicle. For a fleeting moment, she was once again that tall, strong figure who'd waited for her at the altar in her dashing uniform on their wedding day. Before approaching the house, she walked out to the curb and studied the For Sale sign with all the solemnity of visiting a gravestone.

Overcome with longing, Marleigh stepped outside and waved from the porch. It was all she could do not to run to her for a hug.

"How much are you asking?" Zann asked, breaking into a devastating smile.

"For you? I can cut you a deal."

As Zann drew closer, it was clear her smile was forced…and that she too might have been crying, perhaps only minutes ago.

Marleigh couldn't help herself. When Zann reached the top step, she opened her arms and pulled her into a hug. Feeling the hands on her back, the chin resting on her shoulder, she fought to compose herself. The pain of their separation gave way to a deep, familiar comfort.

"I've missed you," Zann finally stated with an emphatic nod, as if it settled everything.

"Me too." Marleigh stiffened and put a few steps between them, fighting the temptation to give in to what she knew would make her feel good at this moment. If she weakened and invited Zann to come back, they'd be on the same dismal track as a month ago—on the verge of ruin and doing nothing to save themselves. "I've got some boxes ready."

In a matter of seconds, Zann's cheerful face contorted through several expressions, ending with grim acceptance. "Fine, let's get to it."

In fairness, Marleigh could hardly expect warmth when she too was afraid to show it. "How'd the meeting with Malcolm go?"

"They settled with Miles Douchebag, so at least that part's over. But they won't bring me back—you'll love this part—until I've seen a shrink. Apparently they don't trust me to work with the public without attacking them. Funny…that didn't bother them the first time they hired me when I'd been attacking people for real for eight years."

"I guess they just want to make sure you can turn it off."

"You sound just like the lawyer," Zann scoffed as she started through the door, decidedly unamused.

"Sorry…I've always thought it was a good idea for you to talk things out with somebody. Believe me, I'm not trying to pick a fight or anything, but it's a fact that you keep things bottled up inside. Maybe it would—"

"Give it a rest, Marleigh," she snapped. "How about for once you be on *my* side?"

The swing from tenderness to hostility felt as violent as a shove. "Come on, Zann. That's not fair. I've always been on your side."

"Well, you have a funny way of showing it," she muttered as she nudged one of the boxes with her foot. "I didn't come here to fight. You want me to haul this crap out?"

"I can help. And it's not all crap. There's a lot of our personal stuff in here. We'll need to go through it eventually and decide what we want to keep."

Zann rummaged through a box and removed a glass globe they'd picked up in Key West. A gentle shake stirred a settling of tiny starfish, flamingoes and shells. "From our honeymoon. Tacky as hell but I still love it."

This time Marleigh was careful with her words, biting back an offer for Zann to keep the memento. It would have sounded like a final disbursement. "Then make sure you take care of that box. It's full of stuff neither one of us wants to lose."

"That's what it feels like though…losing, I mean. If I had it to do over again, I wouldn't have moved out. That's like admitting we give up, and there's no way I'm doing that." With a nostalgic flair, she ran her hand across the bare mantel. "If I got Malcolm to let me come back to work, would that be enough to stop this runaway train?"

The last two weeks had been the most difficult of Marleigh's life as she grappled with the fact that Zann had chosen to leave rather than share her secret. Saying yes would soothe her heartache for now, but she'd be setting herself up for even more down the road when their mutual mistrust reared its ugly head again. Another round of hurtful words could leave them damaged beyond repair. "Right now we need to focus on selling the house. Pete called this afternoon. He's got two showings lined up for tomorrow."

Her pale green eyes flashed with anger as she snatched the fragile box of keepsakes from the floor and stalked toward the door. "I guess that means no."

"One of us has to be the adult here, Zann."

"And it can't be me because I still live with Mommy and Daddy, right?"

They were doing exactly what she'd feared, hurting each other with careless words. "I'm sorry. I didn't mean to say you were a child. It wasn't an easy decision but one of us had to make it."

Zann ignored her apology, wordlessly making one trip after the other until all the boxes were stacked in the cargo area of her SUV. Standing with the driver's door open, she nodded toward the house and asked, "Anything else while I'm here?"

"Please don't be mad." Despite her fear of being rebuffed, Marleigh clasped her left hand and drew it to her lips, flashing back to a similar moment from the first day they'd shared at Wright Park. "You know I love you."

Zann visibly relaxed, the creases in her forehead disappearing as the corner of her mouth turned up in a half-hearted smile. "Yeah, me too you. I'm sorry I've put us through this. But I promise I'm going to fix it, Marleigh."

"What I want you to fix"—she placed a palm over Zann's chest—"is whatever's gone wrong in here. It doesn't matter what happens to us if you're still broken."

She raised up on her toes to plant a kiss on Zann's lips, then gently pushed her away.

CHAPTER TWENTY-ONE

Present day

She found Marleigh's hand in the dark and touched the phone to light up the clock display. Time was running out. Bobby was due any minute to pick up Ancil and his friends. It was clever the way he'd stalled by demanding to talk only to a federal officer. The local police were only too happy to oblige, not wanting such a heavy weight on their shoulders. The nearest fed was probably an hour away in Burlington and Ancil clearly hoped to be long gone by then.

That meant the danger was almost over for everyone but Bridget. Marleigh had warned the dispatcher that Ancil's plan was to take Bridget hostage.

Zann was more concerned about the Colfax police force. They weren't trained to handle such a crisis. If they lost control of the situation, Bridget could end up in the line of fire. And if Ancil managed to escape with her…they'd never see her again.

"Marleigh, listen for God's sake. I have to stop them. I can't let them take her."

"And I can't let them take *you*!"

"They don't want me. Look, I've got this figured out—a new idea. All I have to do is sneak to the back door and open it…pretend I just happened to come in. I just need to get close to them. They won't expect me to attack. You stay here out of the way."

"No way, it's too dangerous. That crazy guy's not thinking straight. He could blow your head off and not bat an eye."

"Shhh. If I don't go—"

From the other room, Fran snapped, "This man needs a doctor now! I don't know how you think you're getting out of here, but they're never going to stop hunting you if he dies."

"Shut up…shut *up*!" Scotty was getting worse by the minute, and it was easy to picture him waving his gun in her face. Marleigh was right—he couldn't be counted on to keep his cool.

"Scotty, Scotty. Come with me," Ancil cajoled. "Let's talk this over…I have something in my pocket I think you will like. David, kill the lights and keep an eye on the window. Bobby should be here any minute."

They entered the break room, again stopping only inches from where Zann and Marleigh hid.

Scotty, shuffling in what clunked like oversized boots, danced excitedly from one foot to the other. "Fuck, Ancil. Why didn't you tell me? I'll take whatever you—"

Then, a muffled *pop!*

Marleigh flinched, causing her foot to thump against the door at the very instant one of the women in the lobby cried out, "Oh, my God!"

A long, low groan was followed by the sound of a body slumping to the floor.

"Ancil!" David warned the hostages not to move, his voice traveling across the lobby. Clearly he was fighting the urge to leave them unguarded so he could check out the commotion. "What the fuck just happened?"

"He left me no choice, David," Ancil called to him calmly. "He pointed his gun at me when I could not give him a hit. Go back and watch the window."

Zann could only pray Ancil hadn't heard the noise from the cabinet, that he'd been too absorbed in his actions. With her legs stretched over Marleigh's, she had no purchase to coil and strike if he suddenly opened the cabinet.

"We need to get outta here right now," David yelled.

"Get the girlfriend ready."

Her mind raced through possible scenarios. With Scotty dead on the floor, there was one less shooter to worry about. She might even get her hands on his gun if Ancil hadn't thought to pick it up. That would be a game changer.

If not, her best bet was to wait for Ancil to return to the lobby and then sneak down the hallway without being seen. Every detail mattered. If she crouched low—and if they were focusing on the action outside—Fran's counter would partially shield her from view. She could overtake whichever one was closest—Ancil or David—using his body as a shield if the other tried to shoot her.

The Marine Corps had trained her for this. How many times had she taken down her hand-to-hand combat instructors and stripped them of their weapons? Could she do that now with her left hand weakened? She had to.

The hostages would be sitting ducks. They were tied up with duct tape, unable to jump into the fray or even run for cover. She had to get the drop on Ancil and David or else—

The cabinet door abruptly opened to Ancil, who was crouched at eye level and aiming a pistol straight at her head.

* * *

The dusky gray light from the window was enough for Marleigh to see the twitch in Zann's jaw, as if she were fool enough to lunge at a desperate man with a gun. Ancil would kill her.

"Zann, do what he says...please."

"Your friend gives you excellent advice." Ancil's smirk was pure evil—and he'd just killed a man in cold blood. "Out."

It was obvious to Marleigh once they stood that Zann could have overpowered him easily had he not been armed—and maybe even then if she'd been quick about it. Short and wiry, his only threat was the pistol he had trained on them. He was dressed in a gray suit and shirt, more businessman than tough guy.

The man called Scotty lay crumpled on his side, blood pooling on the white tile from a wound near his waist. From the baby-like skin of his cheek, he was hardly more than a teenager.

She did her best to block Ancil's view as she sidled away from the cabinet, but he spotted the cell phone she'd left behind.

With his gun sagging in their general direction, he quickly scrolled through the texts they'd sent the dispatcher. "So it appears I was right about Luc Michaux after all. Poor Bridget. He does not care what happens to her."

"You aren't getting what you came for," Zann said. "And now that the building is surrounded, you might as well give up. There's no way you're getting out of here."

"We shall see about that."

Marleigh wanted to slap the smug look off his face. Marching in front of Zann to the lobby, she was horrified to see Clay, ghastly pale from the loss of blood. He lay stretched out on the floor with his head in Fran's lap, a crimson stain covering his shoulder and chest.

Fran and Terry appeared relatively calm considering the circumstances, but Tammy's makeup was streaked with tears. All three sat on the floor with their wrists bound in duct tape.

Bridget's look—a mask of fear and guilt—broke her heart. She was the only one not restrained, and it occurred to Marleigh the others might even be suspicious that she was somehow part of this attack. Surely they were wondering if she knew of Luc's drug dealing. Marleigh didn't believe it for a second. Her best friend for ten years…Bridget hated the scourge of drugs in Vermont as much as anyone.

"I found these two hiding in the cabinet like frightened kittens." He tossed what was left of the duct tape to David. "Tie them up."

"I was hoping you guys got out the back," Terry told her.

"Shut up!" David barked. Unlike Ancil, he looked the part of a drug dealer, at least by the standards she'd seen in her jailhouse reporting of the rural trade. Unshaven and sloppy, he wore ripped jeans and an oversized sweater with loose threads. "Hands together," he snarled as he peeled off a thinning roll of tape.

Zann thrust her hands forward first, her eyes still on Ancil as he walked to the window. Keeping her voice low, she spoke calmly as he wrapped. "You know what he did, don't you David? He murdered Scotty. You heard it yourself—he lured him back there by telling him he had something in his pocket. Scotty never pointed his gun."

He glared at her stubbornly but it was clear he was listening.

"That's right, he thought he was getting a bump. You should have heard him. So excited, so happy. Ancil was his friend who was going to help him get high. Instead he stuck a gun in his gut and pulled the trigger." She made a shooting gesture with her index finger and thumb. "We heard the whole thing. The kid never had a chance…and neither will you. Ancil doesn't give two shits what happens to you. He'll kill you too if he thinks it gives him a better shot at getting away."

"Sit down." He said it evenly, as if he were turning over her words in his head. Earlier he'd referred to Scotty as his cousin. Maybe he felt responsible for him…and maybe he was losing trust in Ancil.

Marleigh held her hands out and allowed him to finish off his roll after only one wrap. It hardly seemed enough to hold her. With her back pressed against the counter, she slid to the floor and pulled her knees to her chest.

Zann held David's eye until he grudgingly returned to the window. Then she began to look around as though sizing up the situation. Marleigh knew her well enough to know she was laying out another plan.

* * *

Zann's training had covered weapons of opportunity. Practically anything in the newsroom could be used against an enemy. A box of paperclips on Fran's counter that she could throw in Ancil's face, the heavy stapler or picture frame that would disorient him for a millisecond if hurled at his head. And in an urn by the door, a large umbrella for striking or dislodging his gun. It was a custom Colt 45, chrome plated with a mother-of-pearl grip. A frighteningly deadly weapon, especially at close range.

In another few minutes, she'd have darkness on her side as well. They'd turned off all the lights so they could see out without law enforcement seeing in.

David had turned his back on her, not noticing that she hadn't sat on the floor as ordered. From her squatting position, she was ready to spring.

There were scissors in the bin on Bridget's desk—not as maneuverable as a knife, but sharp enough to do some serious damage. As handcuffs, the tape was a joke. One powerful swing of the elbows from her chest downward would tear it off.

All of her plans were predicated on not getting shot within the first three seconds. She'd have to get within arm's reach of one of them to execute a takeaway. Both were holding their guns with a finger on the trigger, a finger she'd snap to cause excruciating pain when she forced the gun down. She wasn't worried about her own safety—the biggest danger was the gun going off in the direction of the hostages.

That risk meant the scissors might be safer if she could get close enough. A vicious slash across the gun hand would cause him to drop it. Or the umbrella…driving the sharp end into his eye would disable him instantly.

So many things could go wrong. The scissors could be dull, the umbrella tip could be flat instead of sharp. No, there was only one way to do this—get to him fast and take his gun away with brute force.

No question which one she'd have to take down first. Ancil was smaller, easier to overpower, and he'd already shown his willingness to murder someone. If she managed to get his gun, David would probably surrender.

"Shit, looks like more cops, and these guys aren't staying back," David said, his voice high with panic. "Fuck, Ancil…it's the DEA."

Eight feet. That's how far away Ancil stood, next to Bridget's desk and angled so he could keep an eye on the room, though his main focus was on what was happening outside. Fling the stapler, grab his gun hand and force it down…three to four seconds from the time she broke the tape. Could he react that quickly?

The better question was did she feel lucky.

"Ancil Leclerc, this is Special Agent Robert Warner with the United States Drug Enforcement Agency." The voice blared over a loudspeaker, causing even Ancil to jump. "You are completely surrounded by law enforcement personnel. No one else will be allowed inside the perimeter. You will not be permitted to leave the area with or without hostages. Step outside the building with your hands on top of your head and prepare to be searched."

Zann almost grinned. Ancil hadn't expected the feds to get here so quickly and now his getaway plan was ruined.

"Goddammit!" David grabbed his head frantically, one hand still holding his gun. "What the fuck are we gonna do?"

After several seconds of silence, Ancil replied calmly, "We do what they say. What other choice do we have?"

"Fuck! Goddammit…fuck."

The relief around the room was palpable. Tammy fell sideways against Terry and burst into tears.

"Then go on and do it so we can get the EMTs in here," Fran barked.

The two men raised their guns above their head and slowly walked out the front door, prompting a spontaneous celebration among Marleigh's coworkers.

"Jesus Christ, that was scary as hell," Terry said. "My heart's going a thousand beats a minute. Did he really shoot that other guy?"

"Do this, Marleigh." Zann demonstrated how to break the tape with one swing and handed her the scissors from Bridget's desk so she could free the others.

Outside in the parking lot, Ancil and David had turned over their guns and were lying facedown on the icy pavement.

The two agents directing the arrest wore black jackets with the letters DEA on the back. One of them jerked the thugs to their feet, placed them in handcuffs and marched them toward a black SUV.

She reveled in the humiliation the two gunmen must have felt—surrendering so calmly after their threats and cocky assurances. Ancil had wisely concluded his getaway was foiled by the DEA ignoring his demands and pulling all the way to the front door, especially since they weren't letting anyone else inside the perimeter.

With the lights on inside now, Bridget sat on the corner of her desk, her hands shaking. "Guys, I'm so sorry this happened. I swear I had no idea Luc was involved in drugs. I only met Ancil a few times. I thought they were both stock traders."

As she apologized, the emergency medical team barreled through the door with first aid equipment in tow. One tended to Clay while the other made a cursory check to confirm Scotty was dead. Next a pair of Colfax officers—Rance Fuller and Joey Crisp, whom she knew from town hall—came in to secure the scene and start taking statements.

Watching Marleigh comfort everyone else, Zann was suddenly overcome with emotion. Considering her reason for coming to the office today, the whole scene was almost surreal. Whatever it took, she would win her wife back for good. Their love, their life…nothing would break them apart now. They couldn't live through something so terrifying and throw it all away. "Marleigh, come here."

Marleigh must have known exactly what she was feeling. She fell into her arms without wavering and buried her face in Zann's neck. For this one moment, their old problems didn't even exist.

"I love you so much," she murmured softly so the others wouldn't overhear. "I'm not letting go of you…ever. I promise you, I'm going to fix everything and you won't ever have to worry about me again."

One of the DEA agents entered and stood with his feet apart and hands on his hips. He definitely had the look of a federal agent—clean shaven with short dark hair, perfectly gelled. "Which one of you is Bridget Snyder?"

"That's me."

"Ms. Snyder, we're trying to piece this story together and I understand your boyfriend may be involved. Would you mind coming with us so we can get a statement and have you look at a lineup? We've been tracking this drug ring for quite some time."

Bridget blew out a frazzled breath. "Yeah, I guess. Can my friend come with me? Marleigh, please? I'm about to lose my shit here."

"Sure. Maybe I should follow you in my car."

"No need for that. We'll be happy to bring you back," the agent said with a friendly smile. He had to know how glad everyone was that they'd shown up just in time. "Shouldn't take more than an hour. Two at the most."

Still in Zann's embrace, Marleigh raised up on tiptoes and gave her a peck on the cheek. "Meet me at the house later and we'll figure this out. I'll call Pete and cancel the contract. And Zann...I love you too."

The words left her weak. In that instant, Marleigh had delivered her from a fate far worse than any Ancil or his friends had threatened. Watching her walk away, she vowed silently to become once again the loving, courageous hero Marleigh believed her to be when they married, a partner in every way.

In the parking lot and beyond, more first responders had arrived, their flashing lights causing probably the biggest commotion Colfax had seen in decades. A second ambulance pulled up alongside a pair of newly arrived state troopers. Ancil and David were plainly visible in the middle row of the SUV, while the other agent waited by the open door for Bridget and Marleigh to climb into the back.

Zann acknowledged the heaviness of her legs as she started toward the break room for her coat. Her muscles quivered from being cooped up in the cabinet, and her emotions still roiled from the turmoil of trying to talk Marleigh into saving their house and marriage. As if all that weren't enough, there was the adrenaline crash. Now four years out of active military duty, she wasn't used to operating at such a high level of tension and focus. Nor did she ever want to again. The last few months had shown her that.

Officer Fuller, with a cherubic face and flaming red hair, emerged from the hallway, "Anybody know what we're supposed to do with this body back here?"

"Ask that guy from the DEA," Crisp replied, adding sarcastically, "Looks like they're taking over our case."

"They just left. Did you get their card?"

"No...call in to HQ. They can probably find them in the register. What'd he say his name was? Something Warner. Robert...Bob?"

Bobby! A sickening wave of panic hit Zann's stomach like a physical punch. No wonder Ancil had surrendered so easily. "Son of a bitch!"

She blew past the other officer on her way out the door, where she searched frantically for the agents' vehicle.

"Whoa, there," Crisp said, catching her arm. "We're going to need to get your statement before you run off."

"That SUV, those agents...they're in on it. Ancil called them to pick him up." This was no time for their cluelessness. Marleigh was in the hands of a stone-cold killer.

CHAPTER TWENTY-TWO

"This feels weird as all get-out," Bridget said, her voice barely above a whisper as the vehicle bounced over a pothole known locally as the Crown Street Crater.

That was an understatement. If Marleigh had it to do over, she'd have insisted on driving her own car and having Bridget ride with her. Sitting in what amounted to a rumble seat behind the guys who'd held them hostage at gunpoint was downright creepy. It didn't help to see the men's hands merely cuffed in their laps—they weren't tethered to anything that would keep them from leaping out of their seats and attacking the agents from behind. Ancil had already killed a man today—he wouldn't be afraid to do it again.

"Where do you think we're going?" Marleigh wondered aloud, though not so the men could hear her. There was no federal building in Colfax. All of the local law enforcement offices were in the opposite direction.

"Can't be far. He said he'd have us back in an hour or two. Maybe they have an office near the college…you know, so they can watch for drugs on campus."

The last building of Colfax Community College whizzed by as they left the town limits and started across an open road that would take them to New York State. Toward Chimney Point, Marleigh realized with a shudder. Inhaling deeply to calm her nerves, she raced to rationalize where they might be headed and why. The agent had said they were investigating others, faces they wanted Bridget to identify. Maybe they'd raided Ancil's associates at a hideout in Chimney Point.

Tuning out Bridget's nervous chatter, she studied the agents from behind. Warner's demeanor during the arrest had been friendly but authoritative, almost military. Now he slumped casually in the passenger seat, muttering occasional expletives in response to a game he was playing on his smartphone. The driver had yet to utter a single word. Their lack of vigilance made her uneasy. They seemed way too cavalier about the potential risk posed by their captives, especially given the seriousness of the crimes they'd just committed. Not once had either agent asked how she and Bridget were doing in the back, or even turned around to check on their well-being.

Ancil too appeared overly relaxed considering his predicament, leaning his head lazily against the window as they rode past farm after farm. If he was worried about the feds, he didn't show it. But then he'd been cocky throughout the entire confrontation. Perhaps he had a plan to invoke his Canadian citizenship and demand to be sent back across the border.

David, on the other hand, looked far more agitated, with shaking knees and a sweaty forehead. From his antsy expression back at the newspaper office when Zann had told him about Scotty, he hadn't signed on for murder—his cousin's murder at that. He was in over his head. In her years as a crime reporter, it was her observation that men like David spilled their guts in the interrogation room...a point that made her even more concerned that Ancil didn't appear the least bit anxious.

"Where are we going?" Marleigh shouted so the agents could hear her over the hum of the road. Neither responded, nor even acknowledged her question. Whispering to Bridget, she said, "I don't like this. Something's messed up here."

A techno trill—Zann's unique ringtone—sounded from her shoulder bag, which was tucked between her feet.

Before she could answer, Ancil abruptly turned in his seat and, with his hands still cuffed, leveled the shiny pistol he'd used to threaten them earlier. In a voice that chilled her, he stated flatly, "You will not answer that."

Agent Warner turned around too but did nothing in response to Ancil's threat.

"Oh, my God." Bridget dug her fingernails into Marleigh's thigh and brought the other hand to her mouth.

David was as shocked as they were, stammering, "Jesus H. Christ, Ancil! You son of a bitch. You scared the shit out of me. I thought we were fucked."

With a cynical laugh, Ancil said, "I told you not to worry, did I not? My friend Bobby came through for us exactly as I said he would." He nodded toward the man they knew as Agent Warner.

Marleigh grasped at once the danger they were in. This wasn't merely a personal grudge from a hotheaded drug dealer who'd been burned. It was a drug shipment worth seven million dollars, stakes so high that collateral damage like Scotty—and like her and Bridget—wasn't even an afterthought. If these two were real DEA agents operating in cahoots with a drug ring, they wouldn't be leaving witnesses behind.

Their only hope now was to turn the men against each other. She glared coldly at Ancil and repeated what Zann had said to David. "You murdered Scotty in cold blood. I heard you." As she spoke, she fumbled silently with the phone in her pocket, getting only as far as to open a text window to Zann.

"No, no." Ancil waved the barrel of the handgun from Bridget to Marleigh and back. "Your phones, *s'il vous plaît*. Both of them now."

She hesitated until he snapped the slide with a menacing click. There wasn't a doubt in her mind he would shoot her on the spot if she didn't comply. Her only chance for staying alive was to do what he said and hope Bridget was somehow able to help him find Luc. Even then...

Ancil passed the phones forward to Warner, or whatever his real name was. "Toss these out the window."

How long would it take the horde of law enforcement officers gathered at the *Messenger* to realize they'd been duped? It was possible no one would even miss them until tonight when Zann got impatient that she hadn't returned home. She and Bridget could be in Canada by then.

Ancil got the key from Warner and removed his cuffs, then David's. In the same chilling voice he'd used in his earlier threats, he taunted Bridget, "Let us hope your sense of direction is sharp today, *mon cœur*. Your lives could very well depend on you leading us to the apartment where Luc's father lives. You remember how to get there, *oui*?"

She began shaking her head. "I…it's somewhere in Montreal. That's all I know."

"Do not lie to me. I know for a fact you have been there."

"But Luc was driving," she pleaded. "I never paid attention to how we got there. I hardly know anything about Montreal. All I remember is that it was an old brick building. And there's a wheelchair ramp in the front. Wait—I remember him saying it was in Monkland."

Their scheme was coming into view. Rendezvous with someone at Chimney Point—likely to switch vehicles, since the authorities would be looking for this one—and cross over the lake into New York, where local and state law enforcement wouldn't be so desperate to find them. Upstate was notorious for its back roads where you could cross the Canadian border without a passport. Once in Montreal they'd use Bridget to again pressure Luc out of hiding.

Marleigh was nowhere in their plans, a fact that grew more terrifying by the second. She'd only been brought along to placate Bridget. At literally any moment, Ancil could put a bullet through her forehead knowing it would terrorize Bridget into doing exactly what they said. She had to get out now.

From her seat in the third row of the SUV, the only possible means of escape was through the rear cargo door, which could very well be locked. Each time Ancil looked away, she stole a glance at the latch behind her. Even if she managed to crawl over the seat while their heads were turned, she'd never be able to open the door without them hearing it. And then what? They'd stop the vehicle and—assuming she could still walk after falling out onto the pavement—chase her through the neighboring fields, where she'd be gunned down like an animal.

He jingled both sets of handcuffs. "*S'il vous plaît.*"

As he wrenched them into place, Marleigh acknowledged that she was actually relieved. Why would he bother to cuff her if he intended to kill her? She figured into his plans for now but every minute she stayed alive was a gift.

Lake Champlain appeared through the leafless trees on their left. The vehicle slowed and turned through snowy ruts into a cluster of small cabins she recognized as a sportsman's club for hunting and fishing enthusiasts. It was abandoned except for a single vehicle, a white luxury SUV without a speck of snow on its hood or top, a sign that it was parked there earlier that day as part of their meticulous plan.

David beamed. "Look-a-there. They brought us a Cadillac."

"It's not for you, dumbass," Warner grunted.

The four men filed out and gathered at the front of the vehicle to talk, ducking as a pair of police cars roared by with sirens wailing and lights flashing. Whatever their plans were, David appeared to be the only one out of the loop.

Meanwhile, Bridget was close to hyperventilating. "Please tell me those police were looking for *us.*"

"They must be." That would mean the cops had figured out the ruse only minutes after they left. "Zann would have told them we were headed to Chimney Point. We heard them say so in the break room. Could be they're setting up a roadblock."

"They won't be looking for a white Cadillac."

Over at the other vehicle, the agents traded their DEA jackets for ordinary civilian coats.

"I should have known," Marleigh said with a groan. "Those guys aren't even real DEA. They were waiting here the whole time in case Ancil and his friends got caught. The whole thing was fake."

"Well, they're not faking now," Bridget blubbered. "I don't know about you but I'm scared shitless. What are they going to do with us?"

The answer to that was too grim to put into words. "If something happens to me, Bridget…you need to make a break for it. Run away, yell out for help. Whatever it takes. It can't get any worse than it is now."

Marleigh used her elbow to wipe the condensation off the inside of the window so she could watch them. It was hard to make out details now that it was dark. Ancil and David had retrieved winter gear from the white vehicle—ski suits, caps, heavy gloves.

Warner pointed toward the lake and handed them something from his pocket, an object too small for Marleigh to see. Then he and the driver got in and drove off, leaving Ancil and David in the lot.

It made no sense at all. They couldn't continue in the black SUV—the cops would be looking for it.

David wrenched the sliding passenger door open and tossed the fake DEA jackets on the floor with a bundle of cell phones. "Out. Both of you…follow him." He nodded toward Ancil, who was walking cautiously back toward the highway, checking up and down for traffic.

It was then Marleigh noticed another set of tire tracks in the ankle-deep snow, too narrow to be from either vehicle. They picked up again on the other side of the road.

She elbowed Bridget and pointed down the lake bank. "Look. That's how they're getting us across the border." She hadn't seen it when they turned into the sportsman's club, a motorboat tied to the dock across the road. No more than eighteen feet long, it had a paneled glass windshield with a canvas top, but seating for only two.

Ancil stood in the middle of the road and waved them on frantically. "*Allons-y!* Get on the boat."

On the off chance someone discovered their getaway car, Marleigh took care to lift her feet high with every step so they'd leave distinct footprints in the snow. As they crossed to the boat dock, she saw signs of commotion in the form of flashing lights and a long line of taillights about half a mile up the road near the Lake Champlain Bridge—a roadblock. And in only minutes, their boat would pass underneath, oblivious to those desperate to find them.

"Marleigh, a car!" Bridget suddenly broke back toward the highway and started waving her arms.

"Bitch!" Ancil raced to her and swung wildly at her head, landing a blow that caused her to crumple. He hoisted her limp body over his shoulder and hurried to the boat.

Marleigh hesitated on the dock, buying a few more seconds so the car's driver might see them. A shove from David sent her tumbling into the well of the boat and for an instant she considered diving into the icy water. Drowning in handcuffs ended the same as being shot.

David then yanked her up by the hood of her coat and steered her into the tiny cabin space beneath the bow cover. It was little more than a cramped storage compartment and it smelled of fish. Before she could even get her bearings, Bridget landed on top of her and the boat's engine roared to life.

* * *

Zann paid no attention to speed limit signs as she raced through the twilight over the two-lane road, zooming past slow-moving traffic regardless of the solid yellow line. Every set of taillights in front of her was a potential target until she drew close enough to determine it wasn't the black SUV.

Vermont Highway 125 was the quickest route to New York State, crossing fifteen miles of farmland to Lake Champlain. The last mile snaked along the lakefront and ended at Chimney Point, Ancil's apparent destination. The state police had been alerted to expect them and had set up a roadblock at the Lake Champlain Bridge, a strategic intersection of state highways where they could cut off escape in all directions.

At Willow Point, the lake came into view along the road on her left, barely discernible against the night sky. The sportsman's cottages along the lakefront sat dark, the boat dock abandoned. It would be two months before the lake iced over for fishermen, but few boaters braved the cold this time of year.

She hit the speed dial on her phone for her parents' number. "What did Ham say?"

Per her instructions, her father was in constant contact with the mayor's office, where their longtime friend was monitoring the police chase and relaying updates. "There's no sign of them yet, but you were right about their phones. They found both of them smashed to bits on Crown Street right outside of town."

She had a feature on her phone that would locate Marleigh's, and she'd used it after her call went unanswered. "They must have thrown them out when I called her. But it definitely means they're headed to Chimney Point."

"Ham said for you to pull out, Zann. You can't be in the middle of this. They've got police all over the state watching for that vehicle."

"Not going to happen, Pop. I need to find Marleigh. Where else are they looking?" She had to consider the possibility that Ancil would change his plans after learning she and Marleigh had overheard his call.

"Eight checkpoints in different directions, he said. And every law enforcement officer in six counties around Addison. Ham said to promise you they won't get away."

That wasn't good enough for Zann. There were plenty of back roads where Ancil and his DEA imposter friends could steal a different vehicle, making it more difficult to spot them in a search.

Up ahead, a long line of taillights had slowed to a crawl amid flashing blue lights. She'd reached the Chimney Point roadblock and swung into the left lane to get a better view of about a dozen vehicles in the line. Not one was a black SUV.

"Keep checking in with him and let me know if you hear anything."

"Zann, be careful."

She ended the call and slammed her Jeep into reverse for a three-point turn. There was another way across the lake—the ferry at Larrabee's Point, fifteen miles to the south along Lake Street. Or maybe they'd cut across one of the back roads toward Burlington.

By the time she reached the sportsman's cottages, flashing lights appeared in her rearview mirror. Of course—they'd seen her ducking out of the roadblock and couldn't take a chance she was trying to escape. "I don't fucking have time for this," she muttered, pulling over on the wide shoulder next to the boat dock. It was all she could do not to scream as she leapt from her vehicle and stomped toward the patrol car.

The officer shined a beam of light directly into her eyes. "Stop where you are and show your hands." It was a woman's voice from a car belonging to the Vermont State Police.

"You're looking for a couple of drug dealers, right? So am I," she barked. "I was one of the hostages in Colfax. Those bastards took my wife."

Inching closer, the woman looked at her sternly. She was bundled up in a bomber jacket with a faux fur collar and a matching hat pulled down over her ears. "Show me some ID."

The urge to punch her in the face and take off was almost overpowering, but Zann held her temper in check and produced her driver's license.

"Suzann Redeker...I know you."

Zann checked her name tag—Lieutenant Lisper—and realized she was face-to-face with Marleigh's former girlfriend Troop. "Marleigh Anderhall's my wife. She's one of the hostages. We heard them say they were going to Chimney Point."

"It looks like they changed their mind. We got the roadblock up six minutes after the call came in and we've searched every single vehicle. There's no way they got past us."

"Goddammit!" Zann spun aimlessly, looking up and down the road. "They could have gone south to the ferry. I have to get there before they cross. This guy's a killer."

"I'll radio down there for a unit to intercept. But you need to leave this matter to us. It isn't safe for..."

Her words faded into nothingness as Zann noticed for the first time a set of tire tracks in the snow leading down the bank to the boat ramp, along with several sets of footprints. She stalked past Lisper to cross the road, following the tracks to a parking area behind the cottages. The black SUV was there, abandoned. A second set of vehicle tracks led out and turned east back toward Colfax.

"I'll be damned." Lisper, clearly excited at the discovery, fumbled with her handheld radio as she peered into the SUV with her flashlight, with Zann looking over her shoulder. The beam landed on a couple of dark jackets with yellow lettering, and she threw the door open to check inside.

"That's Marleigh's bag!" Zann whirled around for more clues. Using her phone as a flashlight, she frantically examined the cluster of footprints leading back to the highway, including a small set that could have been Marleigh's.

"This is Unit Seven-Three. Suspects' vehicle has been located point-four miles south…" Lisper went on to describe the scene, including the mention of a second set of vehicle tracks. A garbled reply over the radio confirmed the black SUV had been reported stolen that morning from a dealership in Burlington. "No sign of suspects or hostages."

Burlington. So the guys had come down through Vermont, not New York.

Still combing for clues, Zann trudged through the lot to follow a third set of tire tracks—thin and narrow—that led behind the second cottage to a small boat trailer. "They split up!" she yelled. "Look at these footprints. See how small they are? They could be Marleigh's, and they go all the way to the lake. I'm telling you, they left here in a boat. You need to get patrols out on the water."

As the trooper slogged over to confirm what she'd found, Zann bolted past her to the Jeep. There wasn't a second to waste while the cops got themselves reorganized.

CHAPTER TWENTY-THREE

Icy air seeped through an open seam three feet long where the boat's hull met its bow cover. Making matters worse was the occasional splash of frigid water. Since being thrown into the compact cuddy cabin thirty minutes ago, Marleigh had wrapped herself around her still unconscious friend to generate body heat lest they both succumb to hypothermia.

Bridget finally stirred, moaning as her hand went to her head. Marleigh had felt it already, a bump behind her ear from a blow so vicious it could have been deadly. "Where are we?"

She spoke only loud enough for Bridget to hear over the steady hum of the outboard motor. "We just passed under the bridge, going north. How's your head?"

"Feels like somebody hit me with a baseball bat." Bridget squirmed to peer out the opening, but their view was almost entirely blocked by David, who sat at the steering console. "I can't see a thing. Are they taking us all the way to Canada?"

"I doubt it. I didn't see a spare gas tank, and the one they have won't get us that far." She'd strained to hear what Ancil had told David, who clearly had been kept in the dark about their whole plan. "Ancil said something about Shelburne. It's a harbor on the lake just south of Burlington." She'd gone there once with her college friends to try windsurfing.

"I've been there. One of Luc's clients has a big house right on the water." She grunted. "Clients, my ass. Probably one of his drug cronies…that sleazy bastard."

Marleigh had to agree. "Does Luc have a friend named Everett? When we were hiding in the break room, we heard Ancil talking to somebody on the phone. That's what he called him, Everett. He told him we'd be there in three hours."

"Everett…" Bridget said the name aloud. "That was his name, the guy who had the house. He's rich as all get-out but weird as shit. The place looked like something out of *Rocky Horror*. And he was creepy too. Had about five hookers hanging off his arm…oh, and this huge bodyguard who talked like he was Russian."

A beam of light suddenly lit up Bridget's face and she covered her eyes with her hand. "Shut up, both of you," David snarled.

"Turn that light off, you imbecile!" Ancil's clipped voice and sharp accent made him sound almost effeminate.

"I had to be sure they weren't up to something."

"What can they be up to, David? Are you afraid they will escape through a tunnel in the bottom of the boat?"

Bridget's teeth began to chatter as her consciousness experienced the cold for the first time. "We don't have to worry about Ancil shooting us. We're both going to freeze to death."

In the brief gleam of light, Marleigh had noticed her friend's shining earrings, thin gold hoops that hung well below her jawline. "Give me one of your earrings."

"What for?" Even as she asked, Bridget worked a hoop free.

"Keep your voice down. I want to try something." Though her wrists were bound, Marleigh was able to gently shape the hoop into an L. Feeling her way, she slid one end across the base of Bridget's handcuffs until it scraped the keyhole. Probing blindly for a spring of resistance, she worked it until the soft gold bent too far from the force. "Damn it."

"Here, take the other one."

"No, I can make this one work. I…just…have to…" She bent it in half and used her teeth to twist it into a sharper point. "Okay, let me try again."

Her makeshift key finally caught the locking mechanism in exactly the right place and the claws sprang open.

"You did it!"

"Shhh…we have to make it look like it's still locked, so keep your hands down and act like it's tight."

Bridget presented her other cuff. "Here, do this one too."

"Mine first." She worked her own lock for a couple of minutes, unable to gain purchase to spring it. "Here, see if you can do it. There's a catch inside the hole. When you feel it, try to press against it and they'll pop open."

She could hear Bridget's frustration in the occasional grunt or expletive under her breath. Minutes passed—as if they had anywhere else to be—until Bridget dropped the earring.

"Goddammit."

Marleigh felt along the lifejackets and down into the cold, wet V of the hull. "Forget it. Give me the other one."

This time she lay on her back and worked the probe herself. Occasionally she had to stop and shake out the cramps in her hands, which were also numb from the cold. Giving up wasn't an option. If they got a chance to run, having her hands free could be the difference between living and dying.

When the latch finally released, she almost cried out with relief.

"Okay, so what do we do now?" Bridget asked.

"I wish I knew." She had no real idea what Ancil had planned for when they got to Everett's house. Was there still a chance to make a deal with Luc? Was anyone looking for them on the water? If the answer to both of those questions was no, chances were good they'd be killed.

* * *

Zann forced herself to slow down, as the melted snow was turning to ice now that the temperature had dropped. The secluded stretch of back road was one she knew from her teen years when she'd gone joyriding with her friends. It would take her north of the roadblock to a road that hugged the shore all the way to Burlington.

Steering as best she could with her left hand, she dialed a number she hadn't called in weeks. "Wes, it's Zann. I need you, man—we're talking life and death. A couple of drug dealers took Marleigh hostage about an hour ago and they're going to kill her."

His rapid-fire questions assured her he was darting around his house gathering what they might need to mount a rescue. There was no one in Colfax she'd rather have on her side right now.

"I'm headed up to Button Bay. You know where that is, right? Meet me at the entrance to the park as quick as you can get there." He lived well north of Colfax, meaning he could even get there first if he left right away. "And Wes…I need you to bring all you've got—this is war, man."

Buoyed by her backup, she focused on her plan once they got to the lake. They could steal a boat…assuming they could find one that hadn't been stored already for the winter. Their other option was to track Ancil's movement from the shore and hope like hell he docked on the Vermont side of the lake.

The map on her phone showed just how easy it was to reach Canada by water. Still, only a speedboat could do it in a couple of hours, and that boat trailer she'd found wasn't long enough to haul a vessel of that size. At most, it was a small motorboat.

She placed another call to her father. "Pop, get out your laptop. I need you to check something for me online."

"I've got it right here. I was looking at the map. Ham called and said the state police thinks they got in a boat."

"Yeah, let's hope they're out patrolling the lake by now. I need you to figure something out for me. Say a boat left Chimney Point twenty minutes ago going north. Where would it be right now?"

"Depends on the boat. How many engines are you talking?"

"Probably just an outboard. The trailer was single axle. But it has to be big enough for three or four passengers."

"So about eighteen feet. Probably a cuddy like the one Ham used to have. You'd have to be crazy to go out there in a jon boat as cold as it is."

He was right. They'd freeze to death out on the water in an open boat.

"All right, so do some math for me. I heard one of them tell somebody on the phone they'd be there by seven o'clock. How far can they go from Chimney Point in a couple of hours? I figure it's got to be one of the docks—Button Bay, Kingsland Bay or Shelburne. Call me back as soon as you've figured it out. But mostly I need to know where they are right now."

Fields, barns and silos faded past as she skidded and spun. The narrow back road took her well inland before finally jogging west to intersect with the lakefront highway far north of the Chimney Point barricade. She pulled onto the shoulder and checked the map on her phone. It showed the lake right in front of her but all she saw was inky blackness.

Phone in hand, she zipped up her parka and slid through the snow and underbrush down a steep bank to the water's edge. There she listened, trying to convince herself of the sound of a distant motorboat. As her eyes adjusted to the dark, she scanned the water's surface for anything that seemed to be moving.

Nothing.

The chime of her phone startled her. "Pop, what did you get?"

"New York or Vermont? You didn't say which side."

If they docked on the New York shore, there was no way for Zann to catch them. There were only three routes across the lake—Chimney Point and Larrabee's Ferry behind her, and US 2 just this side of the Canadian border. "It has to be Vermont… has to be."

"Good, Vermont has a lot more landings. But here's your problem—you're looking at anywhere between Kingsland Bay and Burlington. That's a lot of territory to cover. And they might be headed for a private boat dock."

Of course. She might be able to head them off if she got north of them on the shore. "Where would they be right now?"

"Best guess is around Rock Island. You know where that is?"

"Got it." It was on her map about three miles north of her current position. She scrambled up the bank and raced back to her car. Squealing back onto the road, she said, "Keep me posted. I need to get in front of them."

"Zann, the police are all over it now. They're looking in three different states and Canada."

"Wait...Everett!"

"What? Where's Everett?"

"Everett's not a where, it's a who." It was the longest of long shots but it was the only other clue she had. "I heard him tell some guy named Everett they'd meet him around seven o'clock. All the property tax records are online, right? So pull up everything between Kingsland Bay and Shelburne and see if there's somebody named Everett with a house near the water."

"First or last?"

"I don't know. Try both." Ancil had called everyone by their first name. "I've got to keep moving, Pop. Call me if you find anything."

Ignoring the posted speed limits, she pushed past everyone in her way until she reached Button Bay State Park. Wes's pickup, illuminated by its running lights, sat at the entrance. She flashed her headlights and slowed enough for him to fall in behind. At the far end of the park was a boat ramp, where she parked and raced all the way out to the shore.

"I take it we're looking for a boat," he said gruffly as he joined her, raising a pair of binoculars just as a three-quarter moon broke through the clouds to bathe the landscape in contrasts.

"Thanks for coming. If I'm right, they'll be rounding that point any minute now."

"How many we talking about?"

"Probably no more than two. They aren't exactly trained commandos but they're both armed. One guy, Ancil Leclerc... he's real trouble. He killed their other partner, lured him in the back room and shot him in the stomach. It was cold, man." She shuddered at the ruthlessness of Scotty's murder and the knowledge that Ancil would do it again without batting an eye. "They're chasing seven million dollars worth of heroin. Marleigh's friend Bridget…turns out her boyfriend's a mule. He picked up their shipment in New York and ran off with it. Now they're using Bridget to try to lure him out. What scares me is they don't need Marleigh. They could threaten her just to get—"

Wes's hand went up as he peered out across the lake. "I got something."

She eagerly took his binoculars and discovered they were night vision, lighting up the shadows in various shades of green. Sure enough, there was a small motorboat rounding the point with two figures visible at the console.

"That's gotta be them," he added. "They're running dark."

The men were wrapped in blankets all the way to their heads, but one was unmistakably slight in stature—Ancil. "That's them, all right."

"Want me to call the cops?"

"Not yet…I don't want them to panic and do something stupid. If they cross over to New York, we're screwed." As the boat pulled even with their position on the shore, her phone rang. "Pop, we found them. They're passing Button Bay right now. What have you got?"

"Two properties, both of them right on the lake. One belongs to a Stephen Everett, the other to an Everett Percy. Both assessed around a million four. The first looks like it could be a farm, eight and a half acres south of Shelburne. Percy's is a six thousand square-foot house—pretty fancy if it's worth that much."

This was the break Zann needed. She and Wes could lie in wait for the boat to arrive and surprise the captors. "I want you to call Ham and tell him to send the cops up toward Shelburne, tell him you got a tip. But don't give him the exact address until I give you the word. If they show up with lights and sirens, it'll scare them off. I need these bastards to dock."

"Zann, you be careful."

Careful, but focused and determined. Tonight she was a trained combat soldier tracking the enemy. "Don't worry, Pop. I know what I'm doing. Send me everything you can find on both of those guys."

"Leave your Jeep," Wes said. "We'll be a lot less obvious if we don't look like we're having a parade."

Her only reluctance—that he might not drive as fast as she did—proved not to be a problem. Plus his truck was equipped with an elaborate navigation system that allowed him to issue voice commands. Stephen Everett's farm was only twelve minutes away.

"What is it with you guys and your trucks? Is this some kind of...extension?" Her joke was a feeble effort to calm the adrenaline pumping through her veins. It reminded her of Whitney Laird's lame banter, something she'd done to break the tension as their unit entered a village. It was unsettling to have Whit invading her thoughts now of all times.

"Don't knock it. I'll take it over that rusty bucket of bolts you drive any day." He gestured toward the crew cab space behind them. "Check out the hardware. So happens I brought your Legion."

"You mean *your* Legion." It was pure luck she'd sold her guns back to Wes. That meant going in with something she'd trained on, something she'd fired hundreds of times. "How about the Colt?"

"How about a SIG M400 instead?"

A top of the line assault rifle. "You spoil me."

"Only the best for my friends."

His simple acknowledgment of their friendship should have been gratifying. Instead she felt guilty for dropping off his radar after selling back her guns, unable to explain herself or to face the idea of sharing her feelings with the veterans group. What good were their opinions at that point? She wasn't looking for comfort or support for killing her own soldier.

"You realize what we're doing here is a little outside the lines," he said. "There probably ain't a court in the land that's gonna let us off if we go into a man's house and shoot him."

She'd thought about that. They weren't operating under military rules of engagement that allowed them to storm an enemy camp and fire away at anyone who fought back. Even the cops were expected to show restraint. "If you want out, fine. But I'm not going to sit on my ass while these bastards threaten my wife. I'd gladly live out my days in a prison cell if it means she gets out of this in one piece."

"Never said I wanted out. You think I'm gonna sit by while you have all the fun? I just wanted to make sure you remembered this is Vermont, not Afghanistan. There ain't nothing you can do here that's gonna change what you did there."

That was a sucker punch. This was about saving Marleigh, not Whit.

"That's right," he went on, scolding her with a condescending gaze, which he seemed to think showed compassion and insight. "I looked up your commendation. You lost somebody over there and it's still messing with you. That's why you started shooting again, so you'd be ready next time."

Zann felt as if a scab had been ripped off her soul. "How could you possibly know what's in my head?"

"'Cause it's in mine too. I lost three guys to an old, decrepit suicide bomber after I told 'em to show some respect for their elders. You know what that's called? Shit you have to live with. But you think I don't see his wrinkled-ass face every time I pull a trigger?"

What a horrible burden to carry through life, three lives lost forever because he believed in humanity. "Jesus, I'm sorry. That's just so…some days I wonder if we don't all belong in a mental hospital."

He snorted. "Yeah, like the VA's gonna pay for that!"

"You have arrived at your destination."

Zann shook off the heaviness and turned her attention to the farm. The lot was long and narrow, with a two-story frame house at one end and a flat, snow-covered field that fronted the lake at the other.

"This doesn't look much like the castle of a drug lord," Wes said.

She agreed but wasn't going to leave without checking it out. "Stay here. I'll go have a look in the windows."

"Maybe I should do it…nah, never mind." Obviously he'd forgotten for a moment she was a Marine.

Approaching the house, she aimed a penlight at the pair of vehicles parked in the drive, a pickup and a hatchback with bumper stickers touting local produce. A peek through the window confirmed her conclusion this was not Ancil's destination. A woman of about seventy stirred a pot at the stove while a man of the same age wearing nothing but an earnest look piled laundry into a washing machine.

She jogged back to the truck and slid quietly into the passenger seat. "I'd give anything not to have looked in that window."

CHAPTER TWENTY-FOUR

Everett Percy was definitely their guy. It wasn't the house that tipped them off, though it was certainly grand, glittering from bottom to top with up-lighting and floor-to-ceiling glass that allowed one to see through it to the lake. It wasn't even the two luxury vehicles that sat on the circular drive. What gave Percy away was the infrared beam that ran at ground level from each side of the gated entrance to the corners of the property. Drug dealers needed warning when someone entered the premises unexpectedly.

"What do you think?" she asked Wes, who'd just returned from an exploration of the perimeter.

"There's only one clean way in. We have to climb a tree and hop over to the roof of the boat shed. Then we've got a whole new problem 'cause the backyard looks like it's wired with motion detectors."

The best way to beat a motion detector was to move while movement was expected. "Those guys will set off the sensors when they dock. We could hang out on the roof and go in when they do."

He nodded absently. "Like hiding in plain sight. See, that's why they pay captains more than sergeants."

She followed him around the wall through the neighbor's yard to the water's edge, where the thick trunk of a beech tree forked high above Everett Percy's boathouse, leaving about a four-foot drop to the roof. Climbing out on a branch was the easy part. The real trick would be sticking the landing on the steep slope, especially if it was icy.

"Guess we're about to find out how a mountain goat feels," Wes said, grunting as he hoisted himself up to the fork. A strip of bark gave way beneath him and he flailed at a branch to regain his balance. "Last time I did this, I was twelve. You wanna hand up your gear?"

"I'm good." The Legion was tucked inside the pocket of her coat and a strap held the rifle in place across her chest. She pulled herself up to join him, acutely aware her right arm was doing most of the work. Hanging back while Wes walked out on the limb, she studied the hand- and footholds he used. Simple enough. But to reach the roof, she'd have to lower herself and drop, something she wasn't sure she could do given her weakened grip.

Wes was down, girding himself at the apex of the roof to help break her fall should she slip. "Easy does it, Cap'n."

"If I fall on my ass and set off the alarm, I want you to shoot whoever runs over here to check it out."

"My pleasure."

It was hard not to feel exposed, though the bright lights inside the house made it unlikely anyone could see out. She crouched and wrapped herself around the branch, mentally gauging the mechanics of the maneuver and how she'd compensate if her left hand gave way. Before she could start her drop, Wes caught her foot and absorbed her weight as she lowered herself...as though he'd known all along she couldn't do it on her own. "Thanks, man."

"Save that hand of yours for target practice."

They settled on the back side of the slope, a position that kept them mostly hidden but allowed them to watch both the house and the dock. Tall glass doors opened onto an expansive brick patio, where a snowy path had been cleared to the dock. Inside were two men, one a prim-looking man with silver hair who paced the room, cocktail in hand. That had to be sixty-eight-year-old Everett Percy, according to the public records her father had unearthed. Officially, he was CEO of a distribution network for sundries, mundane items that filled impulse displays in grocery stores and bodegas. Probably how he moved heroin as well…a few packs here, a few there…with each layer of the network taking its cut. From the way Ancil had spoken to him over the phone, he was at the top of the chain. Only a powerful man could have pulled the strings for a daring escapade like the one Ancil had launched today.

The second man was a hulking giant whose rigid posture and position near the door made her think he was a bodyguard. A guy his size could be trouble. While holding a phone to his ear, his eyes remained fixed on the dock.

"There's a rifle laying across one of them chairs at the dining table," Wes said as he handed her the binoculars. "And the big fella's probably wearing a piece."

"I expected as much. The old guy is Everett Percy. I don't see a gun on him. He strikes me as someone who doesn't like to get his hands dirty."

"Well, I'm not gonna turn my back on him." He whacked her shoulder gently with the back of his hand. "Hey, you hear what I hear?"

The humming of a boat engine grew louder as the beefy man put his phone away and stepped outside to a flood of security lights turned on by the motion sensor. Inside, Percy set his drink aside in anticipation of the new arrivals.

The boat puttered as it neared the dock and the men aboard came into view. Zann ID'd David as the one scrambling to toss a rope over a mooring cleat, nearly falling into the water as the vessel rocked in its own wake. She watched for Marleigh and Bridget, her anxiety turning to panic at seeing only the men. The women's footprints back at the sportsman's lodge proved they'd gotten on the boat. What if Ancil had pushed them out after Bridget failed to cooperate?

"Sasha! It is very good to see you again, my friend. How is Everett?" Ancil's exuberant greeting sounded as fake as when he'd lured Scotty to his murder.

"Mr. Percy is waiting for you," the hulk replied tersely, his breath leaving a cloud in the cold air. Like Ancil, he spoke with an accent, but it wasn't French-Canadian. More like Eastern European. "He wants to know when you're going to get his shipment back."

"Soon, *mon ami*. I have Luc Michaux's girlfriend, who will lead us to his father. I am certain Luc will do whatever we ask if we promise not to cut off any of his old man's ears."

So Bridget was on board, apparently in the cuddy cabin beneath the steering console. Clinging to the image of two sets of footprints in the snow, Zann told herself Marleigh had to be there too. If Ancil had wanted to kill her, he'd have left her body in the SUV.

She clicked out a message on her cell phone. "I'm texting my dad to wait three more minutes and send the cops. They should be clear of the boat by then. We need to get down there and seal the back." For the second time that day, she thought of her team getting pinned down in the alley in Girishk, how reinforcements had driven the insurgents backward into a trap. That would work here too. When the cops came through the front gate, Ancil and the others would try to escape out the back—where she and Wes would be waiting.

Wes inched backward down the steep roof and dropped to the ground with a soft crunch in the snow, which was muted on the dock by Ancil's continued chatter with Sasha.

"Allow me to introduce my friend David. His cousin was an unfortunate casualty today. A loyal soldier sacrificed to the cause."

Zann scooted to the edge and let her feet dangle. At Camp Lejeune, she'd made hundreds of jumps like this with a full pack, even in the dark. She pushed off and landed in a squat, falling back clumsily. Her right hand struck a snow-covered concrete block and popped so loud she feared the men might have heard it.

"That how you jarheads do it?" Wes whispered.

The pain was like molten lava running through her veins. Her hand was broken. Ignoring it, she scrambled to her feet and peered around the corner, realizing instantly that she couldn't use her rifle at all with just her left hand…which was now her *good* hand. She slid the strap off her shoulder and secured the textured grip of her pistol, managing to cock the slide with her rapidly swelling fingers. The combat soldier in her wanted to rush the dock and stick the barrel in somebody's face. *Four of them, two of us.* The odds didn't faze her, but she wouldn't dare make a move without first knowing Marleigh was safe.

"Mr. Percy wants the girl," Sasha said, spurning the niceties.

"Then I am pleased to present her." Ancil drew his handgun and gestured to David, who kicked at something beneath the console.

Bridget suddenly appeared, her tall frame unsteady as her feet sought purchase on the deck of the swaying boat. She looked terrified. Her wrists were bound in front with handcuffs, and she needed David's support to step out onto the dock.

Zann's gut tightened. What if Ancil had concluded he had no use for Marleigh? He could have killed her in front of Bridget for the thrill of it, or to terrorize her into cooperating.

"What do we do with this one?" David asked. There was more movement in the boat as another figure slowly uncoiled from the cuddy cabin.

"I do believe that's your wife," Wes whispered, his voice sounding like a smile.

Zann felt her knees go weak with relief. Marleigh too was in handcuffs, but unlike Bridget, she showed no trace of fear. Steady on her feet, she shrugged defiantly from David's grasp to take a giant step out of the boat by herself.

Wes caught Zann's arm as she instinctively started forward. "Don't go jumping the gun, now. We got 'em right where we want 'em."

As much as she hated to admit it, he was right. A sudden move could draw panicked gunfire from all directions, putting Marleigh and Bridget at risk of getting caught in the crossfire. One nightmare like that was enough for a lifetime.

"Who's she?" Sasha demanded gruffly.

David hurried to catch up to the group, rubbing his shoulders briskly. "Goddamn, it's cold out here. If you guys want to chitchat, let's do it in the house by the fire."

Ancil ignored him. "She is...how should I put it...extra incentive for our friend here to be forthcoming about her boyfriend." Strolling casually around Bridget, he leaned into her ear. "Your memory of where Luc's father lives...it improves, *oui*?"

"I'll help you however I can. Just don't hurt her. She has nothing to do with this."

Marleigh spoke her first words with a cold, flat tone. "He's going to kill us whether you help them or not. And probably David too, just like he did Scotty. Isn't that right, Ancil?"

He took a menacing step toward her, prompting Zann to raise her handgun to eye level and line up the sights to his chest. But could she trust her aim? Marleigh was so, so close.

"Yes, well...perhaps Luc Michaux will bargain for your lives." He lowered his gun and spun back toward Bridget. "I would graciously consider making such a trade. But first I need to find him."

"Ancil!" Percy appeared in the doorway and bellowed, "What are you waiting for? Come inside. Sasha..."

At the sound of his name, the bodyguard whirled on David and plunged a knife into his gut.

* * *

Sure, there still was a glimmer of hope they'd get out of this alive, but Marleigh didn't like their odds. Montreal was a major world city. It could take days—weeks even—for Bridget to find the building where Luc's father lived. Ancil wouldn't wait that long. He was on the hook for seven million dollars worth of Everett Percy's China Girl that he'd entrusted Luc to deliver.

Watching David get stabbed at the snap of a finger told her all she needed to know about the barbaric culture of the drug trade. Money was god. People were expendable, especially those who screwed up. Everyone linked to the Luc Michaux disaster would be killed eventually, and even Ancil seemed to know it.

"I don't care about dying anymore as long as I get to be warm," Bridget muttered as they entered the house at gunpoint. A fire crackled on a stone hearth that rose from the floor to the cathedral ceiling. The surrounding décor was every bit as tacky as Bridget had described, from the filigreed sculptures to the mounted heads of exotic trophy animals.

"Keep your hands in your lap," Marleigh whispered. They couldn't afford to call attention to their loosened handcuffs.

The tension between the two men was immediately tangible. With henchman Sasha still outside disposing of David's body, Marleigh wondered if this wasn't their best chance to break free. She'd feel a lot braver if Ancil's finger weren't still resting on the trigger of a gun he wasn't afraid to use.

From the couch where Ancil had ordered them to sit, she took a visual inventory of the exits. The carved mahogany front door clearly had a keyed deadbolt. They couldn't take a chance on sneaking over there and finding it locked. The hallway was a possibility, assuming it led to a bedroom with an outside door. But that one too could be locked. The only certain way out was through the same door they'd entered.

They needed a better plan than just to get out of the house. Where would they run? Not back to the boat—there wasn't time to untie it and push away from the dock. Then there was the high wall that surrounded the property. To get around it, they'd have to go through the freezing water to the other side, where there was no guarantee they could escape or even hide. It might buy them a couple of minutes, but then Ancil would kill them in a rage.

Still, they had to try. There was no "bargain" that ended with her and Bridget being freed, especially since they could finger Everett Percy as the kingpin. It was run or die.

"You told me you trusted Luc Michaux," Percy spat as he lounged in a wingback chair, glaring indignantly like a king reviewing his subject. He had an air of eccentricity, not surprising given his odd array of collectibles. "And I trusted you.

Give me one good reason why I shouldn't have you gutted like your friend out there."

Ancil shrugged out of his heavy coat and warmed his hands by the fire, his courage an obvious pretense. "Because you need my help to move your product, Everett. And because I am the only one who can recover our shipment. You seem to forget that Luc stole from me too. I am highly motivated to find him and make him pay for his foolishness."

Percy gestured with his drink toward Bridget. "Young lady, do you know where your boyfriend is?"

She shook her head. "He hasn't called me in three days."

"Then—excuse my bluntness—why are you both here in my house and not outside in a plastic tarp with Ancil's incompetent colleague?"

Ancil stepped between them, regaining the aura of self-assurance he'd shown when he surrendered to the fake DEA agents. Like Everett, he was an alpha male who enjoyed calling the shots. "Because she will take us to Luc's father in Montreal. I messaged my friend who works the border crossing at Saint-Armand. We will go tonight, *mon ami*."

So he intended for them to travel the rest of the way by car. Saint-Armand was north of Burlington on Interstate 89. Police on the US side would be out in force looking for him.

"See, there's your problem, Ancil. You seem to think I'm your friend. I'm your employer and right now I'm extremely unhappy with your job performance."

"As you should be, Everett. But a good employee takes responsibility for his mistakes and makes them right. Together we will send a message to everyone that neither Everett Percy nor Ancil Leclerc will tolerate betrayal."

Marleigh kept her eye on his hand, which still gripped the pistol he'd brandished all day. It rippled with tension, as if at any moment he might end the condescending rebuke with a bullet to Percy's head. Probably the only thing keeping him in check was the threat of Sasha.

The older man grunted. "I won't tolerate incompetence either. I'm sending Sasha with you. You'd best hope he's happy with your results." He craned his neck to see into the backyard. "What's taking him so long?"

* * *

Zann tiptoed into the boat shed behind Wes to find the thug, his back to the door, rolling David's lifeless body into a plastic sheet. With just two silent steps, Wes reached him with a cocked pistol at his temple. "Hey there, big boy. Your mama said for you to take that gun out of your armpit before it gets all smelly."

Sasha barely even turned his head before making his move, sweeping Wes's feet out from under him only to see Zann step forward in his place, her SIG aimed right between his eyes.

"Like my friend said." The gun shook slightly in her left hand, but she was more than confident at a range of only three feet. Her other hand looked like a latex glove someone had inflated and tied off as a joke. "But only if you want to live."

Holding one arm out in surrender, Sasha cautiously removed a semiautomatic pistol from a holster inside his sport coat and placed it on the dirt floor.

Wes scrambled to his feet and patted him down, finding the bloody knife he'd used on David and a snub-nosed revolver in an ankle holster. "You're just full of tricks, ain't you?"

Zann studied Sasha's steely eyes and twitching jaw. The cogs were turning in his head as he gamed his options. Any second, he'd explode with rage, betting he could survive her first shot and kill both of them before they got off another. He still thought he was in control, all the way up to the moment her boot viciously struck his chin and sent his head snapping back.

"Remind me never to piss you off," Wes said as he retrieved a coil of ski rope from a hook on the wall. Straddling the thug's back, he went to work knotting his limp limbs together. "They say it's kinda dangerous to hogtie a fat guy. It'd be a shame if we forgot about him."

With Sasha out of the way, the major threat now was Ancil. Everett had shown no movement so far toward a weapon of any kind—henchmen like Sasha were there to provide the muscle. However, both of the men inside had proved their ruthlessness, snuffing out Scotty and David without hesitation.

"You ready to close in?" Wes asked, ducking low as he sized up their advance.

Zann inched toward the house, careful to keep a support column between her and Everett so he wouldn't see her approach. He and Ancil, whose back was to the door, appeared to be arguing, while Bridget and Marleigh sat side by side on a couch near the fireplace. Marleigh was studying the room, as if searching for an escape. "That's my girl…looking for a way out."

Wes made it all the way to a row of shrubbery beneath the window and waved her over. "What's taking the cops so long? Think we oughta rush 'em before they do something stupid?"

"Not with that gun in his hand." With all the glass, they'd be seen before they could get through the door.

Suddenly the floodlights went dark, their automatic timer expiring after a prolonged period without any movement in the backyard.

"Well, fuck me," Wes muttered under his breath. If they moved now, the lights would come on again and give them away.

Zann peered through the bush to gauge the reaction inside. Everett sat up tall in his chair, straining to see beyond the glass. Clearly he expected to see his man Sasha moving around outside.

Wes yanked her collar backward, pulling her under the hedge. "Get down!"

Not ten feet away, Ancil appeared in the doorway to survey the backyard. His words, though somewhat muffled by the glass, were clear enough to hear. "I do not see him. Perhaps he is in the boathouse."

In the distance, a cell phone rang. And rang. It was Sasha's, which Wes had tossed aside during a search of his pockets.

Everett began to yell, his voice growing louder as he neared the door. "Go find him."

"*You* find him! Do you think I trust either of you after what he did to David?"

Moments later, Everett stormed onto the patio with the assault rifle in hand, triggering the floodlights again. "Sasha!"

They were sitting ducks if he turned around, up against the shrubs in plain view.

He called the name again and continued hesitantly toward the boat shed as a faint blue light began to flicker against the building and the tree above it—a police car in the driveway. The next few seconds seemed to pass in slow motion, as realization dawned and he looked over his shoulder to confirm his fears. When he saw them next to the house, he instinctively raised his gun.

A barrage of bullets exploded from Wes's mighty SIG MCX, one causing Everett to jerk and spray several rounds into the air. Wounded, he scurried behind a stone barbecue pit.

Wes shouted, "I got this one. Go!"

Gun drawn and cocked, Zann raced toward the door and collided with Bridget as a bullet shattered the glass nearby. "Go around to the front!"

If Bridget reached the gate, the cops would be there to meet her.

There was no sign of Marleigh or Ancil in the great room. With her Legion in the ready position, Zann checked potential hiding places, finally starting down the hallway. Her broken right hand throbbed as she tried to steady her left-handed grip. She was barely aware of her trigger finger, such were the deadened nerves in her hand.

Another exchange of gunfire sounded outdoors, ending with two shots she would have bet her life came from Wes's rifle.

"It's over, Ancil," she called. "My partner just shot Everett and the cops are outside."

There was no reply as she kept walking, clearing each room the way she'd been trained, acutely aware she wasn't wearing body armor and her firepower was limited. Swinging into the last room, the master suite, she came face-to-face with a terrifying sight—Ancil's arm wrapped around Marleigh's neck and his gun pointed at her head.

"Let her go. There's no way out of here."

"That is where you are wrong, *mon amie*. She is my way out. You know I am not afraid to kill her. What do I have to lose?"

"He's going to kill me anyway, Zann. Don't let him take me."

Even if she was sure she could aim straight, she had no shot with him using Marleigh as a shield. Too close, too much room for error.

"I am going to the boat." Averting his eyes for an instant, he unlatched the door behind him and peered out onto the patio. "If anyone tries to stop—"

Marleigh's hands parted, one of her cuffs hanging open like a dangling claw. Reaching behind her, she dug it into his groin and yanked upward. He doubled over to clutch his injury, the instinct of self-protection. In the instant his gun was lowered, she threw her weight against his legs and drove him into the glass door.

His gun went off, the bullets setting off puffs of plaster from the ceiling.

With her left elbow locked, Zann raised her arm and reeled off a string of shots, her wrist weak and flailing with each recoil. The glass doors exploded one after the other.

With every pop, Ancil twisted and flinched as if to shield himself from the onslaught, all the while firing back wildly. Then suddenly his neck burst into a gurgling fountain. Bright red, oxygen-rich blood meant for his brain. He slumped forward over Marleigh, the two of them motionless on the floor.

Zann took a tentative step forward, horrified. Seconds dragged by without any sign of movement as the pool of blood crept outward. "Marleigh…oh God."

"Get him off me," a muffled voice finally said.

She stumbled over and shoved Ancil aside, shivering at his vacant stare. Marleigh was drenched in blood. "Where are you hurt?"

"I'm okay. I knew you'd come." With a handcuff still hanging from her wrist, she threw her arms around Zann's neck. "I knew you'd come…I knew you'd come."

Voices filtered down the hallway, police officers fanning out through the house. Trooper Lisper, with her service weapon drawn, was the first to reach them. "Marleigh, are you all right?"

"She's fine. Did Bridget get out? Where is she?"

"Outside in a patrol car—a *real* patrol car." She holstered her gun and put on a latex glove before checking Ancil's carotid pulse. "Marleigh, your wife here...she's the one who figured everything out. Those guys had us chasing our tails."

Marleigh buried her head against Zann's chest. Her breath was ragged, as though she was trying not to sob.

Zann nodded to Lisper, who winked and left the room. "It's over, sweetheart. You're safe now."

"I thought I was going to die."

"I wasn't going to let that happen." For a fleeting instant, she let herself feel like the hero Marleigh believed her to be. Holding her, rocking her, basking in her own stoic pride.

Over Marleigh's shoulder was a notch in the doorframe where one of her errant bullets had splintered the wood. How close had she come to killing the person she loved more than life?

CHAPTER TWENTY-FIVE

Two days later

The steering wheel of the Jeep pulled slightly to the left, making it tough for Marleigh to stay in her lane. If that weren't enough, a spring in the seat dug into her butt, and as she pulled into the driveway, the brakes went all the way to the floor before they grabbed. The Jeep was like a bucking bronco that only Zann could ride.

On the front seat beside her were two parking tickets, accumulated while the vehicle sat abandoned at the boat launch in Button Bay State Park. Too bad it hadn't been stolen.

Wearing jeans and a USMC sweatshirt, Zann greeted her from the front porch with a feeble wave of her left hand. The right was in a sling, immobilized by an inflatable splint until the swelling went down enough to wrap it in a cast. "That didn't take long."

"Because your father drives like a bat outta hell. At least now I know where you get it."

At the top step they kissed, lingering warmly despite the freezing air that was turning the rain to sleet. The last two days had been filled with moments like this one, spontaneous bursts of love and comfort. Whatever problems lay ahead, Marleigh was every bit as determined as Zann to work through them. Being together was all that mattered.

"Cops just left," Zann said. "Correction—it was the commander for the whole state of Vermont getting all his i's dotted and t's crossed. I could tell he was pissed that we didn't call the cops as soon as we figured out where they were headed, but the bottom line is there won't be any charges."

"I can't believe they'd even consider it. You guys practically did their jobs for them."

"I didn't say that but I wanted to. He admitted that we saved you and Bridget, that Ancil might have taken you if we hadn't been there."

In the living room, a fire crackled on the hearth, where a day's supply of dry wood was stacked. It was inconceivable Zann could have managed the wheelbarrow by herself. She would have struggled mightily just to build the fire. "Okay, how'd you do that?"

"Magic?"

"I hope you're telling the truth…because I have a list of things you can do next."

Zann laughed and urged her to the couch. "Wes came by right after you left. I got him to do the breakfast dishes too. Oh, and your old pal Troop called about thirty minutes ago. Guess who got picked up in Stowe with a carload of China Girl?"

"I'll be damned…does Bridget know?"

"I'm sure she does by now."

Marleigh scooted close and lifted Zann's left arm around her shoulder. It was amazing she'd never really noticed all the limitations the war injury had imposed, so much more obvious now that her other hand was out of commission. Zann had gotten around her deficiencies all these years by overcompensating with her good hand while making it appear she was using both.

"What did Wes come by for? Surely not just to do the dishes."

"Funny you should ask." Zann shifted her hip. "Check my back pocket."

"If this is a trick to get me to feel your ass, it isn't very subtle." She took advantage of the opportunity, eliciting a playfully dreamy sigh. Then her fingers extracted a folded piece of paper. A check—*for eight thousand dollars!* "What the hell?"

"It's a loan, which I'll pay back with my Marine Corps pension, plus five percent. First thing tomorrow, we go down to the bank and catch up on our mortgage. And I promise you, we won't ever miss another payment." She painstakingly returned her arm to Marleigh's shoulder. "Which reminds me—you should call Pete and tell him to come pick up his yard sign. It's in the back behind the trash can. I plan on dying in this house and I expect you to be holding my hand."

Marleigh had taken that as a given the moment they'd returned home together after Thursday's harrowing events. You didn't live through an experience like that without realizing what really mattered in life.

The unspoken pact had transformed Zann into a new person. Though her secret still lurked beneath the surface, it no longer seemed to hold her in its dismal throes. Her mojo was back. She was both optimistic and blissful, as if she knew nothing could take her down.

"Are you sure you're ready to start back to work on Monday? You can't drive with your arm in a sling."

"I'll let Malcolm worry about that. You think anybody at town hall is going to give me a hard time after Terry's write-up in yesterday's paper?" She pulled her arm out and examined her fingertips. The swelling already had subsided considerably. "Besides, my thumb still works. I can hitch a ride."

A cluster of embers collapsed and fell into the grate, sending a flurry of sparks upward. Marleigh got up and added another log.

"It's so good to hear you joking around again, Zann. I've missed that."

"Yeah, me too. It finally feels like everything's going to be okay."

Settling back into Zann's shoulder, she laid a hand in her lap and began a gentle massage of her thigh. "Whatever made us think it wouldn't be?"

The subtext of her question was yet another probe at what Zann was hiding. Before the gunmen had taken over the office, she'd sworn she was ready to come clean. Two days later she was pretending it never happened.

That didn't mean Marleigh wanted to risk another fight about it. She could learn to live with the silence as long as Zann wasn't visibly suffering.

Zann kissed her temple and pulled her closer, nestling Marleigh's head beneath her chin so they couldn't see each other. As if reading her mind, she said, "You get the truth, honey. Right now."

* * *

Zann hadn't forgotten her promise. It struck her more than once that she'd even redeemed herself by shooting Ancil before he could hurt Marleigh, a fact that should have brought her a measure of satisfaction. But it made her no less a fraud, a soldier who'd been hailed as a war hero instead of the screw-up she was.

"Remember back when I told you I wasn't who you thought I was?"

Marleigh nodded, a gesture so slight she barely noticed. "Yeah, but…"

"Turns out I wasn't who I thought I was either. Last May—in fact, the same day I went out to the range and told Rocky to hit the road—I got a letter from a woman in Ohio. Vanessa Laird. Her sister was the soldier in my unit who was killed the day we went into that house and found the Taliban."

"Your sergeant, Whitney?"

"That's right, Whit. Vanessa put in a request for her records. In the autopsy, they found out the bullet that killed her came from my gun." The truth felt like a rush of cold wind leaving her body. "I'm the one who shot her."

"Oh Zann! That's so… No wonder you were… Sweetheart, I'm so sorry."

She tightened her grip to prevent Marleigh from turning around to face her. "Turns out the Marine Corps knew all along…but they never told me. That's why I went to DC that day. It had nothing to do with Bethesda. I needed to hear the truth from somebody in the Commandant's Office. They'd hung a medal around my neck and told everybody how brave I was. But Whit…she was the first one through the door that day. Tip of the spear. That's what real valor is."

"So your medal, your Bronze Star. That's why you took it out of the case."

"I tried to give it to Vanessa but she wouldn't take it. That's where I went…that night I left. I drove all the way to Zanesville, Ohio and waited for her to come out of her house. Whit deserved it. I didn't. But her family…they can't forgive me. I don't blame them."

"Zann…"

"It's been eating me up ever since I found out. I started going out to the gun range because I kept seeing it over and over in my head. I felt like I needed to fix it so I wouldn't screw up again. I know that probably sounds stupid…"

Marleigh freed herself and turned to face her. Her expression was pained, a mix of hurt and heartbreak. "You could have told me! What did you think I'd do?"

"I knew exactly what you'd do. You'd tell me everything was fine, that you loved me anyway. But in the back of your mind, something would click. Whether you meant to or not, you wouldn't be able to think of me the same way anymore. I'd never be your hero again." Zann glanced up briefly but couldn't bring herself to hold Marleigh's fiery gaze. "I never realized how much of who I am was wrapped up in that one story."

"Zann…" Marleigh took her face in both hands and forced her to look at her. "I didn't fall in love with you because they gave you a medal—and I don't care whether you deserved it or not. What I fell for is the fact that you were brave enough to be there in the first place. That you were so disciplined, so sacrificing. You had one of the world's most important jobs and you took it seriously. Do you have any idea how admirable that is?"

She hadn't done those things to be admired. "It's what I was trained to do."

"And you don't even realize what an extraordinary person that makes you." Marleigh fell into her lap and squeezed her waist. "I'm sorry if I ever made you feel like you had to be more than that. I love you so much, Zann. There isn't one thing I'd change about you."

She'd convinced herself long ago of what Marleigh would say, how she'd gloss over the worst of it only to see it settled under her skin. But her words carried far more passion than Zann had imagined, more conviction. "I really want to believe you."

"Then do. It's that easy."

It wouldn't end her nightmares, nor her guilt at making an irreconcilable mistake. That would take time and effort in her therapy sessions. But it was a gift, a chance to be free of her greatest fear—losing the love of the only person who mattered. Marleigh believed in her. How had she not known that all along?

Bella Books, Inc.

Women. Books. Even Better Together.

P.O. Box 10543
Tallahassee, FL 32302

Phone: 800-729-4992
www.bellabooks.com